Deer Run Trail

David R Lewis

Deer Run Trail

Copyright: 2012   David R Lewis

Published: Ironbear LLC

ISBN: 978-0-9969038-5-1

Cover Design: Jack W. Davis

JackDavis.com

What Readers are saying about **DEER RUN TRAIL**

5 Stars

Ruben Beeler is a good natured and untested young man on his own since his father died a year ago. His rescue of brutally beaten, robbed and left to die gunsmith Arliss Hyatt sets him on a path filled with danger, violence, friendship and romance.

This book is written in Ruben's voice and you can't help but like him and want to know what happens to him next. There are moments of subtle humor in his conversations and everyday life that just sneak up on you and have you laughing out loud. This exemplifies the author's ability to create a close relationship between the reader and Ruben. It was so engrossing that I was sad when it ended. So sad in fact that I've already read it twice after buying it less than a month ago.

It's a great book and I want to share it with everyone. I'm sure my friends and family would like me to shut up about it and I will if they read it and still don't want to talk about it.

CJ_Mac

An entertaining and fun read   5 Stars

I will be the first to admit I have only read a few Western novels. If they were all as good as this one, I would read a lot of them. I think novelists should be good story tellers and David is!

For me reading Deer Run Trail was like being masterfully drawn through a window in time and I went willingly. The author's creative use of a point of view was excellent and led me to readily accept the book's virtual reality. It was easy to become drawn into the interesting story line. The nice balance between story line and characters made this an easy read. This is a book I did not want to put down and I finished it in two sittings on the same day.

The book's pacing was just right so the story line did not lag and yet the characters were believable and interesting. The dialogue added to the period feel of the book and was very well done. The writing was of very good quality.

In summary I give this book 5 Stars and recommend it not only to fans of the Western genre but to others who are adventurous. --Reviewguru

Titles by David R Lewis

Nosferati Series
BLOODTRAIL
BLOODLINE

Crockett Series
FEAR OF THE FATHER
GRAVE PROMISE
SITUATIONAL FLEXIBLITY
ABDUCTED
WITNESS REJECTION

Trail Series
DEER RUN TRAIL
NODAWAY TRAIL
CALICO TRAIL
PAYBACK TRAIL
OGALLALA TRAIL
KILLDEER TRAIL
CUTTHROAT TRAIL

Stand Alones:
COWBOYS AND INDIANS
ONCE UPON AGAIN
ENDLESS JOURNEY (nonfiction)
INCIDENTS AMONG THE SAVAGES

Read the first 4 chapters of NODAWAY TRAIL
Sneak Peek of book #2 of the TRAIL series, NODAWAY TRAIL by
David R Lewis, at the end of this book!

This book is dedicated to my grandfather,
and those men like him,
who lived what I can only imagine.

PROLOGUE

I never did really meet ol' Arliss Hyatt as much as I just come up on him. I found him, actually, layin' in a dry wet weather creek bed in Osage County where he'd drug hisself after one of them Duncan Brothers had shot him. They took his wagon, ridin' horse, an' team a mules an' left him for dead. I reckon they was a time or two when he'd been sorry they hadden gone ahead on an' finished the job. Judging by the tracks, he'd drug hisself a fair ways to git down into that creek bed an' outa the sun. It was terrible hot for early May, an' unusual dusty, too.

It was the buzzards that made me take notice an' find where he'd been knocked off his wagon. I ain't real good at readin' sign, but it didn't take no Injun to tell purty much what had happened. I seen where his body had hit, an' how the ground was kindly scuffed up an' clotted with blood where they'd kicked him around some afore they left him laying there an' run off with his wagon an' stock.

He warn't no spring chicken, an' he'd been awful used. At first, I thought he was dead, there was so much blood an' all, but he warn't. He'd been shot through the left side of his neck, in an' out, an' grazed heavy on the left side of his head, down low enough toward his ear that a little bit of it had been cut off the top. Heads bleed a lot an' there was so much blood all over his head, an' face, an' neck, an' on his shirt, that them Duncan Brothers must a thought he was a gone beaver.

I took his shirt offa him to see, but I couldn't find him shot nowheres else. He was bruised up quite a bit on his back an' chest. I reckon they'd stomped on him. I cleaned him up a little bit with what water I had left an' give him a sip or two, slow like so he didn't choke, but it just run into his mouth an' out agin. I covered his neck an' the side of his head up with my bandana to keep the flies off, poured on some of a little dab of whiskey I carried, an' left him alone. Night come on an' I built a small fire an' et some biscuits I had with me. I didn't mean to, but I drifted off an' he woke me up, screamin' an' shakin' quite a bit. It didn't last long an' he was out agin. But this time it seemed more like he was sleepin' instead a dyin'. That's when I figgerd he might make it. I give him a little more water an' it ran down his throat. That's when I decided he was one tough ol' sonofabitch. Turned out, I was purty much right.

*   *   *   *

He warn't the first I'd ever seen shot. Back home when I was a kid, there was a fella everbody called Turkey. He warn't but about half smart. He lifted a Henry rifle outa somebody's saddle scabbard, offa horse tied up in front a the dry goods store, one afternoon an' shot hisself in the foot with it. He dropped the Henry an' fell down squalling an' flopping around in the mud quite a bit. Some fellas come out of the store to see what all the noise was about, includin' the man that owned that Henry that was layin' out there in the mud. He was some put off. Picked Turkey up by the collar a his coat an' knocked him down in the mud agin'. In a little bit, two ol' boys carried him out to a shack by the livery stable an' the barber come down an' had a look at

2

him. They liquored him up an' the barber got that slug outa his foot, but it still swelled up an' got rotten after a few days. Took nearly a week afore he finally died from it.

I was afraid that was gonna happen to Arliss, but it didn't. The next morning right after I woke up an' done my business, I give him some more water. He opened his eyes an' looked at me.

"Who are ya?" he asked. His voice was pretty weak. Only about a whisper.

"Ruben Beeler is my name, sir," I tolt him. "You been shot, but I don't think whoever done it has managed to kill ya."

He actually smiled a little. "I'm Arliss Hyatt," he said. "You found me, I reckon."

"Yessir, I did," I said. "You been shot in the neck an' the head, an' you been kicked on some. I washed out your wounds, built a fire, an' set with ya. You carried on a little last night, but you seem to be better this mornin'."

He studied on me with hard eyes for a minute, then they softened. "Rube," he said, "you git me through the next few days an' you got yourself another friend."

"I oughta pour a little more whiskey on them wounds a yours," I said. "You ain't gonna like it."

"Don't make no difference," Arliss said, "I'm leavin' ya for a spell anyways."

*   *   *   *

While he was out, I poured what was left of the whiskey on his head an' neck an' covered it all up agin 'cause of them flies. I took my canteen an' walked down the dry wash a ways 'til I come on a little seep in a low spot. The water smelt kindly bad an' was full a little critters zippin' around. I filled the canteen an' headed back with it anyways, an' flushed a rabbit that run off a little piece then stopped to look things over. I got a lucky with my

Yellaboy, luckier at least than that cottontail, but that 44/40 purty much made a mess of him. At least the hindquarters was still good. When I got back, I freshed the fire, strained that water through the sleeve of my second shirt, an' put it on to boil while I skint what was left of the rabbit. The water was coolin' an' the rabbit was sizzlin' when Arliss come around agin'.

"Can ya eat?" I asked him.

"I can try. I'm awful thirsty."

I took my little pot to him. "It's still warm," I said. "Had to strain an' boil it. Probably gonna taste awful."

I held his head while he took a couple of swallers, an' he passed out agin for a little bit, but come back.

"I pass out?" he asked me.

"Yessir."

"I thought so," he said. "You raised my head an' everthin' commenced to spin. Is my skull broke, I wonder?"

"I seen some blood and such," I said, "but I ain't seen no brains. You got creased pretty deep along the top of yer left ear. I speck that's what's makin' ya dizzy. Little bit off the top of yer ear is gone."

"The hell ya say."

"Yessir. They hit your neck on the left side, too. Hole goin' in an' coming out. They bled quite a bit, but I stuffed a couple a pieces of my neckerchief in 'em an' they clotted up. Yer bruised up front an' back some. Looks to me like they was kickin' on ya."

Arliss kindly smiled then. "Boy, are you trying to tell me that I ain't the picture a health?"

I grinned down at him. "You ain't the picture a good health anyways," I said.

He laughed, gritted his teeth, an' went off agin'. I led my ridin' horse an' my pack horse down the creek bed to that little seep an' hobbled 'em there, then I went back to the fire an' tended to the rabbit.

* * * *

That rabbit was about as done as a fella could stand when Arliss woke up agin. I tore off some little pieces an' soaked a couple a biscuits in water. I'd give him a little bite a rabbit an' a bite a soggy biscuit together 'cause he couldn't hardly chew. It took some time, but he et both biscuits an' near half a haunch a that rabbit afore he had to quit. While he rested up, I et the rest of the rabbit an' my last biscuit.

"We're plumb outa food," I tolt him. "Chamois is about twenty miles behind me. I'm gonna have to ride back there an' git us some bacon an' beans or somethin'. If my horse holds up, I can do it in a long day. Reckon I should leave a little afore dawn in the morning. I could build a travvy an' take you along, but I ain't sure you'd make it."

Arliss studied on me for a minute an' seemed to make up his mind. "My right boot heel," he said, "has a trick to it. There's a nail head into the sole of the boot just in front of the heel. Take your knife and prise up on that nail head. It'll come up a quarter of a inch or so. Then twist on the heel of the boot."

The heels a his boots were durn near three inches tall. I did what he asked, an' that boot heel twisted to one side an' ten twenty dollar gold pieces fell right out onto the ground. Two hunnerd dollars was hiding in the heel of his boot! I never saw the like.

"Rube," Arliss went on, "you saddle up and make tracks. Just leave me your handgun and your slicker. You can be in town before dark and back out here tomorrow by the middle of the afternoon. You get whatever you need for us to stay here for a week or two. I'll hang on until you git back."

"You got any idea who done this to you?"

"Got no memory of it. You said they took my horse, my team, and my wagon. I know that much. Dirty bastards."

I hustled around an' got ready to leave, then took my revolver an' slicker over to him.

"A Schofield Smith and Wesson," he said. "Why not a Colt?"

"I like top breaks," I tolt him. "Faster to load an' easier on horseback."

He smiled. "What kind of rifle you carry?" he asked.

"Yellaboy," I said.

"Why not a Henry?"

"Don't like that top load magazine."

"I admire a fella that knows his own mind," Arliss said.

"I left my packhorse hobbled down the creek bed a little ways," I told him.

"If there's water, he'll hang around," Arliss said. "Now git."

I touched spurs to my sorrel an' he snorted an' wanted to run, but I held him in a short lope. We had a ways to go.

CHAPTER ONE

I'd gone about ten miles or so, retracin' the route I'd come out on, staying a mile or two south of the river as trails would allow, when I stopped for a spell by a near dry little creek to let the sorrel blow an' ketch his breath, an' me to ketch mine. We'd both settled some an' got ourselves a drink, when I heard a horse nicker an' seen a fella come ridin' up through the scrub. When he noticed me, he raised a hand an' said "howdy."

I tossed it back at him an' kept both my hands in plain view an' my movements slow. He done the same as he climbed down off a big ol' ugly blue roan with a long head an' a thin neck. He looked to be a little past his prime with long hair going gray, an' a mustache that drooped down past his mouth on both sides. He wore a gray slouch hat, a white shirt an' a black vest with a watch chain across the front, a short barreled Colt in a cross draw toward his left side, an' another one in a short drop on his right hip. It had a barrel long enough that a couple a inches of it poked out the bottom of the holster. There was a ten or twelve gauge coach gun in his saddle scabbard. He was tall enough to hunt geese with a rake.

"Marion Daniels," he said. "United States Marshal."

"Glad I run across you, Marshal," I said. "My name is Rube

Beeler. I'm on the way to Chamois to git some food an' such for a feller that got bushwhacked. He's about ten miles behind me, shot through the neck an' damn near through the head. Says he usta have a horse, a team a mules, an' a wagon."

"He know who done it?" Daniels asked me.

I shook my head. "He don't remember nothin' about it," I said. "I seen some vultures an' found where it happened. From sign, it looked to me like two or maybe three fellers shot him off his wagon, kicked him around some, an' left him for dead while they made off with his truck an' possibles. I tracked where he'd drug hisself to a creek bed for shelter outa the sun an' found him. I poured whiskey in his wounds an' he come around in a little while. I speck he's gonna make it, but not terrible soon. He give me money an' sent me to git food an' such over in Chamois to keep both of us goin' 'till he gits back on his feet. I left him my slicker an' my Schofield an' lit a shuck."

"You know who he is?" the marshal asked.

"Yessir. He said his name was Arliss Hyatt."

The marshal kindly jerked. "He didn't!"

"Yessir, he did," I said.

"Well, hell," he went on. "I don't like that. I've knowed Arliss for a spell. He's a good man."

I waited while he cogitated on things for a minute.

"Ruben, is it?" he asked me.

"Yessir," I said. "Or Rube."

"Ruben," he said, "you go on with your errand. I'll backtrack you and go set with Arliss until you get back. That all right with you?"

"It'd be a comfort to me, Marshal," I told him. "I hated to leave him in the first place."

Marshal Daniels shook his head. "I seen a wagon with two

8

outriders an' a couple of extra horses a little ways this side of Gasconade County yesterday evening, but I wasn't close enough to recognize it as the rig belonging to Arliss. Can't miss his much. Got the prettiest set a matched mules you ever seen. Big red sonsabitches with tiger stripes on their legs. Unusual for Arliss to be out this way so far. He usually stays on the other side of Jeff City. Between there and over at Saint Joe. Your horse all right?"

"Yessir," I said. "I ain't workin' him too hard."

"Good," he said. "Slap leather, boy. I'll find Arliss. You go git them possibles and chuck."

*   *   *   *

It was late in the day when I come to Chamois. I went straight to the general store an' got a slab a salt bacon, a bag a beans, a bag a flour, some coffee, a little sugar, a little salt, five tins a canned peaches, two three-gallon water bags that I filled from their cistern, a bottle a whiskey, a bottle of laudanum, a bottle of rubbin' alcohol, a clean white sheet, a twelve-inch iron skillet, an' a handful of peppermint sticks. From there, I went to the livery, told the fella what I needed, an' come away with a rented black mare that was a little nippy under a beat up Mexican saddle. I went back to the store, talked the fella there out of a couple a ol' flour sacks an' a piece a rope, put the chuck in them bags, tied 'em together, tossed 'em over that Mexican saddle with a dally around the horn, an' figured on startin' back to where Arliss was. The sky was clear an' a near full moon was comin' up. I could git a bite to eat, take it slow, an' still get back by sunup. My sorrel was a purty stout horse.

*   *   *   *

I seen the fire when I was still a half-mile out. The sky was just starting to lighten in the east when I yelled, "hello the camp!"

"C'mon in!" the marshal yelled back, an' I did.

Arliss was propped up agin' the marshal's saddle a little an' mostly awake. I left the marshal to unload the mare, an' I went over to him. He smiled at me.

"Rube," he said, "what took ya so long?"

*   *   *   *

A hour later, me an' the marshal was eating bacon an' frybread, an' Arliss was halfway through a can of big yella peaches. A little after we finished, Arliss kindly crawled away into the brush a while to relieve hisself. When he come back, he was panting some, but he made it.

"You all right?" I asked him.

"Some better," he said, "long as I don't stand up. How about you, Rube? You look a little pale to me. You had any sleep at all?"

"Nossir," I said. "I figured you might need a big ol' peach. I kin sleep anytime. I spent near fifteen a your dollars. I still got the rest of it."

"You hang onto it, boy," he told me. "You go roll up for a while. Lookin' at you makes me tired."

*   *   *   *

I slept most of the day, I reckon. When I finally woke up, Marshal Daniels had coffee ready, an' beans an' bacon an' biscuits near done. I got a cup outa my kit an' set by the fire. Arliss was propped up agin' that saddle with a peppermint stick in his mouth.

"How are ya?" I asked him.

"Marion found that laudanum," he said. "I'm doin' right well. He cleaned out my head an' neck an' dressed my wounds up. I'll be fine as soon as I can stand up without blackin' out and fallin' down. I'm gittin' better, I can feel it. It's just gonna take a little time."

The marshal spoke up. "Me and Arliss talked it over," he said. "If he's still gittin' better in the morning, I'd like for you to come with me to over around Gasconade to see if we can git a line on his wagon and stock. Winfield Simms is the sheriff over that way, and he ain't worth piss on a grass fire. If I have to tangle with two or three fellas, I'd like to have somebody with me I can use. Can you shoot?"

"Yessir," I said, "some."

"You ever shot a man?"

"Nossir."

"Will you come with me?" he asked.

"Yessir," I said, "as long as Arliss can spare me to go."

* * * *

The next mornin' about a hour after daybreak, me an' United States Marshal Marion Daniels rode out of Arliss Hyatt's camp on the way to Gasconade County, looking for a wagon pulled by a team a big ol' red, tiger-striped mules.

CHAPTER TWO

We rode through some pretty thick scrub an' polk for a ways 'til it opened up an' I could ease along side Marion. I asked him how he come to be a marshal an' such, an' he looked over at me.

"How 'bout you?" he said. "How'd you come to be a marshal?"

I was kindly got. "Me?" I said. "I ain't no marshal."

That was the first time I seen him smile. "Until this here ride we're on is over, you damn sure are," he said. "A deputized United States Marshal. Cain't have no ordinary citizen doin' this with me. Wouldn't be proper."

I couldn't think of much to say about that, so we rode on for a spell.

"Arliss has got your handgun, I reckon," Marion finally said.

"Yessir," I said. "I left my Schofield with him."

He lifted his Colt from the crossdraw and handed it over to me. "Short barrel," he said. "Ain't much good over ten yards. Pulls to the left a little. It'll feel awkward if you're used to a Schofield, but a feller needs a handgun. Where you from, Ruben?"

"I was raised up over in Cahokia," I told him. "Worked with my daddy there 'til he got kilt about a year ago. He was puttin' a wheel on a wagon an' the jack give way. Axel come down on his arm an' just broke it all to pieces. It swole up real bad. The doctor done all he could, I guess. Even cut some pieces off it, but purty soon it turned colors an' dark streak started runnin' up toward his shoulder. Took a while, an' then he passed away from it."

"I'm sorry," Marion said. "What'd you and your daddy do?"

"He was a carpenter," I said. "A finish carpenter. Made cabinets an' tables an' such. I was studyin' on it with him, but that's over."

"So you took to the road," Marion said.

"Yessir. I sold off Daddy's big equipment, took some tools for myself, an' struck out. I been movin' west close to the river. Always somebody building something close to the river."

"Where you headed?" he asked.

"I don't know, sir," I said. "Thought I'd follow along around the Missouri 'til I'd gone far enough, then maybe turn around an' head back. I make enough to take care of myself."

Marion wanted to know how old I was so I told him.

"Just comin' nineteen this October," he said. "Why son, you got your whole life ahead a you, got a trade, got you a rifle, a revolver, a good horse by the look of him, an' a pack animal. Looks to me like you're pretty well fixed to get on with life. Shame about your ol' daddy, but you seem fine to me. Plus, you're the kind a fella that stops to help somebody else in need. That says a lot for a man."

He touched spurs an' eased his roan up into a short lope. I come along behind. Seemed like our conversation was over.

* * * *

We come to Chamois about the middle of the day an' stopped by the general store. The fella there knew Marion an' remembered me. He claimed he hadn't seen nothin' of a team of mules an' a wagon, but he got kindly nervous when the marshal asked him about it. The smith over at the livery wanted to know why I come back without his horse an' saddle, but I explained to him the fella that had 'em couldn't ride yet. When Marion asked him about the wagon an' mules, he got real busy forkin' straw into a stall. The marshal took a stance by the stall door.

"I ain't in no hurry," he said. "I can stand right here 'til you're neck deep in dry grass if that's the way you want it, but you ain't gittin' outa that stall until I get a answer. Make it easy on yourself, bub."

The smith stopped and looked at him. "You can't treat me like this, Marshal," he said. "I ain't done nothin' wrong."

"I decide what's wrong," Marion said, "and not talking to me is wrong. It ain't as wrong as lyin' to me, though. You damn sure don't wanna do that. Lyin' to me is a punishable offense, sir."

The smith stood there for a little while, looking down at the straw, then commenced to sway back an' forth some, kindly the way a horse does that ain't been out for a long time. Purty soon he straightened up an' stood still, but he wouldn't look the marshal in the face.

"Ain't nobody gonner want ta tell you nothin', Marshal," he said. "Folks be afraid to say much in case it got back to them boys."

"What boys?" Marion asked him.

"Them Duncan boys," the smith said.

Marion stiffened up a little. "I thought those boys lit out for Wichita or Lawrence or someplace a few years ago," he said. "If memory serves, there was a bank or two robbed out that way soon after. Last I heard was they had gone out west. Arizona Territory or somewhere."

The smith nodded. "They're back," he said, "at least for a

little while. Their father died around a year ago an' they has come home. I reckon it took some time for the news to find 'em. He run some cattle northeast of Gasconade. Them boys is probably back just to sell off anythin' left, or git whatever he wanted 'em to have."

"You sure it's the Duncans?" Marion asked him.

"The other day," the smith said, "near a hour or two afore this young feller with you showed up needin' a horse an' saddle, one a the Duncan boys come in here on horseback, all cocky like. He asked if I needed a team a mules. He didn't have 'em with him, but he said they was real good mules. I tolt him no, an' he rode off. Could be them's the mules yer lookin' for."

Marion studied on things for a minute before he spoke up. "Grain them horses a little," he said, "but not much. We got to keep movin'. I want a beefsteak. We'll be back for 'em in a while."

He walked out an' on down the street toward a cook tent set up next to a saloon or whorehouse or somethin'. I durn near had to trot to keep up. Like I said, Marion was real tall an' most of it was legs.

*   *   *   *

It was comin' on dark afore we were ready to push on, so we set up in a wash a few miles outside of town an' built a little fire. Marion had salt pork an' coffee, so we didn't go plumb hungry. After we et, we made our places an' stretched out. It was real warm. I kept my saddle blanket handy in case of a heavy dew, but I laid out in the open. I watched the stars until I drifted off. Marion snored some.

*   *   *   *

He had coffee goin' when I woke up. I went off a ways an' took care a things. When I come back, he smiled at me.

"Thought you was gonna sleep the morning away, Ruben," he said. "I reckon these past days have wore you down some. Set an' have coffee. We ain't in no big hurry. I got some flour for frybread, an' a little honey to sweeten it with. I usually keep a little honey with me. Always had a sweet tooth."

* * * *

That frybread an' honey picked me up quite a bit. I had just saddled the sorrel an' tended to his feet when Marion walked over and handed me a badge.

"Put this on," he said.

I did, but it pulled on my shirt kindly funny, so I took it off an' hung it through a cartridge loop on my gunbelt. Marion saw what I done and smiled.

"It's heavy," I said.

"Sometimes it can git a lot heavier," he said.

I thought about what he said for a minute. "I doan feel like no marshal," I tolt him.

Marion full out grinned at me. "I won't tell nobody if you don't," he said, an' swung up on his roan. As usual, I had to hurry some to keep up.

* * * *

Winfield Simms was the town marshal of Chamois. When we got back into town, Marion rode down the main street an' stopped at a little clapboard building set off by itself a ways, down the street from what could have been a small boarding house or somethin'. A couple of folks nodded at us when we tied our horses to a post with a ring set into it. One fella touched his hat brim at me an' called me marshal. I almost looked over my shoulder. Marion chuckled an' opened the door to that little building.

There was a fat fella with near no neck an' cinnamon colored hair under a old derby hat leaned back in a chair with his feet on a desk. He wore his pants tucked into a pair a tall boots with long dog-ear pull straps dangling down on the sides, an' a crossdraw rig with a big ol' open top Remington revolver. The kind that was a conversion from the Army cap an' ball. He grunted an' swung his feet to the floor with a heavy thump an' stood up. He was some shorter than me.

"Marshal," he said. His voice was thin and sorta whiney.

"Simms," Marion replied. "This here is my new deputy, Ruben Beeler. Marshal Beeler, this is Chamois city marshal, Winfield Simms."

I shook hands with him. He had short an' stubby fingers. "Marshal," I said.

"Marshal," he said.

I had to stop myself from wiping my hand on my pants.

"Duncan boys back in this neck of the woods?" Marion asked.

"The Duncan boys?" Simms said. "Last I heard they was way out in the territories."

"Got information they dry-gulched a fella, took his horse and wagon and mules, and left him for dead over west of town the other day," Marion said. "You ain't run across 'em, huh?"

"News to me, Marshal," Simms said. "I'll sure keep a eye open for 'em. They's a tough bunch, no doubt about that."

"I'll git outa your way and let you do your job," Marion said. "You know this neck of the woods a damn site better than I do. We'll hole up at the boardin' house a day or two in case you run across anything. I appreciate your help."

"Glad to do anythin' I can," Simms said, smiling and puffing up a little. "Nice to meet you, Deputy," he said, holding his hand out to me. I took it, nodded, an' followed Marion outside.

"You know where the livery is," he said. "You take the horses on down there while I get us a room."

"We gonna stay at the boarding house?" I asked.

"While we watch Winfield's office," he said. "Old man Duncan run this country when he was alive. I speck Simms will lead us to where them boys are."

I grinned at him. "That's pretty sneaky," I said.

Marion nodded. "Sneaky is just one a the reasons why I ain't dead," he said.

*　*　*　*

I took the horses down to the livery stable, paid the nervous fella four bits to feed an' board 'em an' asked him to check the sorrel's left rear for a shoe I thought might be a little loose. He did an' figured that if I was goin' far, my horse needed shoein'. I give him two dollars an' let him do it as I had never been much of a horseshoer.

*　*　*　*

The room we got was small an' only had one winda. The two cots was pushed up agin' one another to git enough room to walk around the edge an' it was terrible close an' hot in there. Outside the winda was a stretch of roof that was near flat. I clumb out the winda an' set in the shade while Marion walked around town for a while. Right at dark, three things happened. He come back, a breeze showed up, an' it started to rain. I clumb back in the room, took off everthing but my hat an under drawers, an' went back out through the winda to set on the roof while the rain fell. Marion laughed at me some, but pretty soon there he was, nekked as a fresh hatched pigeon wearin' a hat, settin' next to me an' grinnin' into the dark.

It rained for near a hour, nice an' easy with no storm about it. We set out some after it quit to drip most a the water off us,

18

then got dressed. After the rain, it got so thick in the room we went downstairs an' set on the porch in a couple a rockin' chairs.

"You find out anything?" I asked the marshal.

"Naw," he said, "but I really didn't need to. I just went through the motions so Winfield wouldn't git my scent. He'll take out a little before dawn, I reckon. This rain'll make him pretty easy to track. We'll tag along a couple a hours later an' see what we can see."

"You done this kinda thing afore, ain't ya?" I asked him.

"Time or two," he said, then tilted his hat down low an' eased back in his chair.

Warn't long afore he started snorin'.

*   *   *   *

Breakfast at the boardin' house was fatback, beans, an' biscuits. It warn't much, but I did manage to git a glass of sweetmilk. We went down to the office an', sure enough, Winfield Simms was nowhere to be found.

"Duncan place is northeast of Gasconade a half day or so," the marshal said. "We should pick up his tracks pretty easy. You git the horses and meet me at the store. I want to git us some chuck in case we have to be gone an extra day or two."

A half hour later we was horseback. Two hours after that we picked up Simms' trail in the light mud. Lookin' at his prints, I figured his horse was off some in the right front. Marion agreed. Simms didn't seem to notice or just didn't care.

*   *   *   *

Early afternoon Gasconade come in sight, but Simms' tracks veered a little to the north an' kept on. His horse was limping worse, now an' then dragging his hoof a little or crossfirin' with the left front.

"He's slowed down some," Marion said. "Let's go into town."

19

I put the sorrel into a lope an' follerd along.

* * * *

The sheriff's office was a low stone building set back around a corner from the main street. As we got down, a fella a little bigger than me walked outside. He was wearin' a long barreled Colt high up on his right hip, a gray shirt with little brown spots on it, a black hat with a low brim, a sleeve garter on his left arm, an' a badge pinned to the right strap of his suspenders. He spit tobacco juice on the ground by the hitch rail an' grinned.

"You ain't dead yet?" he asked.

"'Bout to ask you the same thing, Homer," Marion replied, steppin' up and shakin' hands.

"Who's this?" the fella said, lookin' at me.

"This here is my deputy marshal," Marion said. "Ruben Beeler, meet Homer Poteet. He's what passes for city law in these parts. You git what you pay for, and Gasconade is short on funds."

The fella advanced on me with his hand out.

"Nice to meet you, Ruben," he said. "Sorry you got to ride with is this ol' buzzard. Maybe things'll git better for ya."

I took his hand. "I'm full of hope an' hanging on," I said.

"Truth told," Homer said, "you could do a little worse. I reckon you got sand, son, or this old stump woulda run off an' left ya. You boys ain't here for no social call, are ya?"

"Duncan brothers," Marion said. "Seen 'em?"

"Never have," Homer said. "They was gone from these parts when I left marshalin' an' come here. Bad bunch by reputation."

"They're back to claim the family fortune. Figure they shot a ol' boy an' run off with his wagon, mules, an' possibles over on the other side a Chamois two or three days ago," Marion said.

"Kill him?"

"Nope," Marion said, "but not from trying. We went by Chamois long enough to tip Winfield Simms off. Trailed him thisaway. He veered north outside of town."

"Simms ain't worth dogshit on a hot iron," Homer said. "Duncan bunch'll know yer comin'."

"Yep," Marion said. "You still got that Sharps a yours?"

"Still do."

"Thought you might like to come along."

"I ain't got no authority," Homer said. "I'm just a lowly town law. Not like you fancy federal fuckers."

Marion smiled. "Reckon I could deputize you," he said.

"Doan know about that," Homer said. "You git yourself two deputy marshals, your head might swell an' ruin that new slouch hat you're a wearin'."

"I'll risk it," Marion said.

"So will I," Homer said. "Been a while."

"You ain't forgot much, I bet," Marion said.

"Cain't," Homer said. "Not even when I try."

CHAPTER THREE

I never spent much time worryin' if I was a coward or not. I just never had to. I tangled with another kid now an' then while I was growin' up, like boys do, but I'd never had occasion to come across nobody that scared me much or tried to do me no serious harm. My daddy was what some folks might have thought of as a hard man, but he warn't never hard on me. My momma run off with a drummer when I was little an' we never seen her again. Daddy just bore down an' took over for her as best he could. He had a trade an' we never hurt for food or nothin' like that. He put me in school an' I learned my letters an' ciphers. He showed me woodworkin' as I got older, how to do rough carpentry an' the finer finish stuff, too. How to git a good miter on corner cuts, an' how to use oil or beeswax to put a purty finish on a good piece of maple or walnut. How to use a mallet an' chisel on mortise cuts an' do delicate stuff like inlays an' such. He also taught me some how to fight if I had need to an' protect myself, an' how to stand up against somebody that might be tryin' to git the best of me. He was some fond of guns an' taught me to shoot a handgun an' rifle pretty good. The Yellaboy I carried had been his. I sold my old single shot after he died, an' his Colt too, me bein' partial to my Schofield an' all. Even in my year a travelin' I had never been tried, never come in close association with what I woulda called hard men. Then again, I had never run up agin' anybody like Marshal Marion Daniels or Sheriff Homer Poteet. Not that I thought either of them was hard men. But in listenin' to 'em I come to realize that they was men who could git terrible tough if they needed to. It scared me some an' made me worry about what might be coming my way. Made me wonder if I would do my part if things got rough where we were goin'. If'n I'd hold up under it an' not freeze or run off, fearful that I might git kilt.

The three of us were settin' in front of Homer's office, them talkin' about the Duncan bunch, an' me, hearing only a little of what they said while I gnawed on not lettin' anybody down or nothin'. Purty soon Marion kindly slapped me on the shoulder with the back of his hand an' brought me back.

"You worried about something, Ruben?" he asked me.

"Yessir, I am," I confessed.

"Uh-huh," he said. "Scairt a little, too?"

"Truth be spoke," I said, "I reckon I am some, yes."

"First time you been tangled up in somethin' like this, ain't it?"

"It is," I said.

He set back in his chair and eyeballed the street, only his eyes seemed to be seein' somethin' father away. "Cheer up, boy," he said. "It don't never git no easier. Ol' Homer over here just pissed hisself."

"Feels good," Homer said. "Right warm."

The laugh that come outa me was more of a whoop than anything else, an' it tickled Homer and Marion quite a bit. They got to laughin' at me laughin' an' it took a minute afore we settled down.

"Rube," Homer said to me, "yer packin' a badge now. When

ya got one a them on for the right reason, it gives ye a little more than most other fellers. You just do what yer tolt until you run outa that, then do what you think is best. Just like Marion an' me, you'll git through it or you won't. Worryin' about it ain't gonna change nothin' or stop nothin' or fix nothin'. All worryin' can do is eat at yer brain. Yer mind can be your biggest disadvantage, boy. You clutter it up with a bunch a bullshit, you ain't doin' yerself nor nobody else no good. Whatever happens, you ain't gonna remember a lot of it anyways. Mostimes, your mind just kinda runs off an' lets you git on with things. I reckon that's best. It knows when to leave you alone if you let it. If that don't work, piss your britches. I find it liberatin'."

* * * *

We stayed in Homer's jail that night, at least until about halfway through. Then we saddled up an' took out under a mostly full moon. An hour or so after first light, Homer, riding a hunnerd yards out front, come on the tracks of a lame horse. We followed him, as he followed them, another hour or so until he went up a low rise, slid off his horse near the top, an' come back down it a ways. Marion dismounted an' handed me his reins when I hit the ground.

"Bring mine, Ruben," he said, "and tie 'em off about halfway up the slope. Then stay low and come on up."

They were on their bellies in scrub at the top of the slope when I crawled up. The sun was mostly behind us, so anybody down below would have a hard time seeing anything agin' the glare. On the flat, near a quarter mile away, was a low cabin of good size, flanked by a barn, a outbuilding, a outhouse, an' a couple of corrals. There was a cistern agin the house an' a covered dug well out front. Marion got one a them pull-out telescopes an' studied the place for a while.

24

"There's nine horses in the corral, plus the two mules and a nice buckskin I believe belongs to Arliss," Marion said. "I can see the front of a wagon stickin' out from behind the barn. I seen movement in the barn mow door and caught a little shadow shift from the edge of the outhouse. At least two of 'em is outside. Probably got a saddled horse or two in the barn. As I recall, there are three brothers in the Duncan clan. Probably got at least two more fellers with 'em. Maybe four or more. Can't tell. Homer, unlimber that Sharps a yourn' an' set up. Whoever is down there is guilty of somethin'. You get a shot at anybody, knock him down. They're waitin' on us. They may as well know we're here."

Homer went down the slope to his horse an' come back with the longest rifle I had ever seen. He noticed me staring at it.

"Forty-five 90 Sharps," he said. "Thirty-four inch barrel. I got this 'un from a buffler hunter after them big shaggies was damn near kilt plumb off. Arliss worked it over for me an' tuned it up."

"Arliss did?" I said.

"Yessir. Ol' Arliss is a gunsmith. Didn't you know?"

"No, I didn't," I said.

"Good as they come. Loads bullets, too. We git all this done, you oughta give him your Yaller Boy to work over. Make it twice as good as it is."

He settled in at the top of the rise, flipped up a tall peep sight that stuck up offa the top of the rifle a ways, an' took sight on the cabin. Me and Marion relaxed an' watched the place. I was thinkin' about Arliss being a gunsmith when that Sharps went off. Ten feet away, I felt the shock of it.

Homer slipped another shell into the breech an' brought the sight back to his eye. "Got the one behind the outhouse," he said. "Never did see him. Figured where he was by a slip of shadow an' shot through the front door. He's down."

"I can just see his foot beside the place," Marion said, that telescope to his eye.

In the quiet that come on after the shot, we could just hear the shot fella screech now an' then, beggin' for help I speck. I waited to feel bad, but mostly I didn't feel anythin'. It was too far away to seem real to me.

In a little bit, another fella come runnin' out from behind the cabin over to the backside of the outhouse an' out of sight. I expected Homer to shoot agin, but he didn't. He just helt his sight an' waited. Pretty soon that fella come hustling out from behind the outhouse an' back toward the cabin with the fella that had been shot slung over his back. He was almost to cover when that terrible Sharps went off again. He fell an' neither one of the men, except for a couple of wiggles, moved or hollered.

"Right through the back of the one carried and through the one doin' the carryin'," Marion said, lowering the telescope. "Got both of 'em with that shot."

Gunfire started up then, from the house an' the barn mow door, but nothing came close to us. I did see one puff a dirt, but it was down the slope in front of us a piece an' off to the right a ways.

"Can't see us 'cause of the sun," Marion said to me, "and can't reach us with their saddle guns neither. Wake 'em up, Homer."

Homer fired four or five more times pretty quick, sending rounds through the barn mow door an' the windas of the house. Marion stood up with his coach gun an' walked down the slope near halfway an' crouched behind some scrub.

"You boys are horse and mule thieves and attempted murderers," he yelled. "C'mon out now and let's stop this killin'. Give yerselves up, and we'll all go back to Gasconade and git ya a legal trial. No need for nobody else to git kilt out here today. I'm Marshal Marion Daniels and you got my word on it!"

Things were quiet for a minute, then the door of the cabin crashed open an' a heavyset fella come runnin' out of it in our direction, his hands over his head. He hadn't gone twenty yards when a shot from the house knocked him down. The Sharps roared agin.

"Got the one that shot from the door," Homer said.

"Gawdammit, boys!" Marion yelled, "that there is enough! Git on out here with your hands up and stop all this!"

About that time, I watched three or four fellas scatter out of the cabin an' head for the barn an' corrals.

"Aw, hell," I heard Homer say. "There he goes!"

Marion was running down the slope an' toward the cabin for all he was worth. I couldn't believe it. It hit me so that I waited an' gawked a little afore I run back down to my horse an' managed to git in the saddle as he danced away from me. I spurred the sorrel up over the top of the hill an' down the slope in time to see a Mexican come out of the barn on a big ol' white horse an' head straight for Marion, reins in his teeth, firing two pistols. I was too far away to help, an' Marion just stood there an' let him come. That Mex was closing with him pretty good when Marion fired his coach gun. The first shot tripped the horse up an' he fell. The second one hit the Mex as he struggled to his feet an' put him on his back. I watched Marion drop the scattergun, take his Colt in hand, an' just stand there, waiting for whatever was next.

I was off the hill in just a little bit, an' on the flat about fifty yards from the cabin when somebody shot my sorrel. He grunted an' faltered, then stumbled some, an' swerved to the right. I grabbed my Yellaboy out of the scabbard an' jumped free afore he fell, landin' on my knees in the dirt. I took aim at one of 'em runnin' after a loose horse by the corral an' hit him in the leg. He went down, then got up tryin' to run in a sideways lope. I shot agin an' he went down an' flopped around some. Homer tore by me on his horse, a pistol in hand, shootin' at anything that moved then, an' it was all over.

Two of 'em had got away on bareback mounts from the corral. They'd shot one of their own, an' five more was shot, the one I'd hit the only one still movin'. I walked over and looked down at him as he squirmed an' grunted. He'd been hit in the leg an' the low belly. There was more blood that I thought there could be.

"Who are you?" I asked him.

"I'm Carl Duncan, you sonofabitch," he grunted at me. "You've kilt me, I guess."

All of a sudden, Homer stood beside me. "He ain't killed ya," he said to the fella on the ground. "I have."

Homer shot him then, just as calm as you please, right in the front of his head.

I throwed up. I couldn't help it.

CHAPTER FOUR

Marion and Homer wouldn't let me stay near them dead folks. Once I got to feelin' better, Marion come over to where I set by the well an' spoke to me about it.

"Yer doin' some better now, I reckon," he said to me.

I looked up at him where he blocked the sun an' stood up. "Yessir," I said, "I am."

"Doan feel bad about gitting' down a little, this bein' your first time," he said. "C'mon with me, now."

I followed him around to the rear of the house. He an' Homer had drug all the bodies up together. Sheriff Winfield Simms was layin' there, backshot. It was him one a them kilt when he run from the house to give hisself up. The buckskin stood tied to a post on the corral under my saddle. There was two canteens an' a canvas bag hanging from the horn an' my bedroll was tied up on the skirt behind the cantle.

"You git on up there and go back to check on Arliss," Marion said. "When he's up to it, come with him back to Gasconade so he can git his wagon and truck. Me an' Homer'll wait there for the two of you. Meantime, we'll git these corpses loaded up and into town and sort everthing out. That all right with you?"

"Yessir," I said. "Is my horse dead?"

"He is."

"I hate that," I said. "There warn't much wrong with him."

"You git gone now, Ruben. Some motion will help settle you out."

I went over to the buckskin an' got on. It took some outa me just to get a leg over the saddle. As I reined him to go, Homer come over an' looked up at me.

"You done fine, Rube," he said. "Just fine. Them was some rank fellers an' you stood your ground. Nothin' to feel bad about. Nothing to be ashamed of. You'll do, boy. You can have my backtrail anytime."

I felt tears comin', but I held onto 'em. "Thank you, Homer," I said, an' I meant it.

"Yessir," he said, an' showed me his back.

I touched the buckskin an' he hit a trot. Them tears come then, slow-like, just easin' down my face, makin' it a little hard to see. Truth be told though, that buckskin had a fine trot to set.

*   *   *   *

I'd been on the trail for about a hour when I realized that it was the middle of the afternoon. I musta kindly lost time settin' out by that well. Dusk was comin' when I got near Gasconade but I passed it by an' made another two or three miles afore I struck camp at a likely spot on a easy slope. I built a fire outa some dead scrub an' opened the poke they'd hung on the saddle. I found two or three cans a beans, some salt bacon, an' seven or eight chunks a frybread inside, along with a little bag of coffee and a plug a molasses an' brown sugar. I took my saddle offa that buckskin, hobbled him, an' built my fire. I warn't terrible hungry, but I made some coffee. When it was ready, I put a little a that brown sugar in it. I don't remember ever tastin' anything so good afore as that hot coffee with some sweet.

I was sippin' on it an' thinking about what I could remember of the gun fightin' an' all, when something shoved my back. It scairt me an' I whirled around. I musta been really deep in my mind to miss that horse comin' up behind me an' pushin' me with his nose like he done. He nickered at me an' shook his head.

"What do ya want when ya act like that?" I asked him. He didn't poke me no more, but stood there in the light of the fire an' waited. I broke off a piece of that brown sugar plug an' held it up. He took it real gentle like, but he didn't chew it. He just rolled it around in his mouth until it went away. It took me as funny an' I laughed at him then, maybe more than I shoulda, but not no more than I needed to. It had been a helluva day.

* * * *

I was up a little afore daybreak. I went off a ways an' done my duty. That buckskin warn't as mannerly an' shit about ten feet from what was left of the fire. I didn't take time to eat or nothin', but wiped the dew offa him an' saddled up as soon as I could. It was some cooler an' cloudy that day, an' we hit it fairly hard. That horse didn't seem to wear down no more than I did, an' it was still a little afore dusk when I smelt a fire. A little while later I yelled for him an' got a answer. I found Arliss settin' up an' leaning back on a saddle, eating more a them peaches.

"Rube," he said, "proud to see you. Good lookin' horse you're settin' on."

I grinned at him as we walked up. "This ol' plug ain't worth a durn," I said. "He et all my sugar."

Arliss chuckled. "He'll do that," he said, "special if whoever has got the sugar is weak-willed. 'Bout time you got here. I'm near out of peaches."

I fussed around settlin' things for a spell, took the buckskin down to the seep an' hobbled him near that rented black mare an' my packhorse, an' got back just as Arliss put bacon on the fire. It was plain to see he was doin' better.

"How come you're on my horse?" he asked me.

"Mine got kilt," I told him. "Feller shot him tryin' to shoot me. I'm fresh outa horses."

Arliss thought for a minute. "I speck you got a fair story to tell," he said.

"Yessir, I have."

"We'll git to that in a minute," Arliss said. "First, I got to tell you the truth about that horse. He ain't really mine."

I was surprised. "He ain't?" I said.

"No he ain't, Rube. That there is your horse. You got yours killed doin' for me and risking you life too, I reckon. Only fair I replace your mount at least. I call him Willie, but it don't make no difference what you call him. Horse don't give a shit what his name is."

Even though I didn't really want to, I started to protest a little, but Arliss cut me off.

"Boy," he said, "I'd be dead if it wasn't for you. Don't you try to tell me my life ain't worth more than one horse!"

"Thank you, Arliss," I said.

"Damn right," he said. "Now tell me about them dirty bastards that shot me."

I leaned back agin my saddle an' did.

CHAPTER FIVE

Arliss was better right enough, but he warn't well. He could git to his feet an' walk some, but if he stood up very long he'd git dizzy like an' lose his balance if he didn't set down real quick.

"I hope I ain't like this for the rest of my days, Rube," he said to me on the second morning after I come back to his camp. "I hate to think how distressin' it would be to just tip over now and then."

The thought of him tippin' over ever so often kindly tickled me an' I grinned at him.

"Ain't very sympathetic, you findin' humor in my distress," he said. "When I was a younger man after the war, I spent a year or so in Abilene. There was a feller down there that had got shot in the top of his skull at Gettysburg. The ball didn't go straight in or nothin', but skimmed along the top and cut a furrow about three inches long. This ol' boy would be settin' real quiet like, just like anybody, and then, for no reason, he'd jump up and sorta hop for a spell, then fall down and shake a while. Purty soon, he'd git up and just go on like nothin' happened. He claimed he didn't have no memory of hoppin' and shakin', but he sure done it. Right queersome to see somethin' like that."

"I speck it was," I said, gittin' a grip on my grin. "You're doin' some better though, ain't ya?"

"Truly I am. Just settin' around like I been these days gives me too much time to think, I suppose. I might try settin' a horse tomorrow. See if I git all wobbly and fall off. I damn shore cain't squat out here for the rest a my life."

"Homer Poteet says you are a gunsmith," I said.

"Yessir, I am," he said. "I spent four or five years at the Remington Plant out there in New York learnin' some a my trade. Then when the war come, I couldn't leave somethin' like that alone. I didn't get in no battles or nothin' but worked behind the lines repairin' rifles and such. After the war, like I tolt ya, I went out west for a spell and started makin' my livin' doin' repair work on guns for folks. I was fair good at it, and most people would rather take a broke gun to somebody than ship it off to some place. Time went on, and I took to loadin' cartridges for sale to folks, then to dry goods stores and such. I even engrave a gun now an' then for somebody with a high opinion of themselves and more money than brains. Now I got me sort of a route I follow. I squat a few days in one spot, work on guns folks has left or bring to me, an' load up some fresh ammunition for sale. I git my supplies shipped in to Jeff City or Saint Joe. Got that wagon set up like a rollin' shop to do my work in. I ain't got no ties or nothin', so I can be gone as long as I care to. I got a little place outside Jeff City a ways. In deep winter, that's where I hang my hat."

"Don't sound like a bad life to me," I said.

"It's the one I got," Arliss said. "I don't mind it much. What do you do, Rube?"

I told him an' he thought on it for a bit.

"You do inlay work, do ya?" he said.

"Yessir, I do. It can git terrible tedious though."

34

"You ever do any wire inlay?" he asked me.

"No," I told him. "Now that I think about it though, it wouldn't be as hard as wood border inlay I suppose. Fella would have to just cut out a groove then lay in the wire."

"I git a call for that type thing now and agin," Arliss said. "Maybe I could git you some business. Folks with a little money like to show off. Maybe git ten or twelve dollars for just a day or two of work."

"Go on," I said. "That much?"

"Wouldn't be surprised."

"What's your cut?" I asked him.

"Ten percent. You got tools?"

"Yessir," I said. "They're in my pack I left here."

"Reckon you could make gunstocks and the like?"

"Never tried to," I said, "but I reckon I could with some practice. I can lay a good finish on walnut an' maple, I know that."

"We git through this mess we're in now," Arliss said, "and you git yourself settled somewhere along my route, I can bring you work. Maybe not enough to support you all by itself, but enough to put away for a rainy day if ya git another job. Extra twenty dollars a month make a pretty good poke after a few years. Gitcha a little wife an' some young'uns."

I musta blushed or somethin', 'cause Arliss looked at me an' began to chuckle quite a bit. It was good to hear him laugh.

* * * *

The next morning I saddled the buckskin an' helped Arliss ease up onto him. I walked along side him an' that horse with my hand aholt of his belt for a spell, but he kept his seat real good. It wore him down a mite an' I believe he was glad to git off. We done the same thing again in the afternoon an' I let go of him for a spell. He rode off a ways an' back agin. When he got down, he stayed on his feet an' went for a walk around camp for maybe a half hour or so before he flopped down by the fire, tuckered out quite a bit.

"Rube," he said, "I believe I'm doin' better than I thought I was. Settin' on that horse done me some good. Maybe we oughta take out in the morning for Gasconade. Might take us a couple a days to git there, but it beats stayin' here. I got this place about wore out. What do ya think?"

I tolt him I thought we should.

The next mornin', that's what we done.

*　*　*　*

Arliss was right. It took us near a day and a half to git to Gasconade. We rode into town late morning, me on the black rented mare an' him on the buckskin. Marion an' Homer was settin' in front of Homer's office when we rode up. They both grinned an' stood up, Homer comin' out to help Arliss off his horse if he needed it. He did.

Once Arliss got set down an' collected, I left my packhorse for Homer to board an' struck off back to Chamois leadin' the black mare. It was durn near dark when I got there. The buckskin was some tired an' so was I when we got to the livery. The smith come outside to meet me.

"Evenin' Marshal," he said to me, takin' the mare's reins. "Good to see you. That mare do right by you?"

"She done fine," I said, takin' notice of his shift in attitude.

"Good," he said. "Yessir, that's fine. I heered about what you an' them other boys done over past Gasconade. Good to have you back, Marshal. Shore is. You an' your horse look a little tuckered."

"We been on the trail a spell," I said.

36

"There's a pallet in the shed out back," he said. "You're welcome to it. I'll brush your buckskin out and grain him. No charge for either of ya. Night's good rest would serve ya well."

I thanked him an' walked down to the store. That little bell over the door rung when I went in an' the fella there come hustlin' over.

"Welcome back, Marshal," he said. "Yer just in time. I was fixin' to close up. What can I do for ya?"

"I need a can a peaches," I said. "I appreciate it if you could open 'em for me an' give me the loan of a spoon."

"Sure thing," he said, an' durn near trotted off. He had them peaches open with a spoon stuck down in the can in next to no time.

"Peaches is on the house," he said. "You can git that spoon back anytime, no hurry."

I tolt him I was much obliged an' he welcomed me back like the other fella done.

"I heard about the gunfight," he said. "You boys done the world a real service. Mighty proud to know you, Marshal. Yessir. Glad to see you back in town."

I got outa there afore he tried to kiss me or somethin' an' drifted back to the livery. I located the shed an' spread my roll out on a old saggy cot, et them peaches, an' stretched out. Mornin' showed up pretty quick.

*　　*　　*　　*

That fella at the livery was good to his word an' wouldn't take a dime for puttin' up me or the horse. Even had the buckskin saddled an' ready to go by the time I was set to travel. I stopped by the store to give that spoon back an' lit a shuck as soon as I could git away from the fella there afore he could throw me a parade or somesuch.

On the ride back to Gasconade I thought some about how good them peaches was, so when I hit town I stopped by the general store, got another can, an' borrowed another spoon. Then I rode on over to Homer's office. The three of 'em was perched out front. I handed Arliss that can of peaches.

"Right thoughtful of ya, Rube," he said.

"You paid for 'em," I said. "I still got a pile a yer money."

"You keep that money," Arliss said. "You been worth a damn site more than that to me."

"You got more money than that," Marion said.

"What?" I asked him.

"I been on the telegraph. There was rewards out on two a them Duncan boys from Lawrence, Kansas, and on that Mex outa Taos. It'll take a while, but you got nine hunnerd dollars comin' your way, Ruben."

"Nine hunnerd dollars! Me?"

"Yessir," Marion said. "Me and Homer is lawmen. We can't accept no rewards. You can, bein' a civilian an' all."

"But I was a deputy marshal," I said. "I still got the badge here on my belt!"

"Funny thing about that," Marion said. "I give you the badge, but I never swore you in. You wasn't legal, boy. That means you git the money."

They was all grinnin' at me like 'possums settin' on a rail fence. "Don't that kick the hog in the creek," I said.

Homer spoke up. "Looks like you're buyin' dinner tonight, Rube," he said. "I doan know what these other fellers want, but a big ol' beefsteak an' some Kentucky whiskey would be just fine fer me."

Marion was grinnin' from ear to ear. "And don't tell us nothin' about that money not bein' here yet. You already confessed to havin' a pile a money," he said.

CHAPTER SIX

Arliss went to the doctor the next day to git his head an' neck looked at. The doc seemed purty satisfied at the way things was healin' up an' took a little snip of ragged skin off his ear. He asked the doc about him getting off balance now and then. Turned out that Arliss was usin' too much a that laudanum. He cut back on it, an' his dizzy spells settled right down. Marion was takin' a drink of water when he heard about the laudanum an' some of that water come out his nose.

Arliss loaned me a Colt an' took my Schofield an' Yellaboy for a couple days. When I got 'em back, the Schofield's hammer action was as slick as butter an' the trigger responded to just a slight touch. The loadin' gate on the rifle took rounds like they'd been dipped in grease an' the lever throwed as smooth as the belly on a catfish. He also give the Yellaboy a new front sight that was a post inside a short tube-like arrangement, an' a new rear peep sight. Made it easy as pie to pick up a target an' hold on it. I thanked him for all the work an' he smiled at me.

"I got somethin' else for ya too, Rube," he said.

He fussed around in his wagon for a minute and come out with a knife an' scabbard with snaps to fit around my gun belt. It was a old-fashioned coffin-handled knife, but bigger with a ten inch blade in hammered Damascus steel an' a wide brass guard kindly like a Bowie.

"Arliss," I said, "that there is a helluva knife. I ain't never seen another one like it."

"There's a smith over by Saint Joe makes some pretty fair blades," he said. "He built this'un for me four or five year ago and I have yet to carry it. It's just been layin' around gittin' in my way. I'd like to git shed of it. Yours if ya want it."

"I want it," I told him, "but let me give you somethin' for it."

"That ain't gonna happen," he said.

"Well," I said, "I hate to just take somethin' for nothin'."

Arliss smiled at me. "Git over that," he said, "'cause I got one more thing for ya."

He reached in a box under the seat of his wagon and come out with the durndest gun I'd ever seen. It started out as a LeFever coach gun I reckon, in twelve gauge, but he'd cut it down, stock and barrels, so the whole thing waren't more than a little over a foot long. I thumbed the release an' it broke open quick under its own weight, just as smooth as you please. Them extractors popped up with a sharp snap that wouda tossed a couple a empty shells two feet. I closed it up with almost no effort an' cocked both hammers. They come back like they was on ball-bearings. I thumbed the right one an' touched the trigger for it, an' it broke away as crisp as crackin' a piece of glass. I released the other one an' looked at Arliss. He was grinnin' at me.

"Arliss," I said, "this here is just fine, it is."

He handed me a holster for that little monster that was set up to snap over a gunbelt. It was heavy mulehide by the look an' feel of it an' had two rows a four shell holders on it, one low an' one high. Countin' the two that would be in the gun, there would be ten shells ready to go when it was put on. A fella wouldn't wear it to go to no dance, but I could shore see how it could be some handy on the trail or somewhere as a saddle gun. Under thirty feet, that thing would turn a bull or drop a cougar.

"It's yours, boy," Arliss said. He was grinnin' like he'd just got new teeth.

"You won't take nothin' for it?" I asked him.

"I ain't got nothin' in it," he said. "Feller brought that to me a couple a year ago when it had a full stock and eighteen inch barrels. He' got it plugged up and touched it off anyways. Blew the end of the right barrel open. Ruint it. I messed with it some now an' then, just for fun, an' it come out like this. Ain't got no use for it. Durn thing keeps gettin' in my road. I was just gonna throw it out anyway."

"You ain't much of a liar," I tolt him.

"Some folks would say that was to my credit," he said.

*   *   *   *

A week or two later I was still hangin' around Gasconade with Homer an' sleepin' in a empty cell. Arliss had been gone for a few days an' Marion had come an' gone once or twice. Folks had mostly stopped treatin' me like I was something special. A couple a ol' boys got a little pushy with me once, but I joked 'em outa it an' we wound up settin' an' jawin' for a spell. My feet was gittin' feathers to tell the truth. I warn't doin' nothin'. Time got to movin' kindly slow. Me an' Homer was settin' out in front of the jailhouse one hot afternoon, to git away from a drunk that was cryin' in the first cell, when Marion come ridin' up on that ugly big blue roan a his.

"By God, boys," he said, stepping down, "I wish the two a you wasn't so busy. Looks to me like yer plumb used up! You oughta git some rest afore ya give out."

"Me an' Rube here decide we need some criticism," Homer said, "we'll go see a preacher, Gawdammit. Yer hair always been that gray, ya ol' fart?"

Marion smiled and eased hisself down into a chair beside me. "Hey, Ruben," he said. "You all right?"

"Yessir, I am," I said. "Where you been?"

"Last couple a days, over in Jeff City. You ever been there?"

"Been by it," I tolt him, "but I ain't never actually gone into the city."

"There's a town, just off the river west a there a little piece, I took a interest in. Place called Deer Run. Heer'd of it?"

"Nossir, I ain't," I said.

"I reckon, the way Jeff City is growin', won't be too many years more before most a them towns around it will be et up. Lots a folks stoppin' over that way. Bein' the state capitol and all, hucksters an' blowflies an' liars an' lobbyists is just natural drawn to the politics an' the politicians. Deer Run is some bigger than a lot of the other towns around there. Caters to folks comin' in offa the river an' such. Three or four saloons, whores, boardin' houses an' the like. Growin' purty fast. Lotsa buildin' goin' on. Place a opportunity for a feller with your skills."

"You tryin' to run me off, Marshal?" I asked him.

"Nossir," Marion said, "I'd like to hire ya."

"What?"

"This time I'll even swear ya in, but you won't be wearin' no badge on yer gunbelt."

"What?" I said again.

"He wants you to be a ringer," Homer said.

"A ringer?"

"A agent a the marshal service to go hang around that town, what was it?"

"Deer Run," Marion said.

"He wants you to hang around Deer Run for some sneaky purpose that he can't git away with," Homer said. "Ain't that right, Marshal Daniels?"

"That'd be it," Marion said. "Folks over that way know me."

"What," I said, "like a spy?"

"More or less," Marion said. "There's work for ya over that way. Give ya a reason to be there. Just poke around a little, see what you can see. Be curious. Doan git yer hoof stuck in no trap or nothin' like that. I just need some eyes and ears on the place. There's the city sheriff over there named Arberry Yont. Come out this way from Saint Louis a few years ago. Got himself more deputies that he oughta need. Been a bank robbery now and then in some of the places around Deer Run. Complaints that a couple of folks have just disappeared out that way in the past. I need you to keep yer ear to the ground. You'll be a deputy marshal, full commission. Sixty dollars a month plus a five dollar stock allowance and payback on unusual expenses. If ya stay in a roomin' house, keep a record of what you pay out. You won't answer to nobody but me. I'll figger a way to git in touch with ya now an' then. Mebbe meet ya out at Arliss' place. He's got a shack over that way. You in, Ruben?"

I cogitated on it for a minute. "Reckon I am," I said.

"Good," Marion said. "Now I can tell ya that I got yer voucher for the reward money. I wanted to git yer yes before I told ya about that fortune. Didn't want you runnin' off to Denver or someplace to spend it all on whores and whiskey."

I felt my ears git warm, an' Homer chuckled.

"That duck cain't float," he said.

* * * *

I spent the next couple a days gittin' ready to go. I got out all my tools an' cleaned 'em up an' oiled everthing. I checked out my riggin' for both horses an' made sure it was all up to snuff. An' I did git my voucher an' go to the bank first thing in the mornin' on the second day. I left most of the money right there, but I did spend a little of it. I went down to the dry goods store an' bought me two pairs of canvas saddle pants, three new shirts, one green, one red, an' one in a kindly stripey brown, a new saddle blanket with a little extra paddin' on the withers, an' a ten X beaver hat in a tan color with a tall crown an' a wide brim. My boots was okay an' I never was partial to wearin' a vest. When I got back to the office, Homer an' Marion was settin' there, Marion pickin' his teeth with a pointy piece of whittled stick. They both grinned at my hat.

"Lemme see that thing," Homer said to me, an' I took it off an' passed it over.

He walked out into the street with it, dropped it in the dirt, then kicked it around an' stomped on it a couple times. I was so got, I couldn't even say nothin' to him. He picked it up, dropped it in a water trough, an' pushed it under for a minute. He drug it out, all nasty an' drippin', beat it on the hitch rail some with water flyin' everwhere, then come over an' pulled it down on my head. He fussed with it a little, kindly puttin' a shape to it I reckon, then backed up an' looked at me. He poked on it some more, an' then nodded.

"Leave it there 'til it dries, Rube," he said, "an' doan mess with it none. It'll fit good when it dries out an' ya won't look like no goddamn dude!"

I thanked him, but I ain't real sure I meant it.

* * * *

That hat dried up purty much by dusk an' I set it on the floor upside down when I went to bed. The next mornin' when I put it on, it grabbed onto to my head like it had been born there. I left it on while I shaved, watched it in the mirror, an' wondered how I might look if I could grow a mustache like Marion had.

By the middle of the morning, I was ready to go. I said so long to Marshal Daniels an' Sheriff Poteet an' headed out, but I did make one stop. I went to the store an' got myself a can a peaches. Hangin' around with Arliss had got me kindly used to 'em I guess.

CHAPTER SEVEN

I took my time gittin' over to Deer Run, spendin' the night at a livery in a little ol' place an' not gettin' where I was goin' until late mornin' on the second day. It was a purty good-sized town. The main street was four or five blocks long an' had several saloons, a dry goods store, some boardin' houses, one real hotel, an' two or three restaurants. I rode through an' down some side streets for a while an' counted three church houses, a hardware store, a feed store, a doctor's office, an' even a store with nothin' but women's clothes. Now an' then I noticed some fella or other eyeballin' me close, an' every one a them boys was well heeled an' wore a blue vest with a silver star on it. Seemed to me like there was plenty of them fellas to go around.

After a while, I stopped at a livery an' this girl come out to see me. I was kindly took aback. She wore a red an' white calico dress, had braided brown hair with some red in it, an' was knockin' dust off her hands.

"Hello," she said. "May I help you?"

I brimmed my hat at her, bein' polite an' all. "Is a stable hand or the smith here, M'am?" I asked her.

She looked square at me. Her eyes was brown. "Until my father returns, I am the stable hand," she said. "I'm not helpless."

"No M'am," I said. "I never thought you was helpless. Just unusual."

The corner of her mouth twitched, but she kept aholt of it. "Do you need to board a horse?" she asked me.

"Yes, I do, M'am," I said. "Two. My ridin' horse an' my pack animal. I'm new to town an' lookin' for work."

"Two bits a day for pasture board, four bits for a stall," she said. "We feed grain to go with the grass. There's a spring, so the water is good and fresh. You can leave your saddle and such on a rack in the barn."

"Pasture would be fine, M'am" I said to her, "as long as they don't git bullied. I don't want neither one of 'em kicked around."

"We watch them if they're fresh," she said.

"That'll be fine. I may need my horse quite a bit for a while. If it's all right with you, I can just collect him an' turn him out as I need to. No point in troublin' you folks with my comin' in an' goin' out."

"That would be acceptable," she said.

I dug in my pocket an' come up with a twenty dollar gold piece that I handed to her. "Let me know when that wears out," I said. "I'd like to leave my truck here until I find a place to stay if I could."

"We can put it in the small shed until you need to get it out," she said.

"Thank you," I said. "Maybe you could tell me of a reasonable an' clean place where I might git a room. I hope to be here for a spell."

"Just off the main street in the second block to the south is a boarding house with a sign out front that reads Clary's. Room or room and board. She's a widow woman, and she keeps a nice house."

"Thank you M'am, I said. "If you don't care, I'll unload my packhorse an' loose him, then ride on down to Miz Clary's place."

She showed me where to put my truck, an' I turned my packhorse out.

"You're looking for work?" she asked.

"Yes, M'am," I said. "I'm a carpenter. A finish carpenter."

"You shouldn't have much trouble," she said. "There's always some kind of building going on in Deer Run."

I stepped up on the buckskin an' my brain caught up to me. "M'am," I said to her, "please excuse me. My manners is awful rusty. My name is Beeler. Ruben Beeler."

She smiled then. "I'm Harmony Clarke, Ruben Beeler," she said. "It's nice to meet you."

"Yes, M'am," I said, "it's nice to meet you, too.

"It's Miss, Mister Beeler. Miss," she said. "Not M'am."

"Yes, M'am, Miss Harmony," I said. "Thank you, again." I reined away afore I messed up anything else, an' she spoke up one more time.

"I admire that hat you have there, Mister Beeler," she said.

I made my getaway.

* * * *

Miz Clary was a nice lady, large of frame with hair that was turnin' gray an' a voice of some volume. She give me a back corner room that was small with a cot an' windows on two walls for twenty-five cents a day an' a extra twenty cents a meal if I wanted to eat an' tolt her ahead of time. I left my stuff there, kept the Schofield on, an' rode down the block a ways to a restaurant. When I went inside, I noticed one a them fellers in a blue vest watchin' me from across the street. I set in the back of the place an' ordered a pounded pork steak with boiled potaters an' peas from a waitress that looked a little tired.

I had just finished a purty good meal when a feller walked in, looked around, an' headed in my direction. He was about my height but some broader, wearin black boots an' pants, with a black flat-brimmed hat, a gray oprey coat, an' one a them blue vests with a big silver star pinned to it that looked like it had brass or gold trim. His gray hair come down around his ears a mite, an' he was carryin' a Colt with a long barrel an' pearl handles in a crossdraw holster. He was left-handed.

He walked up to the table an' smiled down at me.

"Howdy," he said.

"Back atcha, Sheriff," I said, an' toed a chair out a little. "Take a set if ya want to."

"Thank you," he said, holdin' onto that smile, an' backed the chair out some more to give hisself plenty of room afore he took to it.

"I been expectin' somebody to come by," I said. "Your boys been lookin' me over purty good."

"I like to know when strangers come to town," he said.

"Don't blame ya," I said. "Name's Ruben Beeler."

"I'm Arberry Yont," he said," the high sheriff here in Deer Run."

"Nice to meet you," I said. He didn't offer a hand an' I didn't ask for one.

"What brings you to my town, Mister Beeler," he asked.

I smiled. "Ruben or Rube will do fine," I said. "I'm lookin' for work. I'm a finish carpenter."

"Is that right?" he said. "I was talkin' to the mayor the other day, and he was sayin' how he might like some work done on his office. We got carpenters here, but finish work is a little short."

"Maybe I just come to his rescue," I said.

Yont let hisself chuckle at my humor. "Where you stayin',

Rube," he asked.

"Over at Clary's place."

"Wonderful woman," he said, getting' to his feet. "Salt of the earth. Next time I see the mayor, I'll tell him about you."

"Thank you, Sheriff. I appreciate that."

"Welcome to Deer Run," he said, an' walked off like he owned the place. I doan know. Mebbe he did.

* * * *

I had a piece of apple pie that was a little sour for my taste an' a cup of coffee, then went for a stroll. Down at the end of the street I heard hammers an' headed down that way. A gang was puttin' sidin' on a fair sized buildin' that looked to me to be oak that warn't as dry as it should be. That oak would bend an' twist quite a bit as it aged. I walked up to a feller that pointed me out the foreman. I went over to him an' told him what I did.

"This is gonna be a school," he said. "We're gonna need everthing trimmed out, windows hung and set, a cloak room finished out, doors hung, finished trim for a couple a big slateboards and the like. Can you do all that?"

"I'll need one man to help me," I said. "I got my own tools. Can you git good dry one inch stock outa spruce or pine?"

"How much you need?" he asked.

I grinned at him. "Lemme look around," I said.

"Anytime," he said. "Be needin' you in four or five days. How much you gotta have?"

"Three-fifty for a ten to twelve hour day for me, plus whatever my helper'll git."

"That's purty steep," he said.

"Git whatcha pay for," I said.

He studied on things a minute. "Al right," he said. "We'll see what you can do."

* * * *

I went back to the boarding house an' picked up my long tape measure, a pencil, an' my tablet. As I was leaving, Miz Clary was coming in.

"Mister Beeler," she thundered, "in and out are you?"

"Yes M'am," I said. "I found a job of work at the new schoolhouse."

"Isn't that nice," she said.

"Met your sheriff, too," I said.

Her face screwed up some an' she snorted at me.

In a hurry an' figurin' that summed it up, I went on back to the buildin' site.

* * * *

I was in the middle of my measurin' when the foreman walked up.

"By the way," he said, "name's Charlie."

"Rube, Charlie," I said an' stuck out my hand. We shook an' he asked if I'd made any progress.

"I'll have my numbers for ya tomorrow," I said. "What do you figure on coverin' up the inside walls with?"

"Ain't thought that far ahead yet," he said. "Needed to git the thing framed first. They're wantin' to git this built."

"Can you git rough cut cedar that's purty dry?"

"I reckon so," he said. "How come cedar?"

"We run stringers then board an' batten over 'em, paint the cedar with some tongue oil or somethin' like it, maybe linseed, that cedar'll stay nice an' purty, smell good, an' keep the bugs an' mice out. No bugs to bother the kids, no mice to bring in snakes. You probably git a few snakes around here, doncha?"

"Damn site mor'n we need," he said.

"There ya go," I said. "Cedar'll make a good underlayment

for the floor, too. Won't rot."

"By God," Charlie said, "that there is a good idea."

"I don't know if you planned anything along the line of cabinets or not," I said, "but a counter along the west wall under them windas with a bunch a drawers under it would give the kids someplace to put stuff. Keep the place a lot neater an' give 'em a long workspace, too."

He looked at the wall and thought. "You can do that?" he said.

"Sure. Common pine one-by in two an' six inch widths an' a little eight inch if you can git it, all finished on one side. Two-by for the top. Be nice for a school an' all."

Charlie brightened up. "You figger up what we need, and I'll take it to the board for ya. Do my best."

"Need some lightweight wagon wheels, too," I said.

"Wagon wheels? What for?"

"Make oil lamp chandeliers out of 'em," I said. "Hook 'em with rope an' a pulley. Let 'em down to light 'em, then string 'em back up. Little extra light in here when the days get dark an' short in the winter. Won't have to let out so early an' there won't be any lamps settin' around to git knocked over."

"You git me them figgers a your'n tomorrow," Charlie said. "Good thinkin', Rube."

I finished my measurin' in a little while an' walked back out to the buckskin. There was a blue vest waitin' by the rail.

"Afternoon, Mister Beeler," he said.

"Deputy," I said.

"Got yourself a job here, have ya?" he asked me.

"Looks like it," I said. "I'll start in a few days."

"Now ain't that nice," he said. "You'll wanna join the union."

"What union?"

"The Deer Run workers union," he said.

"How much that gonna cost me?" I asked him.

"Be fifteen percent of yer wages. We collect it afore you git paid."

"An' just what does that fifteen percent git me?"

"Right to work in Deer Run," he said.

"Uh-huh," I said. "So if I want to work, I have to pay, that it?"

"Purty much is, yeah."

"And my union benefits that are costing me fifteen cents out of ever dollar consist of what, exactly?"

"Tolt ya," he said. "Right to work."

"What if I refuse?"

"Wooden be good," he said.

I smiled at him. "Nice setup," I said. "How many deputies in town?"

"Quite a few, Mister Beeler," he said. "Welcome to Deer Run."

I watched him walk away an' realized I was grittin' my teeth.

* * * *

I got back to the livery late afternoon an' had just loosened Willie's cinch when a feller walked in.

"You'd be Mister Beeler, I guess," he said. He was about forty with big shoulders an' rough hands. He was mostly bald with quick brown eyes an' a kind face. His voice was a little scratchy. Forge air ain't the best breathin'.

I smiled at him over the saddle. "I'd be Ruben," I said. "You'd be Mister Clarke."

"I'd be Verlon," he said. "That buck a yours is a good looking horse."

"Not so loud," I said. "He'll hear ya."

Verlon laughed an' I pulled off the saddle an' blanket an' put

54

'em on a rack. He and I shook hands. He was gentle on purpose. He opened the short gate to the pasture for me. I slipped the bucksin's headstall an' slapped his butt. He went through the door about thirty feet an' dropped to roll an' fart.

"How long you had the gelding?" Verlon asked.

"Not long," I said. "Feller name of Arliss Hyatt used to have him."

"Thought I recognized him," Verlon said. "I put shoes on him once. 'Bout a year ago."

"You got a good memory," I said.

"You got a good horse," he said.

"I didn't know Arliss done business here in Deer Run," I said.

"He don't hardly."

"Guess he don't care much for the arrangement," I said. He didn't say nothin' so I tried agin'. "How 'bout you, Verlon? You happy with the arrangement?" I asked.

"Not so much," he said.

"I just found out I gotta pay a worker's union tax. What they git you for?"

"Small business tax," he said. "Dollar a day. They collect at the first of the month for the month before."

"What if you don't pay?"

"Water gits bad, barn gits afire, horses take sick maybe. Somethin', that's for sure."

"How long has that been goin' on?"

"Started a few years ago, some after Yont showed up an' got the sheriff job."

"Anybody stand up agin' him?" I asked.

"Three or four over the years. They're not here anymore."

"Where'd they go?" I asked him.

He shrugged.

"He git everbody?" I asked.

"Boardin' houses, saloons, restaurants, stores, purty much everthing."

I smiled at him. "Sometimes even the tall hog don't make it to the trough," I said.

He looked at me for a minute. "My daughter said you was a little different," he said.

"So's Miss Harmony," I said. "She seems like a fine girl, Verlon, but she makes me kindly nervous."

His laugh had some power to it. He looked at me with crinkled eyes. "Hell, boy," he said, "I know'd her when she only weighed about four pounds. She made me nervous even then."

CHAPTER EIGHT

Charlie went in harness with my ideas an' pulled 'em through. In less than a week the schoolhouse was covered on the outside, the roofing was goin' on, an' four big ol' wagons worth a cedar an' pine was stacked outside. I went to work. I gotta admit the reason for me bein' in Deer Run suffered for it. I got a leanin' to git caught up in workin' some, an' for the next couple a weeks I was on site twelve to fourteen hours a day, doin' what I like to do an' tryin' to get that schoolhouse ready for the kids. Charlie watched me some for a day or two, then just kindly backed away an' let me take over the inside while some other boys split shakes an' got the place roofed up nice an' tight. I didn't have one helper, I had as many as I needed an' things moved on purty quick.

One night in about the third week, I was workin' by lamplight fittin' the last two by ten into the top of them cabinets down the west wall. I got it in near midnight. They wasn't finished a course. Scapin' an' smoothin' took full daylight so a fella could git a good eye on things. When I finished settin' that board, I stretched a bit 'cause it was bent over work, hoisted my small bag a tools up by the shoulder strap, an' headed out to Miz Clary's place. I wasn't worried about losin' too much sleep. The next day was Sunday.

I'd work on the Sabbath too, but nobody else would. I could go back as late in the morning as I cared to.

Since I'd been in town for a while, I purty much knowed my way around. I was walkin' down a alley, takin' a shortcut back to the roomin' house when I heard a argument. There was a little ol' house near the end a the alley where a couple a whores from one a the saloons did some business. I'd seen fellas comin' in an' out of there now an' then. I eased back into some deep shadow an' listened.

This woman was sayin' somethin' like she didn't have no five dollars 'cause her monthlies had been terrible bad an' kept her from workin'. Then, this man's voice threatened her an' called her all kinds a foul names an' such. She protested some that she had to eat an' two dollars was all she had. There was a smack sound, an' she hollerd an' commenced to cry. That smack noise come agin' a couple a times, an' she said he'd had his free poke an' if he hurt her she wouldn't be able to work this week either. He laughed then an' I heard a heavy thump sound. The door opened an' a blue vest stepped out, shakin' some change in his hand while he come walkin' in my direction.

I was mad at that fella for the way he done that whore an' for the way the sheriff an' his boys run the town. I guess that's what made me take action. I eased myself down behind a rain barrel so he wouldn't see me there in the dark. As he passed where I was lurkin', I slipped my chisel mallet from my work belt, stepped out behind him, an' smacked him low down near where his skull joined his neck. He never made a sound, just folded up an' pitched over halfway through a step.

I took the money from his hand an' checked his pockets. He had a poke in his shirt that had near forty dollars in it. I put the change from his hand in that poke, added a twenty dollar gold piece, dropped his pistol in the rain barrel, an' went to the woman's door. When I put the poke on her stoop I could hear her cryin' inside. I knocked on the door an' the cryin' stopped.

"Ma'm," I said, "there's some help for you on the stoop. I was you, I'd figger a way to move on purty quick."

I walked by the blue vest then, on my way to Clary's, an' he hadn't moved a muscle. I admit to bein' some fearful that maybe I'd kilt him but not so much that thinkin' about it kept me awake overlong.

*   *   *   *

The next day I was workin' back at the school, smoothin' out them two by twelves with scrapers, when Charlie come by.

"Yer workin' on yer own time, ya know," he said to me. "Looks good, Rube."

I thanked him an' tolt him I thought that counter top would be ready to wax by the end of the day.

"Hear the news?" he asked me.

I shook my head.

"Had a killin' last night."

"What?" I said, my mouth goin' a little dry.

"Yessir," he said. "In a alley back behind the Red Bird saloon. Found one a them deputies layin' out there this mornin'. Face down with a butcher knife stickin' outa his back, no gun in his holster and no money in his pockets. They questioned a whore that lives back that way, but she claimed she's been sick and hadn't heard nothin'. End a the week an all, I reckon he'd been out collectin' an somebody come up behind him, stuck him, and stole the money."

"I'll be dammed," I said.

"I ain't sheddin' no tears," Charlie said, an' walked off.

*   *   *   *

I had to set down an' think that one over for a spell. Didn't take no genius to figger out what happened. At least I hadn't killed him. She'd probably git away with it, if she didn't git too free with that money. Who'd think some little woman would even try to take down a full-growed an' armed deputy sheriff? It come to me then that she hadn't kilt him neither. His conduct had kilt him. She had just been the instrument of a death that he had brung on hisself. Thinkin' about it that way made my part in it seem almost noble.

Almost.

CHAPTER NINE

They was a lotta hell raised about the dead deputy. The high sheriff an' his boys stomped around town like they was killin' ants, glarin' at everbody an' actin' tough. A funeral was held on Wednesday an' townsfolk was encouraged to attend. I went just to look things over. Musta been two or three hunnerd people show up. The mayor, a pale man of slight build name a Eustice Forbes talked for a minute about the loss to the community. Sheriff Yont took over, praisin' the memory a Calib Rooter, goin' on about what a fine young man he was, swearin' eternal damnation on the rotten scum that laid the poor fella low. Yont liked talkin' to a crowd. He puffed up an' thundered for a spell, then give it to the preacher. That preacher couldn't hold a candle to Arberry's toney way of speakin', so things broke up purty quick. The crowd scattered in a hurry. Nobody seemed set on groanin', moanin' an' weepin' over the box. I stayed near the back an' kept from grinnin', then hustled off when the preacher give up.

Nobody was workin' 'cause of the funeral, so I rode back to town an' headed for the Sweewater Café to git a bite. I et at the Sweetwater two or three times a week. Standin' in front of the place was a big ol' blue roan with a long head. Warn't nobody around with a horse looked like that but Marshal Marion Daniels. I tied up the buckskin an' went in, real casual like. He was settin' at a side table where he could see out the winda an' keep a wall behind him. I ignored him an' walked on to the back a couple a tables away where I usually set, shifted that knife that Arliss give me out of the way, an' pulled out a chair. I usually didn't wear no gun on workdays. Funeral days neither, I reckon.

Warn't no time 'til this little blond waitress named Margie came smilin' back to me. She was a purty little thing with blue eyes, a dimple on her left cheek, an' hair leanin' toward yella. Always hurried to see me an' had a big smile on her face. I'd usually tip her four bits on a two-bit meal. Now an' then, I thought about askin' her to go for a walk with me or somethin', but I never was sure if she was smilin' at me or 'cause a that tip she thought she'd git.

"Hi, Rube," she said, tickled to death I'd come in. "We got ham n' beans and cornbread today, or boiled chicken and dumplins with turnip greens and okra."

"I can't bear okra," I said. "Can I trade it for some cornbread?"

"All you want," she said.

"Much obliged, Miss Margie," I tolt her. "I appreciate you doin' for me."

"I was down by that new schoolhouse the other evening, helping my old momma on her walk," she said. "I looked inside. You do that work, don't you?"

"Yes, I do," I admitted to her.

"Well it looks real nice. You should be proud of it."

"Thank you," I said, an' throwed my loop. "Margie, you think you might ever wanna take a little walk with me sometime, or maybe a buggy ride up along the river or somethin'?"

"Why Ruben Beeler," she said, surprised like, "are you askin' to keep company with me?"

My ears got hot right then. "Uh," I said, "I thought a walk or somethin' after you get off work some evenin' might be nice."

"I'll think about it while I get your chicken," she said, an' sashayed away.

I set where I was an' tried to git my breath.

When she come back agin', Margie had two plates. She set one in front of me, an' hustled over to give the other one to Marion. He had a little smile on his face an' give me a sly wink afore he turned his attention to his ham n' beans.

* * * *

Marion finished eatin' afore I did. He took a piece a paper an' a pencil out of his pocket an' scribbled somethin'. Then tossed some change on the table an' stood up. Warn't nobody lookin' his way an' he kindly flipped that paper at me from behind his back. It come at me fast an' I throwed a hand up in front of my face an' caught it. It come so fast 'cause it was wrapped around a five dollar gold piece. I opened it up an' read it. It said "two miles south at the fork after dark." Then there was a line that read "you owe me five dollars." At the bottom was two more words. "Nice Hat."

* * * *

When I finished eatin', Margie come over to git my plate an' the money an' her tip. She smiled at me an' that dimple showed up.

"Tonight would be nice for a walk, Ruben," she said. "Tonight would be just fine. You could come by here around nine, if you wanted to."

"Miss Margie," I said, "I just can't make it tonight. I got somethin' else I got to do. Some other night?"

See looked at me for a second, kindly harsh. "Maybe," she said, an' walked away.

Damn.

* * * *

Along toward dusk I walked down to the livery an' caught up the buckskin. He tossed his head at me some an' hopped around a little bit when I put the blanket on him. "Willie," I said, "I know I been neglectin' ya an' I'm sorry." I give him a chunk a carrot I swiped outa Miz Clary's kitchen an' he munched on that while I throwed the saddle on him. He swole up against the cinch a little, but let it go purty quick. There just warn't no meaness in that little horse.

He bounced around some when I got on him but fell into that shufflin' easy trot a his at a touch. I was passin' by the front of the Clarke's house when a voice spoke up.

"A little late for you to be out by yourself, isn't it Ruben?"

I looked up on the porch about fifty feet away an' seen Verlon's daughter settin' in the swing.

"It is, Miss Harmony," I said. "It's gittin' dark. Kindly scary to be all by my lonesome."

"You gonna be able to bear up under it?" she asked. I could hear her grin.

"I'll be okay tonight, I reckon," I said. "But who knows about tomorrow or the next night?"

"If it gets to be too lonely for you, you might mention it," she said, standin' up. "Could be some way I might be of help to you. Goodnight, Ruben. Be careful out there in the night."

I watched her walk inside. There warn't nothin' I could git myself to say.

Good Lord.

* * * *

There warn't a lot of moon. It was full night when I come on the fork. Marion's voice come at me outa the dark.

"That cute little thing likes her tips, don't she?" he said.

"You git me out here to tell me that?" I asked him.

"Now doan git nasty with me, Ruben," he said. "I mess up your plans for the evening or somethin'?"

"Little bit," I said.

"I'm camped about a mile from here," he said. "Brung ya some peaches. C'mon."

The skeeters was kindly bad, but a breeze kicked up a little an' blowed 'em away. I squatted on my slicker to keep the chiggers off an' started in on them peaches while we set by his fire. Marion mentioned he was in town about the deputy gittin' killed.

"I'm purty sure I know who killed him," I said.

"Ya do?"

"Yessir," I said. "Me partly."

Marion kindly give a jerk. "You?" he said.

"I hit him with my chisel mallet an' knocked him out, but I think it was a whore that stuck that butcher knife in him."

"You knocked him out?"

"I believe so," I said. "I smacked him an' he went down. I might a kilt him with that mallet. I doan know for sure, but I'd bet anythin' that whore stuck him."

Marion took his hat off an' put it right back on. "From the beginning please, Ruben," he said.

"Yessir," I said, an' begun the story.

CHAPTER TEN

"Them ain't taxes on the folks and businesses in town, Ruben," Marion said. "That's extortion, an' it's agin' the law."

"What's extortion?" I asked.

"Extortion is when a business has gotta pay somebody so their windas doan get busted or their building doan catch fire."

"Ain't that what insurance is?" I said.

"No. Insurance pays you money if somethin' does happen. Extortion takes your money so somethin' won't happen. In your case what they're sayin' to you is that if you don't pay 'em money, they won't let you have no job. It's like a fella sayin' to you that if you don't give him a dollar he might punch you in the nose. The problem is a municipality can lever any kind of taxes or tariffs it wants to with the consent of the populace either by vote or through the auspices of elected officials. Is there a city council?"

I didn't know an' I tolt him so.

"But there is a Mayor."

"Yessir. Eustice Forbes." I said. "He spoke a little at the funeral. I'm supposed to do some work in his office on down the road."

"I bet he won't be mayor too long," Marion said. "This

sheriff, Arberry Yont. You can bet he's got his eye on bein' mayor, too. He does that an' can git a city council or town board behind him, he'll be able to git away with most anything. Hell, Ruben, if he's as deep in this as he seems to be, he's gittin' a cut of the money you earn and the money you spend. He's makin' a fortune. An' Jeff City, the seat of state government, is just down the road. No tellin' how big this shit sucker's plans are."

"What are you gonna do?" I asked.

"I got to study on things for a spell," he said.

"You gonna go see Yont?"

Marion shook his head. "No," he said. "I'm gonna hang around and see if that sonofabitch comes to me."

"Can you arrest him?"

"I'm federal, Ruben. That don't apply in this case. He ain't breakin' no federal law."

"Could a county sheriff?" I asked.

"Maybe, if there was one, but I speck Yont's got that sewed up. I ain't even sure what county this is. Anyways, you'd have to have a complainant."

"I'll do it," I said.

"I know ya would, Ruben. You would in a minute, but it ain't that easy."

"Why not?"

They can take their fifteen percent an' call it a city license to work in the city limits," he said. "If it was agreed to by a city council or a vote, it'd be legal."

"And you figger they got enough folks on their side to git away with it."

"I do, Ruben," he said. "Now this whole thing they're doin' with businesses is a different matter. That's real extortion, but ya still gotta have a complainant, an' ya gotta have proof that'll hold up in a court a law."

"I ain't got no proof," I said, "but I shore got my chisel mallet. That worked on one of 'em."

Marion grinned. "Doan you go whappin' folks on the head just yet, Ruben," he said. "Let me cogitate on this some and see if we can't figger a way to work this out. I doan want him to know anybody is sniffin' on his trail just yet. You just keep on doin' what yer doin'. Meantime, you don't know me an' I doan know you."

"All right," I said.

"Don't worry, boy. I ain't gonna leave you outa this. If time comes to root hog or die, you'll be right down in the mud with me."

"Thank you," I said to him.

Marion slapped me on the arm. "The fact that you're thankin' me," he said, "makes me worry about you a little bit, Ruben."

* * * *

That schoolhouse got done in good time, an' I went from there straight to the Baptist church, workin' on the pulpit for their new preacher. He was only a little fella, not much over five feet, but his voice was three times his size. They stuck a ten inch step behind the pulpit for him to raise him up so he could see everbody an' everbody could see him, but the first Sunday he tried it, he got to jumpin' around while he was savin' folks an' fell off the step. His ankle swole up considerable, but it didn't break.

I got some good oak an' built him a nice platform six by eight feet, finished it out an' set it around the back of the pulpit inlettin' it a little so it looked like one big piece. I trussed the floor of it up real good an' put a thirty inch rail all the way around it with a gate in the back so he wouldn't git caught up in the spirit an' bounce off of it. I was some proud of it an' he liked it a lot. He got up on it an' jumped around to test it out. He said it was as good as it could be, an' that, as a Christian, he just knowed I was gonna waive my fee for the benefit of the church. We discussed it for a while but nothin' got settled until I fetched my maul an' headed for it to tear it out. I got my twelve dollars for two days work an' the wood an' such.

I was walkin' back to the boardin' house when I noticed a wagon an' a team a big ol' mules tied off in front of a little building down from the drygoods store. I got closer an' noticed them mules had tiger stripes on their legs. Couldn't be nobody but Arliss! I opened the door an' went in. When he seen me, his eyebrows went up an' he put a finger to his lips. I near choked, stoppin' the yell that was fixin' to come outa me.

"Mister Beeler?" he asked.

"Yessir," I said. "I am."

"I'm Arliss Hyatt," he said. "I'm glad you got my message. I have a little work for you here, if you're free."

"I ain't free, sir," I said, "but I am available."

He started to answer me when the sheriff come through a curtain from the back of the place. He spied me an' spoke up.

"Mister Beeler," he said, nodding at me.

"Sheriff Yont," I said, an' nodded back.

"You're going to be working for Mister Hyatt here?"

"We was just talkin' about that," I said.

"Wonderful work you did on the school. Excellent craftsmanship. Rare in a man so young."

"Thank you," I said.

"Mister Hyatt," he said, "I believe you will be very satisfied with you choice of Mister Beeler here. He has my full recommendation. I, or one of my deputies, will be back when you open for business and discuss with you your possibilities to prosper here in Deer Run. Good day, gentlemen."

"Snake in the grass," Arliss said, when the door closed.

"What are you doin' here?" I asked him.

He grinned at me. "Probably makin' a mistake, Rube. Good to see ya. Let's go git somethin' to eat and I'll tell ya a story.

CHAPTER ELEVEN

Arliss shut the place up an' me an' him started walkin' down the street to the Sweetwater Café. We was in front of the drygoods store when one a them bluevests come up to us an' asked to see me for a minute. I sent Arliss on his way an' looked at the feller. He had a big ol' mustache that went purty much where it wanted to an' a brown spot on his head above one eye where the skin was puckered a bit. He carried a converted open top Remington with a big flat hammer spur in a deep pocket crossdraw holster.

"Mister Beeler," he said, "I believe you owe the city some money."

My ruff come up some then, but I kept a grip on it. "Do I?" I said.

"You got twelve dollars for work over at the Baptist church."

"Nossir," I said, "I did not."

He squared hisself away a little bit. "Yessir, you did," he said. "They paid you today. Twelve dollars."

"They paid me today, right enough, but that didn't pay me no twelve dollars," I tolt him.

He shifted his stance some, straightened up his shoulders,

an' give me stern eyes. "Goddammit," he said, "I just talked to the preacher."

I grinned at him. "Well," I said, "I hope you didn't talk to him like that."

His eyes softened a little an' he glanced away from me an' back, quick like. "Twelve dollars, Mister Beeler," he said.

"Nossir," I said, "they paid me eight dollars. Four dollars was for the wood an' some hinges an' latch, screws, nails, an' the finish oil."

He relaxed a little. "Eight dollars then," he said. "You owe the city fifteen percent. That's uh..."

"A dollar twenty," I said, reachin' in my pocket. "I want a receipt."

He looked at me like I had bird shit on my hat. "What?" he said.

"I want a receipt."

"A receipt?"

"Yessir," I said. "I don't want another one a you fellas stoppin' me on down the way askin' for another jingle in the sheriff's pocket."

"That won't happen," he said, some irritated.

I could feel my face gittin' a little warm. "I'll tell ya what won't happen," I said. "You gittin' a dime offa me without no receipt. You ain't gittin' yours unless I git mine. I ain't refusin' to pay, I just ain't gonna without no receipt. Now, if you wanna slap leather against a unarmed man over a lousy dollar an' twenty cents, go ahead on. I'm just as dumb as you are."

He glared at me for a minute, then kindly sagged. "Oh, hell," he said. "I ain't got no paper or nothin'. C'mon."

We stepped into the drygoods store an' borrowed a piece a paper an' a pencil from the fella there. I wrote out a receipt, date an' all, printed my name at the bottom an' signed under it.

"What's your name?" I asked him.

"Clarence Banks," he said.

I printed his name at the bottom an' he scrawled somethin' underneath it. I got the fella at the counter to sign as a witness, got change, handed the deputy his money, put the receipt in my pocket, an' him an' me walked outa the store. Out on the boardwalk, he looked at me.

"Pleasure doin' business with you, Deputy," I said.

"Yer a feisty fool, ain'tcha," he said.

I smiled. "Feisty yes," I said. "Fool, no. Neither are you, Clarence. You shouldn't be runnin' errands for that puffed up sonofabitch while he lines his pockets. I think yer better'n that."

"Can't help what you think, Mister Beeler," he said, an' walked on his way.

* * * *

Arliss was settin' at a table by the winda when I walked in the Sweetwater. I took a seat.

"What was all that about?" he asked me.

"I was gittin' assessed fifteen percent a some money I made fixin' up a church pulpit. I wouldn't pay without no receipt."

Arliss smiled. "How'd the deputy do with that?" he asked.

"We're both still above ground," I said.

"Your sheriff told me today that I was supposed to hold back fifteen percent a any money I paid out to anybody for labor, and give to him."

"Yessir," I said. "That's the rule. He talk to you about a business tax, yet?"

"No."

"He'll git to it," I said. "I don't know how it works, but near as I can figger, ever business pays money on the first a the month. I guess Yont sets the rates. No way he could keep a accurate total on what a saloon or a whore or somethin' like that makes to take a percentage. He charges the livery smith a dollar a day."

"Clarke?" Arliss asked.

"Yessir," I said. "He said he knowed ya. Recognized Willie when I went there. Said he'd put shoes on him once."

Margie showed up then, all smiles an' wiggles.

"Hello, Ruben," she said. "Ain't seen you in a spell. You all right today?"

"I'm right well, Miss Margie," I said. "This here is Arliss Hyatt. He's a gunsmith come to town. Openin' up a little place just down the street."

"Nice to meet you, Mister Hyatt," Margie said, that dimple showin'. "We got chicken an' dumplings with green beans today or hamhocks and pintos with frybread. Thirty cents for the chicken, two bits for the hamhocks. We got some fresh eggs, too. They're five cents each."

Arliss had hisself three eggs an' some frybread. I et the chicken. Them dumplins' stuck on my teeth a little, but they was good. After he et his eggs, Arliss spoke up.

"Marion has been telegraphin' the capitol some," he said.

"Jeff City?" I asked.

Arliss shook his head. "Washington," he said.

"The capitol a the whole durn country?" I said.

"That's the one, Rube. He's been talkin' to Charlie Devens."

"Who's that?" I asked.

"He's the attorney general."

I just looked at him, an' Arlis shook his head.

"That's the head lawyer for the entire United States," he said.

"Go along," I said. "Really?"

"Yessir," Arliss said. "Been talkin' to him about what's goin' on out here. Now the federal guvmint ain't got nothin' to do with enforcin' no laws here in Missouri. States Rights purty much got that sowed up. Unless sombody's doin' some kind of dirt that stretches across state lines, the fed boys, unless they're asked to step in, purty much stays outa things. Charlie Devens is, more or less, Marion's boss. Marion talked him into gittin' in touch with John Phelps."

"Who's that," I asked.

"John Smith Phelps is our governor."

"You mean over in Jeff City?"

"That's what I mean," Arliss said. "Marion is over there right now, meetin' with some people. Among 'em is Henry Brockmeyer and a man name a Elijah Norton. Brockmeyer is the lieutenant governor of the state, and Norton is, I believe, a member of the state supreme court."

"Them's some high up fellas," I said.

"Yes, they are, Rube," Arliss said. He was grinnin' at me.

"What's the matter?" I asked him.

"Bet you never thought you'd be huntin' with the big dogs, did ya, boy?"

I didn't know what to say, but Margie saved me. She showed up, all bright and shiny, poured Arliss an' me some more coffee an' took our plates away. When she moved past me, she kindly rubbed my shoulder with her elbow. Plumb strange, it was. That spot where she bumped me spread warm out into my chest a ways an' plum down my arm to the wrist. It didn't last long, but it was pleasant in a queer sorta way. She come back in just a minute with the check.

"It was nice to meet you, Mister Hyatt," she said. "Now, don't you be no stranger around here."

"I speck you'll see more a me," Arliss said.

Margie patted me on the shoulder, an' a bunch a warm lit up agin'. "About nine this evenin' Ruben," she said, "would be fine with me. I got a shawl in case it gits cool."

My throat was a little tight, but I spoke up anyway. "Miss Margie," I said, "I'll be by then."

She kindly bounced away, an' Arliss chuckled.

I didn't look at him. I didn't feel like it.

*   *   *   *

Back in his little place, Arliss looked around. "I need a counter under these front windas," he said, "with some shelves under it. An' another one along the wall over here."

"You mean it?" I asked.

"I do," he said. "What'll you charge me?"

"I cain't charge you, Arliss," I said. "Yer my friend."

"You got to charge me, boy," he said, "or it won't look right."

"You ain't actual settin' up no store are ya?"

"I am," he said. "It was Marion's idea for me to come over here and let me git myself took advantage of by the sheriff, but the more I studied on it, the more sense it made. I can work here and sleep in one a them two rooms in the back. I got a nice big shed for storage if I need it, an' a outhouse, too. I can still go on the road some if I want to, but I can sell my place over toward Jeff City for more money than this place cost. I can park my wagon out by the shed an' rent a little pasture for my mules. The way this country is fillin' up, I can make a livin' and never have to git mor'n thirty miles from home. How much you gonna charge me?"

"Three dollars a day an' materials, I reckon," I said.

"Fair enough" he said. "I'll need some rifle an' pistol racks, the front and back doors built up some, a good inside bar for the rear one, and a heavy lock on the front. I'll get the smith to make some bars for the windows and you can put 'em up. When can you start?"

"Tomorrow mornin'," I said.

Arliss grinned at me. "We'll see," he said. "Depends on how much strength you got left after that walk tonight."

*   *   *   *

I et at Miz Clary's place that evening. She served sliced ham an' roasted potatoes an' polk salad. After supper, I filled the water pitcher in my room an kindly had a stand-up bath with some hard lye soap that I don't think ever would have wore out. I got out some clean socks an' used a dirty one to rub on my boots some. I lathered up, stropped my razor, an' shaved the best I could, only cuttin' myself once, up high close to my ear. I put a little alum on it an' it clotted right up. I got into my brand new pair of saddle pants an' my new green shirt, then used that damp washrag to clean a lot a dust offa my hat. I pushed my hair back some an' realized that I hadn't been to no barber since I come to Deer Run. I tied a bright red kerchief around my neck I got for a dime at Skelton's Drygoods on the walk back to the roomin' house, slapped on some Bay Rum I got when I got the kerchief, put a peppermint in my mouth, strapped on my Schofield, set on my hat, an' looked in the mirror over the washstand. A lot of the silver had wore off that mirror over the years, but I guessed I was passable. If I could git off someplace for a month or two by myself, I might try to grow a mustache. I tilted my hat a little to the left, an' set out for The Sweetwater.

*   *   *   *

Margie was settin' at a table inside the front door when I got there, the lamplight makin' her look as purty as a picture. I stepped in an' she stood up.

"Evenin', Miss Margie," I said. "Ain't you lookin' nice."

She dimpled an' give a kinda curtsey or somethin'. "I declare, Ruben," she said, "you look right handsome yourself."

I didn't know what to say, but she took over, openin' her shawl an' holdin' it out to me. I took it by the corners, outa reflex I guess. She turned her back to me an' sorta snuggled up agin' it so I had to kindly drop it over her shoulders.

"Thank you, sir," she said, an' stood up to the door.

I opened it for her an' she stepped out onto the boardwalk an' waited for me. I got up beside her an' she strung her arm through my elbow an' started off. Next thing I knowed, we was on our walk.

We strolled on a ways, her a chirpin' like a sparrow. Her bein' up so close agin' me like she was, my ears wasn't workin' too good an' I missed a lot of what she was sayin', I guess, but it was nice. I had to change my stride some, her takin' short steps like she done, but I got used to it. When we passed by Holman's Ladies Store, she got a little excited.

"I saw the prettiest blue dress in there the other day," she said. "It was a lovely shade of royal blue with white lace trim on a high collar and around the bottom of the hem and sleeves. It had a full skirt and a real snug bodice with a million covered buttons. You think I'd look pretty in a dress like that, Ruben?"

"I think you'd look purty in anything you cared to put on, Miss Margie," I said.

She kindly hugged my arm or somethin' an' laughed.

"Don't you just say the sweetest things?" she said, an' started off chirpin' agin'.

We'd walked like that for a half a hour or more, I guess, when she said I needed to walk her on to her momma's house. She tolt me which way to go, an' that's where we headed, but our route was gonna take us right by the Red Bird Saloon. I woulda crossed the street with her, but the Houston House was over there an' I'd heer'd it was a tough place. I looked over that way an' noticed a couple a whores standin' out front, so we kept on goin' the way we had been.

We was just comin' up on the Red Bird when two fellers come out the front, kindly hangin' on one another an' laughin'. They was cow hands or hayshakers by the look of 'em, an' drunk. I'd been knowed to take a drink now an' then, but I'd only been drunk once an' I couldn't see the use of it. I steered Margie to one side so them boys could git past us, but one of 'em noticed us an' stopped, blockin' our way.

"I know you," he said. "I got some beans an' cornbread from you the other day. Yer that gal what works in that rest'ernt, ain'tcha?"

"Yes, she is, sir," I said. "Nice of you to remember. Excuse us please."

He focused on me in a off balance kind of way. "Cain't she talk?" he said.

"She can," I told him.

"Then why doan you let her?" he said, swellin' up some.

"I'm sure she'll be glad to talk to you when you're sober in the restaurant tomorrow," I said, "but not when you're drunk on the street tonight. Please give way."

"Please give way, my ass," he said. "Who the fuck do you..."

I shook loose from Margie, come up with my Schofield, an' slapped him in the left ear with it at the end of a fair swing. It knocked him plum from the boardwalk an' bounced him off a hitchin' rail an' down between two horses. I knowed his friend would be comin', so, quick like, I swung around an' leveled the pistol while I thumbed back the hammer. That feller durn near run right into the muzzle. It was about two inches from his forehead when he stopped. His eyes crossed some, lookin' at it.

"Nossir," I said. "Not tonight. You collect your friend an' git to wherever you was goin'. When he wakes up, you tell him it ain't nice to use bad language around good women. If he has a problem with that, I am at his call."

That fella swallowed real heavy an' backed away. I took Margie's arm an' we walked on. We hadn't gone ten steps afore a bluevest showed up. It was Clarence.

"Everthing all right, Mister Beeler?" he asked.

Margie," I said, "this here is Clarence Banks. He's a good fella, I think. Clarence, this is my friend, Margie."

"Clarence," Margie said, givin' him a little bob.

Clarence brimmed his hat. "You've served me a time or two in the Sweetwater, M'am," he said. "Nice to make your acquaintance. Sorry about the disturbance."

"It's done," I said.

"I seen it buildin' up from across the street," Clarence said, "but it come up too quick for me to git here. Don't seem like ya needed much help."

"Nice to know you noticed, Deputy," I said. "Have a good evening."

"Yessir," Clarence said, "you two enjoy yer walk."

We went on a way, then took a side street a couple a blocks. Margie never said a word the whole time, just kept hangin' on my arm. Purty soon she steered me to a little clapboard house an' up onto the porch. She eased open the door an' stood there, smilin' at me.

"You're my hero, Ruben," she said. "A hero always gets to kiss the fair maid."

She held her face up then, an' closed her eyes. I didn't know what else to do, so I leaned forward an' give her a little peck on the lips.

She giggled an' opened her eyes. "Aw, Rube," she said, an grabbed me by the back of the neck an' just flat pulled me in.

I swear, she opened her mouth some an' touched my lips with her tongue! It kindly startled me. 'Bout the time I was gittin' used to it, she giggled agin, backed into her house, an' shut the door.

I got off the porch an' out to the street all right, but then I just stood there, sorta locked up. I'm surprised somebody didn't come along an' tie a horse to me.

CHAPTER TWELVE

Arliss had moved some of his truck inside the shop by the time I got there the next mornin'. I come in the door an' he studied on me some, cockin' his head an' lookin' me over.

"What?" I said to him. I was a little peeved at his close inspection.

"I don't see no claw marks," he said. "Guess the stroll with Margie went off all right."

"Neither one of us fell down," I said.

Arliss nodded. "Looked to me like somebody did," he said. "I stopped by the Red Bird for a drink last night before I turned in. When I left, there was one feller tryin' to pick another feller up offa the ground under the hitch rail. The feller under the rail had a purty bloody head. Down the way a little, I seen you and that waitress jawin' with a deputy."

"Shithead got foul mouthed while botherin' Miss Margie," I said. "I won't put up with that."

Arliss' eyes twinkled. "That little gal express her gratitude, did she?"

"Yer life so dull you gotta try to live mine?" I asked him.

"Years ago," Arliss said, "I run across a little chestnut filly that I had to have. Paid good money on a good price for her an' brought her home. Turned her out in a little pasture behind the house and just stood and watched her for a spell. She moved good, kicked up her heels now and then, shined in the sun and was shore pretty to look at. I was proud of her. Next mornin' I brought her up and hitched her to a little high-wheeled gig I had at the time. I got up in the seat, took the reins, and popped a whip at her. Off we went, her struttin', me grinnin'. We was a sight to see. After a mile or so, she lost her pace, a mile after that she couldn't hardly pull her own weight. I couldn't believe it. Little thing was shore pretty, but she wasn't worth a durn in harness. Took a loss just to git shed of her."

"How high you want that cabinet under them windas?" I asked.

Arliss smiled. "Whatever you think is best, Rube," he said. "Anything you decide on will just get me grinnin' like a 'possum."

"I'm goin' down to the yards an' see what's come in by boat," I said, an' walked out.

* * * *

I was about halfway to the livery when I seen Verlon Clarke comin' at me drivin' a wagon.

"Mornin' there, Rubin," he said, reinin' his team to a stop.

"Good mornin' back atcha, sir," I said. "'Nother hot one a comin' I speck."

"That's why I'm gittin' feed this early in the day. Harmony is down at the livery if you need anything."

"When you have time," I said, "Arliss Hyatt is in town. Puttin' in a little place down near the drygoods store on the main street. Said he wanted some bars forged for the windas."

"Arliss got him a place?"

"Yessir," I said.

"Never thought that'd happen. I'll go by an' see him." He

clucked to the team. "Thank ya, Rube."

I nodded to him an' walked on.

* * * *

I went on down to the livery an' caught up Willie. I give him another chunk a stole carrot when I led him into the stable an' tied him to a post while I brushed him down. I was pickin' his feet an' he was fussin' at me about it a little when Verlon's daughter walked in carryin' a pitchfork. She was wearing a long blue skirt with a ragged hem, a man-cut shirt with the sleeves rolled up, a old straw hat, a pair a gloves, an' her hair was loose an' tied behind her head. It hung plumb to her waist.

"Good morning, Ruben," she said. "That gelding of yours needs more exercise than he's getting. His hocks look a little thick to me."

I took notice an' felt of him. "I believe you're right, Miss Harmony," I said. "He's a little warm. It's my fault. I been workin' too much. Ain't had time to git on him enough."

"If you like," she said, "I could take him out a little now and then. No charge."

"That's right nice of ya to offer," I told her, "but I don't know if he'd take a side saddle. Some horses don't like 'em much."

"I have no love for side saddles," she said. "I'd have to use yours. I straddle a horse when I ride."

I felt my face git hot. "That'd be fine, Miss Harmony," I said. "Right nice of ya to offer."

She leaned her pitchfork on a stall, took off her gloves, an' hung her hat on a peg.

"That buckskin broken to harness?" she asked.

"I doan rightly know," I said.

"If he is," she said, "our little carriage rents cheap. Maybe you could give him some exercise on your nightly excursions and save a little wear on Miss Margie's shoe leather. Have a nice day, Mister Beeler."

She left then, an' didn't dally about it. I throwed a blanket an' saddle on my horse an' got the hell outa there as fast as I could. I was halfway to the lumberyard before it come to me that I'd disremembered my spurs.

* * * *

I unloaded the wood from Arliss' wagon about noon, then I had to sharpen my rough saw so my day got slowed down some, but by dusk I had planks cut for the top a them two cabinets an' ones to lay over the inside a the doors. Arliss had been gone with the team for a spell. I was puttin' my tools away when he come in, carryin' a box or two outa his wagon an' a brand new broom. He looked at the boards.

"Oak ain't it?" he said to me.

"Yessir. Stouter for them doors an' better for the tops. Pine would dent too easy. I'll use it for the shelves an' such. It's all purty dry. Shouldn't warp much."

"You like stayin at that roomin' house, Rube?" he asked.

"It ain't so bad," I said. "Got a room an' a cot. Ain't much privacy an' the food ain't real plentiful, but it doan cost too much, I reckon."

"Why don't you live here?"

"Here?" I said, kindly surprised at the notion.

"I been out in that shed, boy. It's right stout. Gotta good floor, level an' such. I got these two back rooms here in this building. I can stay in one and store in the other, plus still have space to reload and such. Hell, I'm used to doin' a lot of what I do in that wagon. As far as I'm concerned, this here is right spacious!"

"I never even looked at that shed," I said.

"Roof is good I believe," he said. "Didn't see no water spots on the floor. There's a couple a mud dobber nests and such and some mouse turds, but it's been empty for near a year. It looks to me to be about twelve by eighteen or so. It might be right cozy if them walls was covered on the inside an' it had a couple a winders and a flu for a stove. You know a good carpenter?"

Him askin' about a carpenter struck me kindly peculiar an' I grinned at him.

"Rent free," Arliss said. "We git along purty good. I'd even throw in outhouse rights."

"Lemme think bout it," I said.

Arliss looked a little offended. "You do that," he said.

I wiped my saw down with oil, an' spoke up. "If the offer still stands," I said, "I'm in."

Aliss snorted at me. "Took ya long enough to make up your mind," he said.

*　*　*　*

I went after Arliss' job as hard as I could, workin' ever day as long as I had light to see by. In less than a week, them cabinets was in, the doors was all built up, an' there was shelves on the back wall. Arliss had this ol' box with some deer antlers in it. I loaned him Willie an' he took off for a two or three days to ride part of his route an' let folks know where he was an' what he was gonna be doin'. While he was gone, I cut some lengths a pine in kindly curly shapes, beveled the edges, an' scraped 'em out real smooth. Then I set pieces of them antlers in 'em so they stuck out, oiled 'em a little, wiped that off real good, an' rubbed the wood with beeswax. When Arliss come back he had six long gun racks on the walls. He was kindly got when he seen 'em.

"Good Lord, Rube," he said, "would you look at that? Them racks shine, boy. They surely do."

"On the house," I said.

*   *   *   *

On Saturday I went to the hardware store an' come up with a big ol' lock set for the front door. When I got back, Verlon Clarke was there with them bars for the windas an' some extra heavy hinges for the doors. I got them doors hung an' the lock in afore I quit, doin' some a the work by lamplight. Sunday mornin' I hung bars on five windas, settin' 'em in with big ol' lag screws, an' Arliss' place was sewed up tight. He walked around, kindly proud-like, lookin' it all over, then took me to the Sweetwater to buy me dinner. We hadn't been set for a minute when Miss Margie sashayed up.

"Mister Arliss," she said, "nice to see you."

"You, too, Miss Margie," Arliss said.

She turned to me, lookin' pretty an' kindly stern. "An' you, Ruben Beeler," she said, "you haven't been in here in days. You ain't tryin' to avoid me, are you?"

"Truly I ain't, Miss Margie," I said. "I been workin' real hard to git Arliss' place fixed up. It's his fault. He kept me locked in."

"Well, you're loose now," she said. "I have tomorrow off, Ruben, if that means anything to you."

"It does, Miss Margie. I'd be right proud to call on you late mornin'. Maybe we could go for another walk, say over to the Crystal Restaurant for dinner, then take a stroll around town for a spell to see what we can see." The Crystal was at the other end a town an' some toney. I'd never et there, but I'd heered folks said it was real nice.

Margie brightened up quite a bit. "That would be just fine, Ruben," she said. "Around noon?"

"Around noon it is," I said.

"Sunday an' all," Margie said, lookin' right prim and cute,

"we got fried chicken with mashed potatoes an' sweetcorn. That all right with the two of you handsome gents?"

"That'll be fine," Arliss said, an' she flounced away.

* * * *

I spent the rest of the day sweepin' up at Arliss' place, then stompin' around in that shed studyin' on what I'd need to fix it up. Arliss was wrong on the size. It was closer to sixteen by twenty feet. He was right on the condition, though. It was in purty good shape. I was gonna need wood an' nails an' that kinda thing, but I was also gonna need a cot n' bedclothes, an' a couple a coal oil lamps, an' a stove n' pipe, an' some winda glass an' a bunch a stuff I never really considered before. It was gonna take more money than I had with me. I was gonna have to go on a little trip soon.

* * * *

Monday morning around eight I went to the Deer Run Drygoods store an' bought me a gray colored town coat in some kinda linen material, an' some bootblack. Even though I didn't care for 'em, I let the feller there talk me into a vest to go with that coat, a black one with thin little gray stripes runnin' up an' down the front of it. He asked me what color shirt I had for it, then sold me a white one with a stiff collar that stuck up my neck about a inch all the way around. From there I went to Holman's Ladies Store and bought a lace handkerchief with little purple flowers stitched into it. The lady there folded it up real nice for me an' put it in a little flat box lined with some tissue paper.

* * * *

I went to Clary's, worked on my boots, shaved my face, fought with that chunk a lye soap agin, put on my new clothes, an' headed out on my walk to Margie's place. I hadden gone a block afore that coat an' vest had me sweatin' like a robber. I went back to Clary's, took 'em off, put on my red shirt, an' struck off agin.

* * * *

Margie come out a her house afore I got all the way up on the porch. She was wearin' a yella dress trimmed in white an' looked as pretty as she could, which was considerable. We said hello an' I give her that box with the hanky in it. She opened it up an' squealed a little, then kissed me on the cheek, sayin' how pretty it was, how much she liked nice things, an' how good it made her feel that I thought a buyin' her somethin'. She kept on chirpin' about this an' that while she tucked it up her sleeve an' left the box on her porch swing. She kept talkin' all the time it took us to walk the six or seven blocks to the Crystal restaurant.

We went in that place an' this fella come up an' led us to a table, holdin' the chair out for Margie so she could take a seat. Quick as a wink he showed back up with big ol' cardboard menus for us with everthing they had to eat writ fancy on 'em. No sooner had he left than this waitress, name a Pauline, arrived with water in fancy glasses, a basket of rolls, an' a square chunk a butter on a little silver plate.

Our table was covered up with a white cloth about as thick as buckskin, with big ol' floppy napkins on it an' two or three forks an' spoons on each side a this shiny white plate. There was a crystal chandelier hangin' down from the ceiling, an' the chairs we was in kindly wrapped around a feller so I had a little trouble gittin' comfortable with my belt knife.

Margie ordered pheasant, but for the life a me I never could figger out why anybody would prefer to eat a pheasant when chicken, which was raised to eat, tasted so much better. I had a beefsteak. They had three or four kinds. The one I took was called a Kansas City Strip, an' I gotta say that it was as good a piece a meat as I ever tasted. We had some wine, too, mostly 'cause the feller said we should, but it tasted kindly sour to me an' I had no likin' for it. After the meal, they brung us some poofy little pillow things made outa pie crust. When I stuck a fork in it, it kindly split open an' the inside was a type of thick creamy stuff with berries in it. It was terrible good. I coulda et two a them things if I'd had another one. After about a hour an' a half we finished up an' that feller brought the check. Eight dollars. Eight dollars! I coulda et every meal at Clary's place for a week an' a half for that much. I paid for it anyway an' left a dollar on the table, but I couldn't see no good reason to spend three days hard work on one meal, no matter how good the beefsteak was.

We walked around town for a couple a hours, Margie window shoppin' an' sayin' how much she'd like to have this an' that, an' how flattered she was I'd got her that hanky. Truth be told, I got kindly tired a her chirpin' all the time like she done, wantin' this necklace or that hat pin or whatever. Ever now an' then she'd squeeze my arm an' git up on her tippy toes to give my cheek a little kiss, especially if she was talkin' about somethin' she'd like to have. After a while, I walked her home, declined the pleasure of settin' in the porch swing with her, an' went on my way. To be honest, I was some glad to git shed of her. I wondered if the Deer Run Drygoods would take back that shirt an' coat an' vest.   Turned   out,   they   wouldn't.

CHAPTER THIRTEEN

The next mornin' I went over to the livery, said good mornin' to Verlon Clarke, didn't see a bit of his daughter, an' collected Willie. I took him back to Arliss' place, tied on my slicker, bedroll, an' saddle bags, borrowed a three gallon water bag, hung my Yellaboy in the scabbard, tied that little shotgun Arliss give me to the horn, put on the Schofield, hung my knife on the other side a my gun belt, an' swung up.

"When ya gonna be back, ya reckon?" Arliss asked me.

"Quick as I can without ruinin' this poor ol' horse," I said.

He grinned at me. "Never did ask ya how your fancy meal went with that little gal," he said.

"Eight dollars an' she wouldn't shut up beggin' for foofarah," I tolt him.

A laugh blowed outa him then, an' he had to bend over a little afore it got the best of him. I waited.

"By God, Rube," he said, "you are a caution, you are. You learn anything?"

"Some," I said, feelin' a little put off.

"Then it was damn sure worth the eight dollars. You take as long as you need on the trip. I'll keep a eye on your tools an' such."

"Thank ya, Arliss," I said, an' turned Willie away.

* * * *

On the way outa town, I stopped by the Sweetwater Café an' bought myself half a dozen biscuits left over from breakfast an' some frybread. From there I went to the general store an' picked up two cans a peaches, a slab a salt bacon, a little bag a coffee, an' three or four cans of pinto beans. Goin' out the door, I almost run into Miss Harmony as she was comin' in.

"Hello, Ruben," she said, glancin' at my load. "What's all this? Are they finally running you out of town?"

It took me funny an' I laughed a little while she smiled. "You ain't that lucky, Miss Harmony," I said. "I'll be back in a few days."

"I can stand it," she said, an' went on inside.

* * * *

It took me nearly two days a easy goin' to git to Gasconade. I hit the main street late afternoon. I dropped Willie off at the livery, lifted that shotgun offa the saddle, took the Yellaboy out of the scabbard, put up with the feller there sayin' how good it was to see me, an' walked over to the sheriff's office. Nobody was around, so I put the guns inside on the floor, set down in one a them chairs out front, propped my feet up on the rail, an' waited.

A little later, Homer Poteet come walking down the way, pickin' his teeth. He stepped up on the porch, set down, eyeballed the street for a minute, an' finally spoke up.

"Rube," he said.

"Homer," I said.

He took a pouch an' papers outa his shirt pocket an' twisted one up. He offered the pouch to me, but I shook my head. He struck a match with his fingernail an' lit up.

"How ya been," he said.

"Fine," I said. "You?"

"Passable. What brings ya back thisaway?"

"I need to git my money outa the bank," I tolt him.

"You spent that left over fortune already?" he asked me.

"That there wouldn't be a whole lot a yer business, would it?" I said.

Homer let that one drift for a minute afore he spoke up.

"Good to see ya, boy," he said. "What in the hell is goin' on in yer life?"

Over the next few minutes, I tolt him a lot of it.

* * * *

"That explains some things," Homer said. "A day or two ago, I got a telegraph from Marion askin' if I'd care to be a Marshal agin for a while. I ain't answered it yet. Marion, as you know, has a way a gittin' people in dangerous situations."

"That's true," I said.

"He is, however," Homer said, "a good feller to be in dangerous situations with. What's he fixin' to do, ya 'spose?"

"Arliss tolt me he was in Jeff City talking to the governor or somebody an' one a them court justices."

"Izzat right."

"Yessir," I said. "Seems like he'd been exchangin' telegraphs with the lawyer for the whole country, out in Washington."

"The attorney general?" Homer asked.

"He's the one," I said.

"That's ol' Marion," Homer said, shakin' his head. "He gits the damn bit in his teeth he'd tear through hell in a handcar 'til he found some cold water. You remember how he took off down that slope on foot while we was tanglin' with that Duncan bunch. I swear, when he gits like that, the ol' bastard is bulletproof.

Scares the hell outa me. Ten or twelve year ago, when I was young, he an' me was out in the territory. We come on this little place that'd been burnt out. Near as we could tell, one feller an' his wife an' daughter had been kilt. Wife and daughter had been stripped nekked. Lord knows what had been done to 'em before they got burnt up.

"We tracked five riders for three days afore we come up on 'em in a night camp. We're layin' up on a hill a hunnerd yards away, watchin' the camp, tryin' to figger out how we was gonna handle things, when ol' Marion pipes up. 'Goddam dirty bastards,' he says, 'fuck this shit,' an' jumps on his horse. Afore I can even stand up, he's tears off an' rides direct into the middle of 'em, guns a blazin'. Right outa a damn dime novel!

"When the smoke clears, his coach gun an' Colt are empty, an' five fellers are down, three of 'em dead an' the other two bad wounded. He takes their guns an' such, an' grabs the lead line on the remuda. 'That'll learn 'em,' he says, an' rides off into the dark with their horses. I hung around until both them other fellers died an' set out after him. I caught up around dawn. He never spoke a word to me about it. Still ain't. He's a bad sonofabitch, Rube, an' a helluva feller to have on yer side."

I couldn't think a one thing to say.

"If he intends on straightenin' things out in that town, Rube, I'll be real surprise if he don't git it done. If he wants me to come along, I prob'ly will. It ain't like I'm no smarter than I ever was. I speck he'd take on a grizzly with a willow switch if he figgerd it was the thing to do. He don't think much a most folks, but he thinks some of you, boy. I can tell. When Marion Daniels thinks high of ya, you doan wanna waste it."

*　*　*　*

I spent the night in the jail, got my money outa the bank the next mornin', an' agreed with Homer that, sooner or later, Marion would let us know what was goin' on. I rode out then, an' it come to rain a little. I got in my slicker an' kept on. The rain stopped in the middle a the afternoon, an' I made camp a hour or so before dusk. I was kindly nervous, like. Findin' it hard to settle. I warmed up a can a beans over the fire, an' made coffee. I was just fixin' to eat when Willie let out a nicker. I eased back on my saddle an' put that little shotgun down beside my leg, when come a shout outa the dark.

"Hello the fire!" it said.

"Hello yourself!" I yelled back.

"Smelt yer coffee," come another shout. "They's two of us. Could yew spare a cup or two?"

"Wouldn't deny no man a cup of coffee if I had extra," I said. "C'mon in. Slow."

They did, one of 'em on a little scrub of a horse, the other'n on a mule. In my head, I wondered what Marion would do.

"Bring yer cups," I said.

They come walkin' in on the other side of the fire. They warn't no cowhands nor hayshakers. They moved some like coyotes, kindly slinky, an' was dressed in dirty castoff clothes.

"Evenin'," one of 'em said. "Thank ye kindly fer the coffee. Yew all by yerself out chere?"

"I ain't never needed no comp'ny but my own," I tolt him.

He kindly grinned at me then, an' I couldn't see no teeth.

"Git your coffee an' take a set right there where yer standin'," I said. "I'd appreciate it if'n you boys would keep close together."

"Close together?" he said. "How come yew want us close together?"

I lifted that little stub shotgun up where they could see it.

"'Cause I hate to waste shells," I said. "Either one a you gits froggy, I don't wanna have to use mor'n one barrel to hit the both of ya."

He looked back an' forth between my eyes an' the muzzle a that shotgun a time or two afore he replied to me.

"We'll be goin'," he said, an' then backed off an mounted up. In a minute, from out in the dark, somebody called me a sonofabitch. I trailed 'em on foot for a ways, but they kept on goin'.

CHAPTER FOURTEEN

Maybe it was the fact that it still felt like it was gonna rain. Maybe it was my run-in with them two fellers. Maybe it was not knowin' what Marion had on his mind. Maybe it was that Willie seemed a mite nervous. Maybe it wasn't none a them things, but I didn't rest well that night. I was up some afore dawn. I had enough coals left to warm up half a cup of coffee a little. I et two stale biscuits an' finished that coffee, then saddled up, strung that shotgun on my belt for a change, an' went on. By the time the sun was full up, I had gone a ways past the south side of Chamois an' swung back north a little to pick up the road. Willie was still some full of hisself, fussin' at the bit an' tossin' his head, wastin' energy in a unaccustomed manner.

By the middle a the afternoon I was gittin' purty close to Deer Run when I met a fella an' a young girl, by the sight of her his daughter, headin' east. I sidled off the path to give their buckboard wagon room to pass easy. He tipped his ol' hat an' gimme a thank you. His girl, who looked about twelve or so, smiled at me shy-like, an' they went on their way. Willie turned like he wanted to follow along, but I checked him back an' off we went. We rode on another mile or two an', all of a sudden like, I knowed somethin' was just plumb wrong. I turned Willie around an' he liked to jumped out from under me, tryin' to git on down the way. I give him his head, an' that little horse laid his ears back an' flat run. I'd never turned him loose afore an' he surprised me some, belly down an' a goin' for all he was worth.

We was eatin' up the ground when I heard a pistol shot purty close. Another one came right after. I showed the buckskin the bit an' he slid to a stop. I swung down an' dropped the reins, hittin' the ground at a lope, followin' on toward where them shots come from on foot. Warn't but a minute an' I heard laughin' an' a female's cries an screams. Then I heard a fella yell something like "she's a hellcat ain't she Chet! Grab onto her. Git her!"

I pulled the Schofield, busted through some brush, an' come out behind a wagon. That ol' boy that'd tipped his hat at me was layin' on the ground beside it bleedin', while another fella, about forty feet away was wrestlin' with the girl that had been ridin' on that buckboard. Another fella was out there between me an' them two, laughin' an' yellin' at 'em. So I wouldn't risk hurtin' the girl, I shot him first. The one that was grabbin' on the girl let her loose when he heard my gun go off an' turned toward me, tryin' to git some kinda hogleg outa his belt. I took aim quick an' shot him in the belly. He went over backwards landin' flat an' commenced to scream. I turned to the first feller, thumbin' my hammer back as he was pullin' his gun, an' shot him agin, the bullet takin' him up kindly high on the left side of his chest. He give up on shuckin' his piece an' fell back.

That girl was layin' in the dirt, cryin'. I left her there an' crossed to the feller I'd gut shot. He was wailin' somthin' awful. I pulled his old Colt out his belt, conked him on the head with it to shut him up, an' tossed the gun back toward the wagon. I hustled over to the other one. He'd been hit in the hip an' again up there on his chest. He was lookin' at me an tryin' to say somthin', but he passed out instead. I went to the fella they'd shot. He was bleedin' some from a wound between his right shoulder an' his neck, but not too much. I knelt beside him an' slapped his face a little. His eyes popped open an' he started to struggle. I kindly held him down an' spoke to him.

"Settle down, Mister," I said. "You ain't in no danger. I shot them fellers that hurt ya. I'm gonna go check on the girl now. I believe she's all right. You just lay still." He looked up at me an' relaxed some. I left him then an' went over to where she was layin'.

She was curled up on her side, her dress purty much tore apart, cryin' in the dirt. I leaned down over her, but I didn't touch her.

"Now then, Missy," I said in a low an' quiet voice, "yer all right. Them fellers cain't hurt you no more. Yer daddy, I believe it is, has been shot, but he ain't hurt too bad. Yer safe now, an' so is he. Just lay still for a minute an' I'll git somethin' to cover you up."

Willie had come on up to see what was what, like I knowed he would. I pulled my slicker offa my saddle an' hustled back to where she was an' put it over her, then kindly lifted her up a mite an' wrapped it around her some for modesty an' such. When I done that, she clutched at me an' hung on. I stood up with her, snapped the slicker closed up at her neck, an' walked her over to where her daddy laid. He was full awake an' strugglin' to set up. She fell to her knees beside him an hung onto his good arm. He looked at me an' spoke up.

"Thank you," he said.

I smiled at him. "Yer right welcome, sir," I said. "Them's a pair a wrong fellas."

He laid back down then an' settled.

During the next few minutes I poured water over his wound, front an' back because the round had gone clean in an' out. His collarbone was twisted up some an' his shoulder sat low. I figgerd the bullet broke that collarbone on the way through. I tore up my green shirt an' made a pad of it so the girl had somethin' to hold up agin them holes. I eased him up into the back of their wagon an' stretched him out, an' she clumb up there with him.

"What's yer name, girl," I asked her.

"Martha Ponder," she said.

"Martha, my name is Ruben," I said. "Did them fellers hurt you serious anywhere?"

"Nossir," she said. "They woulda if'n you didn't come along. You moved off the road for us today, didn't ya?"

"Yes, I did," I said.

She started to cry some then. "You just settle in up there an' hold that cloth up agin' yer daddy's wounds," I said. "I'll take care of them bad fellers an' git you an' yer wagon back into Deer Run. Don't you worry none. We'll git yer daddy fixed up. He'll git through this fine. So will you, sweetheart. Rest easy now."

Them boys was ridin' a broke down little horse an' a ragged ol' mule. When I seen that, I was sure they was the two that come beggin' coffee from me the night afore. It took some effort, but I hoisted both of 'em across their mounts, face down, an' tied 'em there. They was both alive when I lifted 'em on an' one of 'em complained some about it. I didn't cry for 'em none. I tied that horse an' the mule to the back of the buckboard, then hitched Willie's reins up around the saddle horn. I knowed he'd follow along. I clumb up on the wagon an' slapped reins on the team. They tried to go, but couldn't. That mule was balked, his legs set against the ground, refusin' to move. I wasn't in no mood for a stubborn damn mule. I got down, walked back to him, an' pulled on the reins. Nossir, he said, I ain't a goin'. I lifted that shotgun up an' thumped him with the barrels, right smart an' between his eyes. I got back up on the buckboard an' slapped reins agin. Off we went, purty as you please, that mule comin' along like a family dog.

* * * *

It took over a hour to git to town. By the time we got down the main street, around the corner a block or two from the Houston House, an' down to the doctor's office, we had quite a herd a folks taggin' along. Two bluevests were in the pack. One of 'em was Clarence Banks.

"What's goin' on here, Mister Beeler?" he said.

"Them two fellers on the mule an' the horse shot this feller in the wagon an' was fixin' to use his daughter, Martha," I said. "I stopped 'em. They was both alive when I tied 'em on. I don't know what shape they're in now."

A voice from the crowd spoke up. "They're dead," it said.

"You shoot these men, Mister Beeler?" Clarence asked.

"Yes, I did, Clarence, an' I wish you'd call me Ruben," I said. "After all we been through together, you oughta use my first name."

I stood up in the buckboard an' looked at the crowd. "A couple a you fellers ketch aholt a this man in the wagon an' git him toted into the doctor's office. Be nice if one a you ladies was to help his daughter out. She's been knocked around some an' could use a woman's touch an' comfort."

The crowd kindly surged forward then an' got to it. I jumped down an' walked out into the street to where Willie was standin' an' collected him. Clarence followed along.

"Mister Beeler...uh, Ruben," he said, "the Sheriff is gonna

want to see you about this."

"Clarence," I said, "you tell Arberry if he wants to talk about anything, I'll either be at the gunsmith's place or in the Sweetwater. I've had a hard day. If'n Arberry wants to talk he can, by God, come to me. You can also tell the Doc that I'll stand good for this fella's bill, an' the lady at the dress shop that I'll pay for the girl to git a couple a new dresses. As for the undertaker, he's on his own with these two pieces a shit."

I clumb up on Willie then, an' rode down to Arliss' place. He was standin' out front watchin' me come.

"Welcome back," he said. "What's all the fuss about?"

"Not much," I said. "I just saved a fella from dyin', his daughter from bein' raped an' kilt, an' shot two fellas to death this afternoon. You buy supper an' I'll tell you the whole heroic story."

"You wanna go back to the Crystal?" he asked.

"Aw, hell," I said.

"You go clean up a little," Arliss said. "I'll take your horse down to the livery for ya an' meet you at the Sweetwater."

I thanked him an' walked to Miz Clary's.

*   *   *   *

Didn't take me long to wash my face an' change shirts. I left the shotgun behind but kept the Schofield an' walked on down to the Sweetwater. There was several folks inside when I got there, an' a few nodded at me when I come in. I nodded back an' took a seat back from the window a ways. I hadden more than set, when here come Margie, big ol' grin on her face, near skippin' in my direction.

"Ruben!" she said, like she hadn't seen me in a year, "folks in here sayin' yer a hero!"

"Me an' Bill Cody is about the best there is, I guess," I said.

"Don't be like that," she said. "They claim you saved a family from a bunch a outlaws!"

"I cain't help what folks say," I said. "Wasn't much to it, at least not near as much as there will be a couple a days from now, the way people talk."

Arliss showed up then, an' set.

Margie smiled at him. "Arliss," she said, "I guess you know yer settin' with a hero."

"Shore I do," Arliss said. "He's a rare one, no doubt about that. A privilege just to be in the same room with the boy. I wanna be just like him when I grow up."

Margie appeared to be some confused. "We got some good roast beef tonight," she said, lookin' for familiar ground. "It comes with taters an' carrots."

"That'll do for both of us," Arliss said. "Me an' the hero here thank ya."

She skittered away an' I looked at Arliss.

"You havin' fun?" I asked.

"I'm havin' a great time," he said. "How 'bout you?"

I couldn't help it. I laughed. "Goddammit, Arliss," I said.

"You ain't fixin' to draw down on me are ya?" he said.

I purty much fell in the well then. It took a minute for me to settle down.

About the time I got a grip, High Sheriff Arberry Yont showed up an' strutted over to the table.

"Ruben!" he said, "are you doin' all right?"

"Arberry!" I said, "I am. Thanks for askin'."

"I hear you had a helluva day, son."

"Yessir," I said. "I did. And I'm plumb tired to be honest with ya."

"Are you fit enough to tell me what happened?" he asked.

I give him a short version. When I finished, he kindly puffed up.

"That goes along with what that poor little girl told me," he said. "I don't think it'll be necessary to have a formal hearing on charges against you or anything like that."

When he said what he said, my ruff come up an' I got some mouthy. "Ya damn right there won't," I said. "Everthing that happened was in the county. You ain't got no authority out there. You're the city law, Sheriff, an' that's where it ends."

Arberry flinched a little when I come at him like that. "Now hold on," he said. "Yer settin' in my town. My town, my rules. You need to remember that, son."

"You'll have to excuse me, Sheriff," I said. "I've had a hard day. But you need to understand somethin'. I know who my daddy was, an' you ain't him. An' unless you can show me a deed, this town don't belong to you no more than it does to anybody else."

"I will excuse you this time, Mister Beeler," he said, "but this time only. And you need to understand that."

"Thank you, Sheriff," I said. "I always appreciate a good threat. I'm in Deer Run an' I will play by the rules an' not give you no trouble, 'cause that's what I want to do. But as long as both of us is bein' so understandin', understand that the Duncan gang over by Gasconade didn't scare me much when we took them down. Damn near nothin' else does neither, sir."

That stopped Yont for a minute, then he opened his mouth agin.

"You got sand, Ruben, I shore do give you that. I'm always lookin' for good men with sand. Would you ever consider being a city deputy?"

"That's a right kind offer," I said, knowin' I should just shut up, "but I never liked wearin' a vest. Green is more my color anyway."

"Suit yourself, son," he said, an' thumped out.

Arliss looked at me. "I don't believe you made a new friend here tonight," he said.

"I doan speck I did neither," I said.

"Ruben, what the hell is the matter with you?"

"I'm hungry," I said.

"That's a relief," Arliss said. "For a minute there, I thought you might just be stupid."

CHAPTER FIFTEEN

It took me a while to settle down that night, but when I did, I slept hard. I plumb missed daybreak the next mornin'. When I come down from my room, Miz Clary was in the kitchen. She got my attention when I walked by.

"Mister Beeler," she said to me, "you c'mon in here now and set yerself."

I hadn't mentioned I was gonna want no breakfast or nothin'. It was a house rule you had to give her advance notice on meals. I set down at that little table she kept in the kitchen, an' she put a cup a coffee in front a me along with a little pitcher a pale yella cream an' a sugar bowl.

"Thank ya, M'am," I said. "This here's right nice."

"Yer a little late for breakfast, Mister Beeler," she said, "but I saved back a couple a biscuits that'll still be good. There's some bacon fried that I can heat in the skillet for ya. How do ya like your eggs?"

"Well, M'am, I didn't give you no notice on breakfast or nothin'," I said.

"That don't make no difference this mornin'," she said. "Fried sunny side up all right with you?"

"Yes, M'am. That there would be just right," I said.

"A man that does what you done for that father an' his poor child yesterday deserves a good meal after a long night's sleep. You saved them folks from them heathens. That was God's work, Mister Beeler, God's work. And you done it. The least I can do in the face a all that is feed you a good solid breakfast. Truth be spoken, I'm a little drawn to you. My boy Archie woulda been about your age if he'd have lived."

She turned her back on me then, an' got to shakin' her head some while she fussed over the stove. It come to me that she was cryin' a mite, an' my chest got kindly heavy at the thought of it. Them eggs was poppin' in the skillet when I spoke up.

"Miz Clary," I said, "I don't have no memory of my momma. Even though I never really knowed her, sometimes I have felt like I kindly miss her. I would be right pleased if you would call me Ruben, M'am."

It was another minute or two 'til she set that plate a biscuits, bacon, an' eggs in front of me. She put it down an' stepped behind me toward the door.

"You eat up now," she said, "an' clean your plate. I'm real proud of ya, Ruben."

She left then, an' I could hear her goin' toward the back a the house. I cleaned my plate, but I wondered how a fella could feel so full an' so empty at the same time.

*   *   *   *

After I et, I struck off down to Arliss' place. It was only two or three blocks, but on that walk several fellas spoke to me an' tipped their hats. One ol' boy come up an' had to shake hands with me. Not only that, but a couple a real ladies nodded to me. One even throwed a "God bless you" my way. When I passed by the drygoods store, the fella there come outside and stopped me.

"Mister Beeler," he said, "the town is grateful to you for what you did for that man and his daughter. It took courage. You are a valuable and valued member of the community. I would like to shake your hand."

I shook with him an' thanked him for his words.

"Son," he said, "anything you might need from my store today is twenty, no, make that thirty percent off."

"Thank you, sir," I said. "I'll take you up on that offer. I had to cut up that green shirt I bought from you folks so that girl could hold the cloth on her daddy's bullet holes."

"I recall the shirt and your size," he said. "I'll pull one out for you. You like pale yellow?"

"Yessir," I said. "Just fine."

"I'll get you one in that color too, no charge. You can pick them up later in the day."

"That's awful nice of you," I said.

"You deserve it," he said, an' went back in the store.

*　*　*　*

Arliss was at his bench, takin' the grips offa Colt when I went in his place.

"Sleep in, did ya?" he asked.

"I did," I said. "Then Miz Clary gimme a breakfast of bacon an' eggs, an' biscuits. Said I put her in mind of her son. He died for some reason."

Arliss smiled as he took out a little spring with some tweezers.

"Several times when I was walkin' over here folks paid some attention to me," I said. "The man at the drygoods store gimme a shirt to replace the one I had to cut up, an' another one, too."

"That make you feel good?" Arliss asked me.

I tolt him that it did, an' then agin, it didn't.

His smile come back an' he nodded some. "Appreciation can be nice," he said. "Recognition can get a little worrisome. It'll pass, Rube. You ain't the kind a feller that covets fame."

I wasn't too sure what he meant, but it was good to know that he had a handle on things. I hung around for a while, watchin' him pick at that Colt, then figgerd I'd go to the bank with my money when this lady come in. She said her name, but I disremember what it was. She brung me a apple pie. To the best a my memory, I'd never even see'd her afore, but she still brung that pie. She said she'd come back in a couple a days to git the pan, an' left.

It set me sideways a little bit that she done that, but Arliss just said somethin' about folks appreciatin' what I done. Then he took his Barlow knife an' cut hisself out a few bites an' carried the rest a that pie in the back. I went on to the bank an' opened up me a account. Them folks there went on about what I done an'all some. I got out as quick as I could. When I got back to Arliss' shop, I had four big ol' cinnamon rolls waitin' on me, an' a tall white cake. Arliss allowed as how, if things kept up the way they was, we could open a sweet shop an' git rich.

I asked to borrow his wagon to go git some cedar planks an' he agreed. Just as I was fixin' to head for the livery, damn if Arberry Yont didn't walk in the place.

He nodded at Arliss an' spoke to me. "Mister Beeler," he said, "could you spare me a moment of your time?"

"Yessir," I said. "A course I can, Sheriff. What can I do for ya?"

"Mister Beeler," he said, "I don't care for the way you and me left things last evening. You had a day that would have knocked the stuffin' outa almost anybody. And I came at ya like a bull instead a takin' into account everthing that you'd been through. The plain truth is, you did this world a service, and I didn't give that the respect it deserved. Instead, you and me both, I believe, said some things we probably should not have said and behaved in a manner that we regret. At least I do. I came to exchange apologies with you if you can see your way clear to do that."

"Sheriff," I said, "I shot two men yesterday an' I am afraid I took some a my bad feelin's about that out on you. I shouldn't a done that. As far as I am concerned, if we had a hatchet, I'd help ya bury the durn thing."

Yont actually smiled an' stuck out his hand. I shook with him.

"They was one thing that I said to you last evening that I will not take back," he said. "I told you I thought that you had sand, Mister Beeler. My mind ain't changed on that one bit."

"Much obliged," I said. "Comin' from you, I consider that to be quite a compliment."

He looked at the baked goods on the counter. "Don't you boys founder on that cake and get cast in your stall," he said, an' went out the door.

I looked at Arliss. "Butthole," he said.

"Wonder what made him do that?" I asked.

"You're popular right now, boy," Arliss said. "Word has no doubt got around how he come at you in the Sweetwater, an' how you didn't back down. Made him look bad. He's tryin' to fix that. If you an' him can git along, he'll look better."

"Still, it kindly surprised me for him to come in here an' say what he said."

Arliss grinned. "You and him gonna be goin' on long walks in the evenin' now?" he asked me.

"Aw hell, Arliss!"

"He ain't got no use for ya, Rube," he said. "He'd just as soon backshoot ya as look at ya. He just don't want public opinion turnin' against him. He's a little scared of ya, boy. And he don't like that one little bit. If ya was to disappear, it would suit him just fine."

I looked out the winda an' seen a lady comin' at us from across the way, carryin' a covered dish.

"Disappear is right," I said, an' headed for the rear of the place. "I'll see ya later, Arliss," I tolt him, an' ducked out the back door.

*   *   *   *

When I got to the livery, Miss Harmony had Willie cross-tied an' was brushin' him out.

"I had a feeling you'd be here this morning," she said. "Willie will be done in just a minute. I already picked his feet. He's got some kind of bug bite on his withers, but it doesn't seem to vex him."

"Thank you, Miss Harmony," I said, "but you shore didn't have to do that."

She give him a quick brush on the pastern an' looked at me. "You're right," she said. "Maybe I should have just brought you some fried chicken or fudge."

I grinned at that. "Lord, no," I said. "I already got a pie, a cake, an' some sweetrolls."

"There will be more," she said. "Maybe even a couple of invitations to dinner. That's how ladies show their appreciation, you know. You're young, you're not bad looking, you're single, and you're a hero. You're fair game now, Mister Beeler."

I didn't know what to say, so I tossed the blanket up on Willie's back. Miss Harmony stepped back an' watched. I had the cinch tight an' was givin' him the bit before she said anything else.

"Doing what you did to help those people," she said, "was a brave and selfless thing, Ruben. You may be the man I hope you are." She showed me her back an' left.

I stood there, fixin' to think about what she said, but Willie tossed his head an' started nosin' me for a piece a carrot. Just as well, I reckon. Sometimes, thinkin' just gits the water muddy.

CHAPTER SIXTEEN

I made myself scarce until late in the day. When I left Willie at the livery, warn't nobody around. On the way back to Arliss' shop, I stopped by the Doc's office. He had gone somewhere, but the fella that got shot an' his little girl was there. He was propped up on a cot in a back room an' she was settin' with him.

"Why hello, Martha," I said to her. "That shore is a purty new dress yer wearin'."

"Thank you," she said, just ketchin' my eye for a second, then lookin' mostly at her daddy. "The man at the drygoods place give it to me. They's another one, too."

"Warn't that nice of him?"

"Yessir," she said. "He give me a shirt for daddy, too, 'cause his other one got ruint."

"An' you, Mister Ponder," I said. "Yer doin' some better, I speck."

"I truly am, sir," he said. "Me an' Martha owe you a real debt of gratitude. I don't believe either one of us woulda made it if you wasn't there."

"That debt'll be paid in full when you git well an' you an' Martha strike off to where you was goin'," I said. "You eatin' good an' everthing?"

"The folks from over in the café send us meals. Won't accept no payment."

"I expect that lettin' somebody do for ya when you really need it is payment enough for 'em," I said. "It don't take much to feed a good heart. Yer team an' buckboard in good hands, are they?"

"Somebody has 'em at the edge of town. The doc set that up."

"Good," I said. "Is there anythin' I can do for ya?"

"You have done more for us than anybody could ever expect," he said. "Martha and me both thank you."

"I'll stop by tomorrow an' check on ya," I said. "You git yer rest. Martha, you get yer rest too."

"That lady from the roomin' house said she'd come over this evenin' and collect me," the girl said. "She's gonna feed me an' has a pallet for me tonight."

"Miz Clary is a fine woman," I said. "She'll be good to ya."

I left then. When I got outside I had to stop a minute an' kindly ketch my breath.

The next mornin' I took Arliss' wagon an' picked up a load a rough cut cedar boards for the inside a that shed. On the way back, I stopped by the hardware place to git few pounds a nails. The ol' boy that had the place was a little fella with carrot hair name a Jeter. He was a jerky kinda guy, an' he talked real sudden. I had trouble not grinnin' at him all the time. The way his words chased each other around, listenin' to him could wear a fella out right quick.

"Mister Beeler," he said when I walked in, "folks is makin' a fuss over you right now, ain't they? I bet they shore is, ain't they, Mister Beeler? Ain't folks makin' a fuss over you?"

"Some, Mister Jeter," I said.

"And why wouldn't they, why wouldn't they after you done what you done. Why wouldn't they? Sure they would, they surely would you doin' what you done and all. What can I do for you this mornin', Mister Beeler? Is there anything can I do?"

"I need about five pounds of finish nails, five pounds a number six commons, an' some winda glass if you got any."

"You are fixin' to build somethin', aintcha?" he said. "Whatcha fixin' to build, Mister Beeler? Is they somethin' you're fixin' to build?"

"The fella that's openin' that gunsmith place has offered to let me live in that shed he's got, if I care to. I thought I might finish the inside in cedar."

"Cedar would work real good for that," Jeter said. "That'd be fine with some cedar. Cedar would just be real good. You gonna put some windows in it are ya? You'll need some windows for light and ventilation. Windows would be real good too, yessir. Good to have windows in a place."

"It is," I said. "That there is my intention."

"Well then, Mister Beeler," he said. "I got somethin' you might be interested in. You might be interested in somethin' I got. They're right outside in the back. If you care to come out back, they're right outside."

I followed him out the back of the store to a little storage building. He key'd the lock an' opened the door.

"They're leanin' up against the back wall there," he said. "They are right there in the back leanin' up against that wall. You look 'em over an' let me know. You just let me know after you look 'em over."

He darted back into the store an' left me there, feelin' like I needed to set myself down for a minute. In the back a that shed was three double-hung windas, complete with pulleys an' weights to keep the bottom sash where you put it. They was in purty good shape, too. The bottom panes was clear an' not too wavy lookin'. The top panes had about a six-inch strip a stained glass along the upper edge in little cut an' fitted squares of green an' yella, an' brown, all leaded together like they was in a church or somethin'. I was tickled. It would save me hours a labor to have them windas, an' light comin' through that colored glass would be right handsome.

I carried 'em outside, wiped some a the cobwebs an' dust offa 'em, an' looked 'em over. I believe the frames was made outa maple. Put a little soap on them slides, re-hang the weights on fresh rope, clean up them brass latches, an' a fella would have windas to be proud of. I went back inside to face Mister Jeter agin'.

"Did you look 'em over? Look 'em over, did you?" he said.

"They ain't bad," I said. "How much you gotta have for 'em?"

"I don't know how much they're worth. Don't know if they're worth much," he said. "They was here when I took over the place, right out there in that shed. Yessir. They was right out there in the shed when I took this place over. Make me a offer, Mister Beeler. I'd like a offer if you'd care to make one. Could you make one?"

Lord. I couldn't build nothin' like that if I wanted to. I tossed him a offer so low, it drug in the dirt.

"Two dollars each," I said.

His eyebrows durn near flew up into his hair. "Two dollars!" he said. "I don't know about two dollars. Two dollars don't seem like hardly enough. That just ain't hardly enough, is it? Two dollars? Two dollars is awful low, awful low. Would you go four? Would you care to give four apiece for them windows?"

"I could go three," I tolt him.

"Three?" he said. Three. Three's better than two. Yessir, no doubt about that. Three is better than two. Would you go ten dollars for all three of 'em? Whatdaya think? Ten dollars for all three of them windows? Could you go ten? Could so see your way to do that? Go ten?"

"Ten it is," I said.

"Then we got us a deal, Mister Beeler," he said. "Yessir, a deal is what we got. Ten dollars for all three of them windows, all three of them windows for ten dollars. Ten dollars it is, yessir. Ten dollars."

I got my nails an' laid them windas in the wagon on top a that cedar, paid Mister Jeter, an' headed back to Arliss' place. I kindly felt like I needed a nap.

* * * *

By afternoon two days later I had three walls covered in that shed. I like workin' with cedar. It's light in weight, saws good, an' smells nice. It also throws splinters somethin' fierce. Most times I didn't wear no gloves when I did rough work 'cause they slowed me down, but not as much as pullin' splinters outa my hands. It was hot, an' I was sweatin' some. Time was passin' unnoticed like it usually done when I was workin' on somethin'. I was deep into what I was doin' when a voice come at me.

"Hey there, pistolero," it said.

I turned around and there stood about six an a half feet of Marion Daniels, a smile lurkin' under that mustache a his.

"Howdy, Marshal," I said, pullin' off a glove and acceptin' his hand. "Good to see ya. You all right?"

"I'm still able to kick a clod outa my way," he said. "From what Arliss has been tellin' me, you ain't doin' too bad, neither."

"I'm able to be up an' take nourishment," I said, grinnin' at him.

"I left my shotgun with Arliss to give me a excuse for comin' by," he said. "I cain't talk with you much here. I'm camped out where I was before. I speck to see you an' Arliss out there tonight after dark."

"We'll be there," I said.

"Ya done good, Ruben," he said, an' walked away toward the front a Arliss' shop.

I give him a minute to git gone, then I went in through the back.

"Tonight after dark, huh?" Arliss said.

"I know the place," I tolt him.

"I gotta git me a ridin' horse," he said. 'Willie might get overly concerned with the two of us on him. They got anything for sale over at the livery, you think?"

"I doan know," I said to him.

"Maybe I'll hike over there," he said. "I imagine they've gone through what I give 'em to board my mules. You wanna come with me?"

"I could do that," I said.

Arliss smiled at me. "Sure you could, Rube," he said. "Be a fool not to."

* * * *

Verlon Clarke was workin' on the forge when we got there, an' Harmony was pumpin' the bellows for him. She had a dirty face an' some hair stuck in sweat on her forehead. I kindly liked the look of it. It come to me that if Miss Margie had sweat an' dirt on her face, she'd a run rather than let me see her that way.

"Hello, boys," Verlon said. "What are the two of you up to today?"

"I come by to give you some money for boardin' my mules," Arliss said, "and to see if you have any ridin' stock for sale."

"I got one mare I could let go," Verlon said. "She's twelve or so, ain't no spring chicken. Big gal, sixteen hands. Stout, too. She's black with a offside rear white foot. Got a nice way about her, good natured as long as you leave her tail alone, well broke and willin'. She's in the west pasture if you wanna take a peek at her."

"I do," Arliss said, an' the two a them wandered off.

Miss Harmony wiped her face on her sleeve an' looked at me. "I put some sweet tea in the springhouse last night, Ruben," she said. "Would you care for a cool drink?"

"I would, Miss Harmony," I said. "Thank you."

"You go sit up on the porch," she said. "I'll be up there in a minute."

It was some more than a minute, but purty soon she come out the front door, handed me a short glass of tea, an' set at the other end of the swing. I took a sip.

"That's real good, Miss Harmony," I said. "I appreciate it."

It was some cooler up on the porch than down in the forge, an' a couple a big ol' oak trees shaded the front of the house good. The wind was up a little an' it was right nice settin' there.

"I noticed you working at that shed behind Mister Hyatt's place yesterday," Miss Harmony said.

"Arliss told me I could have the place to live in if I cared to fix it up. I'm doin' the inside in cedar. I got some windas for it the other day that got stained glass trim along the tops."

"That sounds nice," she said.

"A course it ain't very big an' just one room an' all. Ain't gonna be like no real house, but it'll be plenty good for me when I'm done with it."

"It will be like part of a real house, won't it?" she said.

I studied on that for a minute. "Why, yes it will, I guess," I said.

She smiled at me then. "Ruben," she said, "if you decided to walk from here to the ocean, what would you do?"

"Well, I doan rightly know," I said, "I'd have to git me some supplies an' such, I reckon."

"You're not thinking about it in the right way," she said. "Right this minute, you are going to start that journey. What do you do?"

"Commence to walkin', I guess," I said.

"And how do you do that?" she asked me.

"Well, ya just walk, Miss Harmony," I said. "Put one foot in front of the other an' step off."

"That's right," she said. "How many steps can you take at a time?"

"Well, that's kindly foolish," I said. "A fella can only take one step at a time."

"Right again," she said, smilin' at me some more. "Just one step at a time."

I thought on what she said, an' then it kindly come on me what she meant. I shook my head an' grinned at her. "I see," I said.

"More than you think you do, Ruben," she said. "They'll bring the mare up in a minute. Why don't you and I take some steps down to the barn."

* * * *

Arliss bought that mare. She was some bigger than Willie, an' wide across the withers. He figured his saddle wouldn't fit her too good. Verlon had a saddle that come with her, an' he an' Alriss did a even-Steven trade. She was a likely mare, set up good, not too long in the back like some big horses git. She held her weight good an' seemed sound of legs an' feet. That evenin' he an' me et a late supper at the Sweetwater, watched Miss Margie show off, an' headed out to find Marshal Daniels.

CHAPTER SEVENTEEN

On the ride out Arliss, like he done from time to time, got a little mouthy.

"You an' Miss Harmony have a nice visit up at the house, did ya?" he said to me.

"We jawed some drinkin' sweet tea from the springhouse," I said.

"Uh-huh," Arliss grunted. "Pretty nice gal, doncha think?"

"She's all right enough," I said.

"Feels a little bit more, uh, substantial than Miss Margie, would you say?"

"She's a nice girl," I said.

"You and her git along fair, don't ya?"

"Dammit, Arliss," I said to him, "quit pickin' at me."

"I ain't 'zactly pickin' at ya, boy, as much as I'm concerned about ya."

"Why don't you concern yerself about keepin' a seat on that new horse," I said. "Tall as that mare is, if you fall off, you could hurt yourself."

He shut up for a little bit, but only a little bit.

"That Harmony gal," he said in a minute, "seems right settled for a woman a her age. How old is she, ya think?"

Lord. That ol' man just wouldn't let nothin' go. "I don't know how old she is, Arliss," I said. "How the hell would I?"

"You could ask her," he said.

"Oh, hell," I said. "Arliss, I ain't gonna ask her how old she is. It ain't none a my business."

"Could be," he said.

I didn't answer him back or nothin' an' he shut up for about a minute. Then he started in on me agin.

"Bet if you was workin' on somethin' and needed help, she'd be out there holdin' onto the end of a board for ya," he said.

"She might," I said.

"Bet that Margie gal wouldn't. She got a spinter or somthin', she take to the bed for a week."

"Arliss," I said, "she's a sweet little gal an' terrible purty too, but I ain't got no interest in Margie."

"I know it," he said.

"Then how come you keep on a bringin' her up?"

"Just makin comparisons, that's all," he said. "If a fella is lookin' for a horse an' there's two in the damn pen, he's well advised to study on both of 'em for he shakes a loop out for either one of 'em."

"I ain't lookin'," I said. "I ain't shakin' out no loop, I ain't in the market fer nothin'."

"Hell you ain't," he said. "Yer a man, aintcha?"

"I piss standin' up," I said.

"Then yer lookin'!" he said. "I ain't talking about homesteadin' and growin' up a passel a young'uns. I'm just talkin' about lookin'!"

"Hard not to look," I confessed.

"She's lookin' too, boy. She ain't got no loop shook out neither, but she's is damn sure leanin' agin the fence. She sees more in you than you see in yerself, Rube. So do I. So does Marion. You'll ketch up to the rest of us, eventually. Meantime, when she sets her cap for ya, don't git all rattled and jump the damn gate."

"Mary an' Joseph, Arliss!" I said, "you are gittin' to wear on me some."

"That gal is solid, boy. She's solid and she's patient. Just keep that in mind."

He never said another word to me on the whole rest a the ride. If I was to tell the truth, I might say I missed his mouth. A little.

*   *   *   *

When we come on Marion's camp, Arliss announced us. We went on in an' set. There was coffee on his little fire.

"You boys et?" Marion asked.

I allowed as we had, an' he went on.

"Here's the deal," Marion said. "I got to telegraphin' Charlie Devens. He's the Attorney General. He set it up with a bunch of Army riders, an' I met one a them boys up by Saint Louis, an' sent him a dispatch with everthing I thought he needed to know about what was goin' on out thisaway. Boys, they was riders spaced out plumb across the country hustlin' that paperwork from railine to railine. I got a telegraph back in Saint Louis that they took the matter up an' sent some dispatches an' telegraphs out to Jeff City to Governor Smith an' Henry Brockmeyer, the Lieutenant Governor. They give me orders to git back out here. I hit Jeff City about four days ago. Them ol' boys is worried some about this Arberry Yont feller. Part of it is because a what he's doin' out here, an' part of it is to protect theyselves in case he gits hisself involved in state politics. They don't want some ol' boy with lotsa cash tryin' to join in their fun."

124

He stopped for a minute an' freshed his coffee.

"Phelps and Brockmeyer," Marion said, "went to the Missouri Court an' jawed about the mess with Elijah Norton. Him an' a couple a other judges, John Ward Henry an' Tom Sherwood, got together with Henry Brockmeyer an' come up with what they call a special dispensation of lawful authority. There's all kinds of legal foofarah around it, but what it means is, they is organizin' what they call a special executive for police action within the State of Missouri. I am still a U.S. Marshal, but I have been vested with indeterminate leave from the Marshal Service to be in charge of that special executive for police action for the state. Now what that means is, I am, by whatever necessary and reasonable means, charged to run Arberry Yont an' his bunch off."

"Damn," I said.

"Ruben," he said, "that don't mean I gonna git fifty men an' chase that sumbitch out to the Arizona Territory or nothin'. What it does mean is authorized legal power, as a officer of the State Court of Missouri, to take action against him. This is all sort of secret. Very soon I will be the head officer in what they call the Missouri State Special Police Service. This is a temporary organization. The state don't have near enough money to build a whole police force. They don't want one, anyway. They also don't want the can a worms around the political shit-storm that would come with tryin' to organize one. I'll have a state police commission. So will you, Ruben, so will Homer Poteet, who has agreed to join in our little game, an' so will Arliss, here, if he decides he want's one."

"I ain't no gunslinger," Arliss said, "but sign me up."

"The object here is to avoid a pitched battle anyway," Marion said. "You boys'll git commissions, an' badges too, but you won't wear 'em. At least not yet. You'll also git paid a decent wage. Fifty a month for no more than six months. If we don't git it done by then, the whole thing is quits. So now, what we havta do is figger out a way to, without hittin' him with a brick, make Yont get outa hand. We need to piss his ass off. You fellers think about that some while I git back over to Jeff City. I should be back in a week or ten days. We are also gonna need some way to account for Homer showin' up an' bein here. He oughta git over this way in a week or less. I don't need no reason for anything. I'm a goddam marshal. I go where I damn well please. Plus, Arliss an' me is old friends. I can hang around his place for that reason if I care to. You boys put your heads together. I'll see you in a few days with your commissions. Now, go home. I am terrible tired."

*   *   *   *

Arliss an' me didn't say much on the way back to town. We rode down past by his place and I spoke up.

"Why don't you go on, Arliss," I said. "I'll take your mare back to the livery for ya."

"Thank ya, Rube. Right nice of you."

I grinned at him. "My daddy always told me to be kind to old folks," I said, an' reined Willie away. I could hear Arliss chuckle as I rode off.

*   *   *   *

When I got to the livery, there was a light burnin' in the barn. I led the horses in an' there, settin' by the light of a oil lamp, wearin' boots, what I can only believe was her night clothes, an' holdin' a book in her hand, was Miss Harmony.

"Well, what in the world are you doin' up out here this time a night?" I said.

She smiled. "Ruben Beeler," she said, "you don't tell me when to put the lamp out."

126

"I reckon I don't," I said, an' flipped a stirrup up over the horn. She stepped up and started to git the saddle off the mare. "You just wait up to help me loose these horses?" I asked.

"I'm curious," she said. "You and Arliss are up to something. What is it?"

"Up to somethin'?" I said. "What makes you think we're up to somethin'?"

Miss Harmony shook her head and locked eyes with me.

"Ruben," she said, "I can see straight through you. You and Arliss weren't out hunting 'coons tonight. What's going on?"

"Yer Daddy gonna be around in the mornin'?"

"He usually is," she said.

"I'm gonna need to talk to him a little."

"About what?" she asked, liftin' the mare's saddle over a rail. She was stout.

"About takin' on a hired man," I said. "One that don't want no wages."

She turned the mare out an' looked at me agin.

"Are you going to tell me what all this is about?" she asked.

"Maybe," I said, "soon as I figger out if I can trust ya."

That made her laugh, then she turned serious. "Everything is all right though, isn't it?"

"Yes, it is, Miss Harmony," I said. "And with a little luck, things'll soon be some better."

"All right," she said. "That's enough for now, but I will get the truth out of you, Ruben."

"I don't think there's much doubt about that," I said, as I watched her pick up that lamp an' walk off toward the house. Her walkin' away, holdin that lamp in front of her in the dark, was somethin' to see. I knowed right then that I'd never forget the sight of it.

* * * *

I was out to the livery at about eight the next mornin'. Verlon was workin' on the edge of a big ol' hinge with a heavy file.

"Mornin', Rube," he said. "Harmony told me you'd be out to see me. What can I do for ya?"

"Mister Clarke," I said, "I got a unusual request. There's a fella comin' to town soon name of Homer Poteet, although he may not use that name."

"If he's tryin' to hide, he better not," Verlon said. "I have heard that name before."

"Yessir," I said, "I don't doubt that. Homer will need a place to work. This would be a good place. He probably won't be much help to ya, but you won't have to pay him nothin' either. Homer is a friend of mine an' part of a very small law force called the Missouri Special State Police. He an' me, an' U.S. Marshal Marion Daniels, an Arliss Hyatt are all commissioned by the Missouri State Court an' the Governor as members of that police force."

"I'll be damned, Ruben," he said. "You was with Daniels an' Poteet when that bunch got took down over by Gasconade, wasn't ya?"

"Yessir, I was," I said.

"You boys is here after Yont too, ain'tcha?"

"Yessir, we are," I said.

"Hell, son, I'll do anythin' I can to help out. Count on me."

"Thank you sir," I said. "I appreciate that."

"An' I won't say nothin' to anybody," he said. "Not one soul."

"I knowed ya wouldn't," I said, "or I never woulda tolt ya. I know Harmony won't neither, will ya, Miss Harmony?"

"Not a word from me," she said, poppin' up over the edge of the loft.

"Harmony, dammit!" Verlon said, an' I started in laughin'.

Harmony come down the ladder an' grinned at us.

"Let this be a lesson to ya, Rube," Verlon said. "Women are a sneaky breed."

"I'm going to hitch the team and go get some feed," Harmony said. "Give you a ride back if you want."

"Why, thank ya, Miss Harmony," I said. "Ain't you nice."

*   *   *   *

I helped her hitch the team an' rode to the feed store an' helped her load them bags. On the way to Arliss' place she looked at me an' smiled.

"Not exactly a buggy in the moonlight is it?" I said.

"This will do for now," she said.

She reined them horses in front of Arliss' place an' I jumped down.

"We'll have our time for buggies and moonlight, Ruben," she said. "Don't you get scared and run off, now."

I walked in the shop an' Arliss studied on me like I had a dirty face.

"Oh Lord," he said. "Like a 'possum in a bear trap."

CHAPTER EIGHTEEN

When I went over to the doctor's office after breakfast the next morning, I found Mister Ponder settin' outside on the boardwalk in a rockin' chair. He looked some feeble an' pale.

"You appear to me," I said, "like you are about ready to go fishin'!"

He smiled real big and nodded. "Let's go tonight," he said. "I love catfishin' of a night."

"Seems like yer doin' fine," I tolt him.

"Doc says that I can maybe go home in two or three weeks," he said. "Martha can handle the team all right. All she'll have to do is try to keep 'em awake."

"Where is Martha?" I asked.

"She ain't come back from the boardin' house yet. She'll be along purty soon, Miz Clary with her, bringin' me breakfast on a tray."

"Looks to me like you got the bull by the nose ring," I said. "Settin' out here in the sun, waitin' for somebody to bring your vittles to ya. That'd be a hard habit to break. Maybe you oughta consider a relapse."

"I'm spoiled rotten, no doubt about that. Everbody has been real good to us, Mister Beeler. Everbody has been just fine."

"You an' Martha earned it the hard way, Mister Ponder," I said. "You two deserve it. It's a gift to see you gittin' better. You say hello to Martha for me. I'll see ya afore you give all this up an' go."

*　*　*　*

I walked on over to Arliss' place an' found him jawin' with the bluevest, Clarence Banks. They was lookin' at a old Henry rifle with a broke stock helt together with wood screws.

"It was my daddy's," Clarence was sayin'. "It works fine, but I'd just like to have it fixed if it can be done."

"Can it be done, Rube?" Arliss asked.

I said hello to Clarence an' looked at the gun. "Well, it can be done," I said, "but I don't know if I can do it. I ain't never done anything like makin' a gunstock."

While I was talkin', Arliss fussed with it an' took the stock off. I looked at it for a minute, then turned to Clarence. "Can you leave it for a while?" I asked him.

"Yessir," he said. "It ain't been shot or even loaded in years."

"I got some other stuff I gotta do that'll take some time, but I should be able to get to it in two or three weeks. I cain't make ya no promises I can make new stock though."

"You damn sure can't hurt it none," Clarence said.

"All right," I said. "I'll take a try at it. How long you been a deputy, Clarence?"

"Be four years this October," he said. "I got hired on right after Arberry won the election."

"He's elected? I didn't know that. I thought he was just hired."

"No," Clarence said. "He got elected near six years ago, an' re-elected four years ago this September.' An' agin two years ago this September."

131

"The elections are in September?"

"Third Thursday of the month, ever two years," Clarence said. "Got the Fourth of July comin' up before very long. We'll be closin' down two blocks of the main street. Have bingo an' cakewalks. Box dinner an' supper auctions, big cookout, games for the kids, shootin' contests an' the like. All kinds of things. Oughta be a time."

"Sounds like it," Arliss said. "Lookin' forward to it."

"Thanks fellers," Clarence said. "I'll leave ya to do whatever ya can."

He went ahead an' left, an' I caught Arliss studyin' on me.

"What?" I said.

"I was about to ask you the same thing," he said.

"What?" I said.

"That's it," he said. "What. What is goin' on in that mind a yours?"

I grinned at him. "What makes you think there's somethin' goin' on in my mind?" I asked him.

"'Cause I'm gittin' nervous," he said.

"Well, you can git nervous all by yourself," I told him. "I'm goin' to work."

* * * *

It took me near two days to finish up the cedar an' set them windas. I had a mind to git some bricks an' frame out a hearth for a stove, an' maybe put a little porch outside the door an' roof it so I'd have someplace to set in good weather, but that gunstock kept callin' to me. I went down to the yards an' looked around a spell. Back in a corner in some weeds I found a chunk a wood, all dark an' moldy. It was about thirty inches long, five inches thick, an' went around ten inches wide on one end an' four on the other. I took it to the feller up front an' asked about it. He said it'd been layin' around for two or three years. It was the tag end off a piece cut for a fireplace mantle. He thought it was birdseye maple. He took two bits an' I took it.

That wood was hard. I spent a couple a hours fussin' at it with my big drawknife an' got it down to a reasonable size. Underneath all that dirt an' mold, it was birdseye maple, sure enough. Even on a rough surface, a feller could see all the whirls an' squiggles a grain inside that wood. I took it up to the shop an' Arliss helped me trace the outline of the stock on it. I locked it up in the big ol' wood vise on his bench, got my heavy copin' saw, an' went to work.

It took me that evenin' an' all the next day to git it worked down with my rasps an' files to where it looked like it might be a gunstock someday. It took me another day to git it all cut out an' inletted so the rifle fit in it right snug an' screw in tight. I cut it off about a half inch short, then worked a slice of center-cut black walnut into kindly a butt plate an' filed it down into a shallow curve to fit on a feller's shoulder right comfortable.

The next mornin' I was workin' on it with my scrapers, takin' that wood down to where it was as smooth as glass. I was honin' a curved scraper on a oil stone when Arliss come back an' dropped a coil a brass wire on the bench, an' left. I looked at that wire, an' then I looked at the stock, an' then I fetched my pack of little gouges an' cutters an' went at it. It was the middle a the afternoon when I finished. That maple was as slick as I could git it, an' on the right side a the stock, all fancy an' in curlicues, was a C an' a B for Clarence Banks inlet inta that wood in brass wire.

I went to the Sweetwater an' asked for a cup of strong tea. They fixed it for me, an' I brung it back to the shop. I spent some time rubbin' that tea on the stock an' wipin' it off 'til it set in an' that blond wood stained up some an' the grain with them figgers an' curlicues just popped. I give it a light rub with tongue oil, an' took it up front. That's when I come to find out that Arliss had been working on the gun. He slicked up that action twice more than Henry done it at the factory, an' polished up that brass receiver til' it gleamed. I laid the finished stock on the bench beside him.

"Hook her up," I said.

He picked up that stock by the ends an' rolled it over, looking at it. "By God, Rube!" he said. "This here is a piece a work, boy. It looks like light is just dancin' inside that wood! I don't believe I ever seen a more handsome thing in my life!"

I was kindly got. "Thank ya, Arliss," I said. "It was a terrible good piece a wood."

"That may be true, son," he said, "but you turned its heart loose. A thousand dollar fiddle ain't worth nothin' if nobody can bow it. You played this gunstock like a violin, an' that's the durn truth of it."

Real careful like, he put the whole thing together an' hung it on the wall. I looked out the winda an' seen Clarence walkin' down the other side of the street. I whistled him over. When he come in I looked at him an' said, "it's done."

He looked kindly confused, an' Arliss pointed to the Henry where it hung on the wall. Clarence spied it an' walked close to take a better look. He studied it for a minute, then kindly staggered back a step.

"Oh, my," he said, his voice sorta whispery. "Oh, my," he said agin, then looked to me, to Arliss, an' back to me again. "What you done?" he said.

He stepped forward an' studied the rifle some more. "Why, lookee there," he said. "Them's my initials, ain't they?"

"Yes, they are," I said.

He kindly lurched to a chair then, an' flopped into it. He set there, his elbows on his knees, lookin' at the floor an' shakin' his head. When he lifted his face to us, he had slow tears rollin' outa his eyes.

"I'd give a year a my life," he said, "if my ol' daddy could see that gun the way it is now."

A lump come up in my throat then, an' Arliss got sudden busy at his bench, arrangin' things that didn't need to be arranged. Purty soon, Clarence snorted, wiped his face on his sleeve, an' walked over to look at the Henry some more.

"Arliss worked over the innards for ya," I said. "Give it a try."

"I'm almost afraid to touch it," Clarence said.

I chuckled at that an' he grinned at me. He looked at it a little more then eased it down off the rack like it was made outa glass. Purty soon his courage come up an' he threw the lever a couple a times.

"Why it don't feel like there's nothin' in there at all," he said. "It's so smooth."

"Arliss is real good," I said.

"Fellers," he said, "what you two done here is a miracle. It ain't nothin' less than a miracle."

He swallerd an' settled down some, then got kindly sheepish.

"How much does a miracle go for these days?" he asked.

Arliss looked at me an' I winked at him. He smiled an' said, "ten dollars."

"Nossir," Clarence said, "I cain't give ya no ten dollars. I can give ya all I got right now. I can give ya sixteen dollars."

"The price is ten," Arliss said.

"I'll give ya sixteen," Clarence said, "or you are gonna have the best ten dollar rifle there ever was hangin' on yer wall. I'd give you boys a hunnerd dollars if I had it, but I don't. I do have sixteen. You'll take that or you will keep the gun."

"Did I say ten?" Arliss asked. "I meant to say sixteen."

Clarence paid up and an' stopped in the door with his rifle. "You fellers is damn good people," he said. "Don't think I don't know that."

"Clarence," I said, "next day or two, you an' me need to talk. I think I got a proposition for ya."

"I'll git with ya, Ruben," he said, an' left.

I looked at Arliss. "We could use the help," I said.

CHAPTER NINETEEN

The next mornin' I got to work on my place. I was sawin' on one a the posts that was gonna be a corner for my porch an' roof when this voice come up behind me.

"By God, it's true," it said.

It was Homer. I'd a knowed that voice anywhere. "What's true?" I said, not botherin' to turn around.

"That there was a shavetail out here playin' with dangerous instruments."

"I heer'd that they was a dangerous instrument just come to town," I said. "One by the name a Homer Poteet."

"You heerd right, young'un," he growled.

I turned around an' grinned at him. "Oh," I said, "it's only you."

He laughed, grabbed me by the shoulders, an' shook me a little bit. "I leave you alone for a spell, an' they tell me you run off an' killed a couple a fellers. You gittin' to be a hard man, are ya Rube?"

"Mean as a snake," I said.

"It's a mean world," Homer said. "I also heer'd that you got me a job a work that don't pay nothin', but that I don't havta work too hard at, neither."

"Yessir," I said. "Over at the livery. Fella named Verlon Clarke is the smith. I believe he is a good man."

"Arliss mentioned that he had a daughter too. Zat right?"

"He does," I said.

Homer grinned. "I felt the hickory come up in ya there, Rube," he said. "That's good. Feller oughta be some protectful of his woman."

My ears got hot. "She ain't my woman exactly," I said.

"Well then," Homer said, "mebbe I should give her a invite for a little evenin' walk down by the riverside."

"Well," I said, "if she wanted to go with ya, I reckon she would."

"Settle down, honey," Homer said. "I'm just funnin' ya. I ain't in the habit a takin' a run at no woman that's spoke for, special by a feller I consider to be my friend. She purty, is she?"

"Dammit, Homer!" I said, an' then had to laugh.

"Good to see ya," Rube," Homer said. "Damn shore is. Why doan you head on over to the livery. I'll be along shortly."

I put up my saw, got back into my shirt, an' strapped on the Schofield. "See ya over there," I said.

I'd gone about ten steps when Homer spoke up. "Nice hat ya got there, Rube," he said.

*   *   *   *

When I got to the livery, Verlon was on the forge an' Miss Harmony was on the bellows. Verlon kept firin' some strap iron for a minute, then took it out the coals an' over to the anvil an' commenced to hammerin' on it. Miss Harmony motioned me outside so we could hear ourselves think. She smiled at me.

"You got dirt on your nose, Ruben," she said.

I wiped at it. "It's gone," she said. "Now you're perfect."

I couldn't think a nothin' to say, so I just grinned. She

138

laughed.

"Speckled pup under a red wagon," she said. "What brings you by?"

"Homer Poteet is in town. He'll be here in a little bit."

"I see," she said.

"He's a tough cob," I said. "Ain't no fear in him. But he's a awful good feller, an' he's my friend."

"Point taken," Miss Harmony said. "I imagine he'd say the same about you. I know I would, Ruben."

I was tryin' to put together what she just said, when Homer come up the lane. He was on a dapple gray with the top a one ear missin'. He seen us an' come our way, stopped the gray, got down, an' stepped to us.

"Miss," he said, brimmin' his hat real firm, "you'd be Harmony Clark, I reckon. Rube here speaks real high of you. That there is good enough for me. I'm Homer Poteet. My pleasure to make yer acquaintance."

"He also speaks very well of you, Mister Poteet," Miss Harmony said. "And that is good enough for me."

"We keep talkin' like this where he can hear us," Homer said, "he ain't gonna be able to git that good lookin' hat on."

Miss Harmony laughed. "If you'll come with me, Mister Poteet," she said, "I will introduce you to my father."

They walked off toward the forge. I collected Homer's horse an' follerd along.

*　*　*　*

I didn't stay much but went on to the shop and got back to work on the porch. Arliss come out.

"Marion come by while you was gone," he said. "We got a meetin' tonight."

He walked off then, an' I tried to keep my mind on my work,

but it took some effort.

*   *   *   *

We was ridin' out to Marion's camp after dark when Homer slid back beside me. "That Harmony gal," he said, "how old would she be?"

"Must be this path," I said. "Arliss asked me the same thing last time I rode out this way."

I could hear Homer's grin. "What'd you tell him, Rube," he said.

"I tolt him I didn't know an' it warn't none a my business!"

"She seems to me like a thirty-year-old woman stuck inside a eighteen-year-old girl," he said. "She's steady, boy. Planted firm in her mind. That's real rare for a young'un like she is."

"She ain't much flighty," I said. "She goes an' gits feed in the wagon, she works the bellows for the forge, she can set a full saddle on a chin high rail, too."

"She thinks a passel a you, Rube."

"She does?" I said.

"She shore does, boy," Homer said. "She got me a tarp to lay down on some straw to pitch my bedroll an' we jawed a mite. She talked some about you."

"What'd she say?" I asked.

"I didn't memorize her words, Rube. It wadden what she said as much as it was the way she said it. Women doan talk straight, boy. She's better'n most, I'll give ya that, but when yer talkin' with a woman, you got to pay attention to how they say what they say more than ya do just what they say. If ya don't, you'll always be ridin' drag in their dust. It's ruint more'n one good man."

I thought about that quite a bit while we rode on. I don't think I ever quite caught up to it, but I was glad Homer run it by me.

*　*　*　*

"Try to git a little peace an' quiet," Marion griped after we come up on him, "an' injuns find yer durn camp, anyways."

"You got a sour stomach or somethin'?" Homer asked.

"I do now," Marion said.

"Maybe it's the epizootic," Homer said. "Maybe yer gonner die."

"Where is thy sting?" Marion said, an' started to chuckle. "Well boys," he went on, "I got your commissions an' badges. I'll give 'em to ya before ya leave."

"You got any extras?" I asked.

"I do," he said. "I have two. How many you need?"

"Maybe one," I said. "I got my eye on a fella. One a Arberry Yont's deputies."

"The hell ya say."

"Yessir," I said.

"Doan git in no hurry with him," Marion said. "We got time. Vet him out real good."

"Me an' Rube done some work for him on his daddy's ol' Henry," Arliss said. "The fella said he'd give up a year a his life if his daddy could see that rifle. Had tears in his eyes. It struck me, boys, an' that's the truth. We'll watch him."

"Be good if'n we had one a them deputies on our side," Homer said.

"Speakin' a that," I said, "you was a sheriff, wasn't ya?"

"I still am," Homer said.

"How long was yer term?"

"Didn't have no term," he said. "I was hired by the city council, not elected."

"What if a fella was a elected sheriff an' somebody run agin' him an' it looked like the sheriff was gonna lose. Could he go to the mayor or somethin' an' git his job switched over from elected to hired so he could keep workin'?"

"He could," Homer said, "but not unless he was more than six months away from the comin' election. All of them kinda things is registered with the state an' subject to state statutes."

"What you got goin' on in your mind, Ruben?" Marion asked me.

"You said once," I said, "that it might be good if'n we figgerd a way to light a fire under Sheriff Yont. He's stealin from the town. Everbody knows it an' doan nobody like it none. I stopped a rape an' two murders when I shot them fellers. It has become known that I was in on the raid on them Duncans an' their bunch. Folks around town is very nice an' respectful to me. We got a city celebration comin' up for the Forth of July. What if, durin' that celebration when a lot of the town was on hand, I was to announce that I was runnin' for Deer Run City Sheriff?"

"Jesus God O'mighty!" Homer said.

"You wanna do what?" Arliss said.

"Word has spread that I already come up agin' Yont at the Sweetwater that night an' backed him down a mite," I said.

"Boy," Arliss said, "he'd already just as soon shoot you as eat a ham sandwich! You pull a stunt like that, an' he'll be on you like ugly on a Flathead!"

"I ain't afraid a him," I said.

"That there is just one a your problems," Arliss said. "You damn sure do need to be afraid a him!"

"Folks in Deer Run is lookin' for relief," I said. "Relief from him, relief from his herd a deputies, relief from his taxes an' dues. I go in there an' tell folks that them bluevests'll be gone, that ever person or business will pay a tenth of what they are payin' now to fund the Sheriff's Department, an' Yont'll be out the door an' they'll elect me!"

"Can't elect no corpse," Arliss said.

"We wanna git under his skin, by God, I'm the way to do it," I said.

"Dammit, Rube, yer gittin' under my skin," Arliss said. "Use your head!"

"Hold on a minute," Marion said. "When's the election?"

"Third Thursday in September," I said.

"Too late now for Yont to do anything but go through with it," he said. "Ruben, let me study on this for a day or two."

"Forth of July is comin' up," I said.

"I know it is," he said. "You keep this under that good lookin' hat a yours until I think it over. You hear me?"

"I do, sir."

"All right then."

He passed out our commissions an' badges an' me an' Homer an' Arliss went back to town. Warn't much said on the ride.

* * * *

Arliss finally spoke up when we was walkin' back to the shop from the livery. "Rube," he said, "if you go ahead with this, I'm afraid for ya."

"Thank ya, Arliss."

"How come you wanna risk your life for this town?"

"I live here," I tolt him. "That makes it as much my town as anybody else's. I hate to see that sonofabitch settin' on his ass an' drinkin' on the life blood of this place. He takes an' don't give anythin' back. The bible would say that he toils not, neither does he spin. An' that there is just wrong, Arliss. Just plumb wrong. By my way a thinkin', if ya see somethin' that is wrong an' you can do somethin' about it an' ya don't, you are just as wrong yerself. I don't want to be like that. Special now. I got Miss Harmony to live up to."

"What the hell," Arliss said. "I'm with ya, Rube."

"I knowed ya would be," I tolt him.

CHAPTER TWENTY

I worked on the shed the next day an' got the porch an' roof all framed out an' a brick hearth layed in a wood frame. The day after, I went down to the yards in Arliss' wagon an' got some tar paper for the roof, then I went by the drygoods store an' got me a nice little sprung cot with a feather mattress, two coal oil lamps, an' a little ol' woodstove with a nice flat top for beans an' coffee an' flue pipe for it with two collars. I got back an' Arliss helped me unload that stove an' set it on them bricks. We went to the Sweetwater for dinner.

Miss Margie was there, struttin' around, but not so much in my direction no more. Arliss an' me were both about halfway through our baked chicken an' greens when, big as life, Marion Dainiels walked in.

"Hey, Marshal," Arliss said, "I got your coach gun ready. Set with us."

Marion made out like he was surprised, walked over an' took a chair while he nodded at two or three folks, an' set with his back to the wall. Arliss went through the motions of makin' sure that Marion an' me knowed one another, an' Marion stopped Margie's advance by raisin' his voice an' tellin' her he just wanted coffee. He an' Arliss visited quite a bit while I mostly ate, an' I left first to git back to work while they stayed behind.

They come back to the shop while I was nailin' felt an' tarpaper on that little stretch a roof. I went ahead an' worked some, finishin' it up after Marion left afore I went inside. Arliss met me in the back.

"Marion don't think you should make your announcement to the whole town on the fourth," he said.

"Why not?" I asked him.

"Too much pressure on Yont at one time," Arliss said. "He thinks ya oughta leak it to somebody you can trust to let it out or accidental-like to somebody that'll run straight to Yont with it. Be some sneaky about it. See what Yont does when he thinks that yer intention to run ain't common knowledge yet."

"That makes sense," I said. "Today is collection day, ain't it?"

Arliss sighed. "I think so," he said. "I don't know how much I owe yet."

"I'll be out back," I said. "If Clarence is the one that comes by, tell him I wanna see him."

"You think he's ready?" Arliss asked me.

"I believe he is," I said.

"Fine with me," Arliss said. "I'll tell him."

* * * *

I was layin' the floorboards on my porch when Clarence come by.

"Yer gittin' you a nice little place back here," he said. "Is that there church glass in the top a them windas?"

"Yes, it is."

"That'll be purty with the sun shinin' through," he said. "Mister Arliss mentioned that you wanted to see me."

"I got a question for ya, Clarence," I said. "You tired a helpin' Yont steal from the folks around here yet?"

He looked at his feet for a minute, then at my windas, then back at his feet. Finally he set his eyes on me.

"I don't like it none," he said. "I just had ta git five dollars from Mister Arliss."

"If you don't like it, why do ya do it?"

"Ya don't just quit on Sheriff Yont," he said. "Fella named Bailey quit about three years ago, an' he just wasn't around no more."

"What happened to him?" I asked.

"I don't know," Clarence said.

"What do you think happened to him?" I asked.

Clarence went back to lookin' at his feet. "I'd hate to say," he said.

"So you just keep on."

"Sometimes I do git to be a real deputy," he said. "Sometimes I do git to help folks. I like that. I was fixin' to help you out that one night, but you didn't need no help."

"Would you like to be a lawman, Clarence?" I asked. "A real one?"

"I would, Ruben," he said. "It would make me some proud to do a good job for folks."

"I need your help," I said. "I need you to do a favor for me, an' I need you to keep a secret. If ya doan keep the secret, could be that some good people might suffer for it."

He looked straight at me then, an' helt my eyes. "You need my help," he said, "you got my help. You need a secret kept, it'll go with me to the grave. I swear it will."

Hearin' what he said an' seein' the way he looked at me, kindly give me a chill. "All right," I said. "Here's what I want ya to do. On the fourth when there's a lot of people millin' around an' havin' fun, you go to Yont an' tell him you heard folks talkin' an' somebody said they heard I was fixin' to run for city sheriff in the next election."

"You want me to tell him that?" Clarence said.

"I do."

"He ain't gonna like that much," he said.

"That's what I'm countin' on. I'm a lawman, Clarence. I'm commissioned by the state an' sworn to get rid a Yont an' let these people have their town back. You can help with that. Once this gits settled, you can be a real deputy if you want to."

"That would be just fine, Ruben," he said. "I'll do it. I thank you for the chance to help."

"I thank you," Clarence," I said, "and I appreciate your help."

"You shore got it," he said, an' walked away. I watched him leave. He seemed some taller.

*   *   *   *

The Forth of July come on a Monday, but folks started gittin' ready the day before, after church an' such. Red, white an blue banners was hung on the front of stores for two blocks of the main street east of the Red Bird an' the Houston House. Little stands was throwed up for kids to play ring-toss games an' the like. Three big ol' freight wagons was brung in an' set side by side with boards laid across 'em to make a stage, an' anybody that had a bench or table brought 'em outside to set in front of it.

That evenin' folks walked around a lot, lookin' things over an' jawin' with one another. Firecrackers was throwed, little kids zipped around like waterbugs, laughin' an' squealin', dogs wagged an' barked, an' Arliss' shop was right in the middle of it. We stood outside, grinnin' a lot. I went for a walk an' several people I didn't know spoke to me or nodded an' smiled. There was a lady with a cart sellin' them little fried pies. I got me a cherry one, but she wouldn't allow me to pay for it. I run into

Mister Ponder an' his daughter, Martha. He thanked me agin an' tolt me they was leavin' for home the next mornin'. Martha even give me a little hug. It was a evenin' that was hard to resist, an' I enjoyed it.

* * * *

The next mornin' I needed some more rough cedar, but the yards, an' durn near everplace else, was closed for the day. Me an Arliss took chairs outside an' watched everthin' gittin' set up. In the street just a little east of us they put up a stand where you could git lemonade an' root beer as cold as they could be. They brung up a big ol' block out of the icehouse down by the river wrapped in a tarp an' settin' in the back of a freight wagon full a sawdust to keep everthin' chilled. I got each of us a root beer. It shore tasted good. There was ladies sellin' pie an' cake an fudge an' the like, little kids pitchin' pennies at bowls an' glasses, tryin' to win somethin' for mama.

* * * *

When it got on towards noon, ladies, girls mostly, started arrivin' for the box dinner auction. All kinds a decorated boxes was set up under a sheet along the front of the stage. It was supposed to be kept secret who brought what box. Then fellers would gather around an' bid to buy the purtiest box. Once one of 'em got that box bought, he an' the gal what made it an' the meal inside it, would go off a little ways an' have dinner together. I hadn't been payin' much attention, then, almost outa nowhere, Miss Harmony showed up. She was wearing a light blue dress that was fair stylish, with a little matchin' hat, an her hair was all done up. She had on these white gloves with a pearl-lookin' button on the wrist. I'd never seen her like that afore.

"Good morning, Mister Hyatt," she said.

"Ain't you just a picture, Miss Harmony," Arliss said. "And

good morning to you."

She turned to me an' smiled. My dusty ol' clothes come to mind an' I felt kindly awkward.

"Hello, Ruben," she said.

"Miss Harmony," I said. "You look real purty today."

"Just today?" she asked.

I felt my face git all hot an' she chuckled at me.

"Green with yellow flowers," she said, an' went on her way.

"What'd she mean by that?" I said.

Arliss looked at me like he kindly felt sorry. "That's the colors of the box she made, Rube," he said. "The biddin' for them boxes is gonna start in about fifteen minutes. She want's you to buy hers so the two of you can eat together."

"I ain't dressed to take dinner with a girl," I said.

"That's true," Arliss said, an' walked off.

I hustled over to Clary's place, washed up a mite, put on some clean pants an' my new yella shirt, strapped on the Schofield, an' got back as quick as I could.

* * * *

Mister Jeter, I guess 'cause he talked so fast an' kindly like a auctioneer when he warn't even tryin', was up on the stage.

"Now ladies an' gentlemen," he said, "we got us some boxes up here on this stage, yessir, right up here on this stage we got us some boxes. Purty ladies made these here boxes, boys, an' ever box here was made by one a these purty ladies you see standing down there on my left. Now then, I'm gonna pick out one a these boxes an' you are gonna bid on that box. Whoever digs deep enough to give me the highest bid is gonna git that box an' him an' the lady what made it, the lady what made that box an' him, is gonna go off a ways an' have dinner together. They are gonna set together n' have dinner."

150

He stopped long enough to draw breath, picked up a red an' white box, an' started in agin.

"Here we go," he said. "Boys, I got me a purty little box here, yessir, what I got here is one purty little box. Now is your chance to git this box for yourself. Now don't forgit that ever dime we raise here today goes to the consolidated church fund for our old folks. What kinda bid am I gonna git for this box, what are ya gonna bid for it? Can I git a two-bit bid on this box, can I git a box bid a two bits? There it is! Let's take it up to four-bits, boys. Four-bits would be a good bid on this box, can I git a four-bit bid on this box right here? Hey, well all right! That's a brave young man over there, yessir that young man over there is right brave. I got four-bits, boys. Now I know there are some deep pockets out there, and I know you boys can reach plumb to the bottom. Let's go fellers, afore these gals git away from ya!"

Mister Jeter chanted away up there an' sold three or four a them boxes, an' the biddin' picked up quite a bit. Then he reached down an' picked up one that was green with yella flowers.

I took the first bid at two-bits, an' a fella went to four. I got it back at six bits, an' somebody else went to a dollar. I bumped it up to a dollar an' a half, which was the highest bid of the day, an' I'll be durned if another fella didn't yell out two dollars. I kindly got caught up then an' hollerd three dollars! Everthing got quiet.

"Well, boys," Mister Jeter said, slowin' way down, his eyes scannin' the crowd. "What we got us here is a bid. Mister Beeler has laid a three-dollar bid out here. Now, who out there is gonna dig real deep an' give me three an' a quarter? Anybody?"

The bunch was quiet as a tomb. The crowd shifted, kindly nervous like.

"Not one a you boys can do better that three?" Mister Jeter

asked. "All right. I got three dollars for this box right here. I got three dollars goin' once."

Nobody said nothin'.

"I got three dollars goin' twice!"

You could hear a pin drop.

"I got the last an final bid goin' three..."

"Four dollars!" come a yell from back a me. I turned around an' there stood Arliss, grinnin'.

The crowd roared.

*   *   *   *

Arliss run that bid up to seven dollars afore I got that box bought. Me an' Miss Harmony et some cold roast beef sandwiches an' raisin pie over in front of the shop, jawin' an' smilin' at each other. It was the best seven dollars I ever spent.

*   *   *   *

After the box lunch was all done an' over, bingo was set up. Cards was a penny each, an' you could git up to ten a game. There was this wire cage up on the stage with a bunch a little numbered balls in it an' a big ol' board to set them balls in when they come outa the cage. Mister Jeter caught me an' talked me into announcin' the numbers when he pulled out a ball. If ya won, you got half the pot, the other half goin' to the old folks fund. Almost all the players was women.

The third game I called, Miss Harmony won. The crowd got to yellin' that I was cheatin' an' laughin' an' such. It was fun. When we got to the seventh game, Miss Harmony won agin. Some a them ladies got outa hand, gigglin' an' throwin' them dry beans at me they used to mark their cards, claimin' that me an Miss Harmony was in cahoots to rob the festivities. I confessed that me an' Miss Harmony had been caught red-handed, but that it had all been her idea, an' took my leave to go down a ways an' watch the cakewalk. Miss Harmony caught up with me before I got there an' took my arm.

"Folks around here like you, Ruben," she said.

"Just folks?" I asked her.

She kissed me on the cheek then, an' went back to the bingo.

It was a fine day.

CHAPTER TWENTY-ONE

As the day went on, the bluevests showed up, hangin' around the edges a things an' watchin' everbody. Some fellas showed up with banjos an' fiddles an' such an struck up music. They was several cakewalks, more folks played bingo, a turkey shoot was set up at the edge a town, kids had sack races, an' three-legged races, an' a pet parade. A bunch a young'uns come with their dogs all dressed up with bows an' things, one even had on a pair a pants. A pig on the end of a rope that was wearin' a hat was the most unusual, but he made a break for it in the middle a the judgin'. Some kids chased him around for a while afore he made his getaway an' run plumb off.

Late in the afternoon a fella showed up from Jeff City that done magic tricks an' told jokes to the crowd. He was right entertainin'. Several times durin' the evenin' I noticed Arberry Yont starin' at me from a distance away. He did not look happy. I reckon Clarence had talked to him.

When it come on dark, everbody went out to where they'd had the turkey shoot an' a bonfire was lit. The crowd gathered around an' some of 'em commenced to singin' songs. Miss Harmony showed up an' stood with me, holdin' on to my arm an' leanin' into my shoulder some. After the fire burnt down quite a bit, I walked her back to the livery an' said goodnight. She kissed me then, an' hugged me for a minute. Then she smiled at me, touched my face, an' went in the house.

I kindly floated down the steps an' back to the center of town. The street by Miz Clary's was deserted. I was fixin' to go inside when Homer showed up, kindly outa nowhere.

"I know how a woman can mess up yer mind, Rube," he said, "I shore do, but you need to git yer head outa yer ass."

"What?" I said.

"One a them bluevests trailed you out to the livery. I seen him from the barn. When you headed back, he was purty much on yer tail. I innerduced him to the butt a my Colt afore he could close with ya. Left him in the weeds. Don't think I kilt him or nothin'."

"I never noticed a durn thing," I said.

"Hard to hear with yer ears up inside yer butt like they was, boy."

"I feel some stupid," Homer," I said.

"We all been there. She kissed ya goodnight, didn't she?"

"Yessir, she did," I said.

"That explains it," Homer said, an' kindly disappeared back into the dark.

I went up to my room an' took to the bed, but I didn't sleep much.

*　*　*　*

The next mornin' I went to the Sweetwater for breakfast. I just got my eggs an' ham when Arberry Yont came stompin' in. He seen me an' come over.

"Come with me," he said. "I wanna talk to you." Him growlin' at me like that didn't help my humor a lot.

"I'm eatin', Sheriff," I said. "Maybe later."

"What are you tryin' to pull, Beeler?"

"I am tryin' to eat my breakfast, Arberry," I said. "I'd like to do that alone. I'll be down workin' on my shack in a while. Why doan you drop by then?"

He glared at me. "Don't you think I won't, boy," he said.

"Yer welcome anytime, Sheriff," I said. "By the way, you see a boy around here, Yont, why don't you buy him a stick a peppermint?"

He heavy-footed it out then. I looked at my plate, but I didn't have much use for food any more.

CHAPTER TWENTY-TWO

Arliss was in the front of the shop when I come in. He took one look at me and spoke up.

"Hell's the matter with you, boy?" he said.

"Yont just ruint my breakfast," I told him. "He come into the Sweetwater an' tried to start up with me. I tolt him to see me later when I wasn't eatin'. He oughter be along soon. Sonofabitch."

Arliss smiled. "Settle down, Rube," he said. "If a feller gits ya all pissed off, he's controllin' ya. You got to understand the rule a opposites."

I shifted my weight an' shrugged. "The what?" I said.

"You got the bit in yer teeth, doncha?"

"Well hell, Arliss" I said, "that butthole come in there an…"

"He come in there an' you got pissed off the minute you see'd him, didn't ya?"

"Well a course I did!"

"An' now, yer pissed off 'cause I'm calm about the whole thing."

Sayin' that like he done kindly pulled me up short. "I damn shore ain't pissed off at you!" I said.

"Sure you are," Arliss said. "I'm controllin' ya. Not much fun, is it?"

I looked at him for a minute an' felt my shoulders settle some. "No, it ain't," I said.

"There ya go," Arliss said, smilin' at me. "Now that yer more ready to listen, I'll go on. The rule a opposites is real simple. When yer dealin' with somebody in a confrontation a some kind, just do the opposite a what he expects ya to do. If he git's loud, you git quiet. The faster he goes, the slower you go. He gits to wavin' his arms an' spittin', you fold yer arms an' lean back agin somethin'. The more excited he gits, the more calm you git. The nastier he gits, the nicer you git. Don't participate in the bullshit. You do that, an' he won't git the upper hand on ya. You do that, and you'll drive that sumbitch nuts. Don't do what he expects you to do."

I thought on that fer a minute. "That makes some sense," I said.

Arliss shook his head. "That makes a lotta sense," he said, "yer still just too pissed off to admit it."

I stared at him an' he blew a kiss at me. I couldn't help it, I started grinnin'

"What's Yont's number one malfunction this mornin'?" Arliss asked.

"Last night I walked Miss Harmony home after the bonfire," I said. "Turns out that there was one a them bluevests follerin' us. Homer see'd him closin' up behind me when I was walkin' back an' smacked him out with his Colt. Said he didn't think he kilt him."

"You didn't notice him followin' ya?"

"Nossir, I didn't, I'm ashamed to say."

"Uh-huh," Arliss said. "That gal kissed ya goodnight, didn't she?"

"Gawdammit, Arliss!" I said.

He grinned at me. "Let this be a lesson to you, boy," he said. "You wanna go out an' git to smoochin' on that gal, take a bodyguard with ya."

I went out back.

* * * *

A little later I was workin' on the railing of my porch with a mallet when Yont an' a bluevest come showed up. Yont was struttin' some , an' the deputy was tryin' to look mean. I stopped my poundin'.

"Hello there, Sheriff," I said. "Purty mornin'. What can I do for ya?"

"I got a deputy with a bandage around his head," he said. "The doc thinks he's got a fractured skull!"

"Well, that ain't good," I said.

"You damn right it ain't," Yont said. "What do you know about it?"

"What makes you think I'd know anything about that, Sheriff?" I asked him.

"'Cause it happened over by the livery, an' I know you walked that Clarke girl home last night!"

"How would you know somethin' like that, Sheriff?" I said. "You have one a your hounds on my trail?"

"What?"

"I'm sorry," I said. "I don't believe I stuttered. You heard me."

"Goddammit!" he yelled. "I know you had somthin' to do with my hurt deputy!"

"This ain't about yer deputy, Sheriff," I said, keepin' my voice low an' calm like. "This here is about you. Everthing is about you. These people, this town, it's all about you. I believe the pressure a bein' town law here is gittin' to be some hard on ya."

"Now you listen to me, you sonofabitch!"

"Whoa now," I said. "You don't know my mother."

I could see in his face that he knowed he'd stepped in it. The deputy knowed it, too.

"So far we just been jawin," I said. "Now yer gittin' personal. I won't have you talkin' about my mother, Arberry. I'm sure you wouldn't want me talkin' about yours."

Yont didn't have no place to go but back. I warn't totin' no gun, but he was in arm's reach of me an' I still had my mallet.

"Yer right," he said. "I wouldn't."

"Arberry," I said, "I'm gonna tell the truth to ya. Yes, I walked Miss Harmony home last night. No, I did not see a deputy. No, I had nothin' to do with anybody gittin' their head busted. Now, judgin' by what you've said to me, somebody was followin' me around last night. I don't care for that. I'm sure you wouldn't like it much either. I don't expect it to happen again, but if I notice somebody followin' me, I will put a stop to it."

"That a threat, Mister Beeler?" Arberry said.

"Yessir, it is," I said. "It is also a fact. Somebody doggin' my backtrail is enemy action. I don't take kindy to something like that. I got a way a goin' right straight at that kinda thing."

Yont curled his lip then. "You think yer kinda tough, doncha?" he said.

I smiled at him. "There's tougher men than me, Sheriff," I said. "I'm friendly with a couple of 'em. I ain't particular tough, but I am terrible determined. So far, that's been enough."

Yont stretched up to as big as he could git, which was considerable. "We'll talk again," he growled.

"You betcha, Sheriff," I said. "Lookin' forward to it. I enjoy our little chats. Drop by anytime."

He left then, his boots kickin' up little puffs a dust. I set my mallet down an' just breathed a while.

CHAPTER TWENTY-THREE

I went ahead back to work on the railing an' just got it finished when Arliss come out.

"Ya need a rockin chair, Rube," he said. "Give ya a good place to set an' watch the lightnin' bugs of a evenin'."

"That'd be nice," I agreed.

"Got the place lookin' real good," he said. "Bout done, aintcha?"

"I still got to hook up the stove pipe an' git the collars in," I said.

"Collars?" he said. "Mor'n one?"

"Yessir. I'm gonna put me in a ceilin' an' fix me a vent for it up at the peak of the roof. Then I'm gonna cut some holes in the soffet. I'll cover everthin' with screen wire to keep the birds an' bugs out. That way, in summer weather, the roof will vent some of the hot air out an' kindly be like shade for the place, an' in the winter, the ceilin' will keep the heat from the stove a little closer in the livin' space."

"Now that there makes a little sense don't it?" Arliss said.

"Then I'm gonna build a cabinet with drawers to put things in an' my clothes an' such, an' a coat rack a some kind by the door. Then a small table an' a couple stools, then git a rocker you mentioned, or maybe a swing for the porch. I'll put in a couple barrels to ketch up some rainwater. I don't fancy diggin' no cistern. Not in this rocky ol' dirt."

Arliss smiled. "Be a right nice place for ya, Rube," he said.

"Yessir," I said. "Miss Harmony said it was just the first step on my journey."

Arliss' smile jumped up into a grin. "That's what she said, did she?"

"Arliss," I said, "Doan you go makin' nothin' outa that, dammit. She was just talkin' about no matter how far a fella has to go, he cain't take more than one step at a time at it."

"Smart girl," he said. "What'd ol' Arberry have to say to you durin' his little visit?"

I tolt him an' he studied on it some.

"Didn't say nothin' about you runnin' for sheriff, huh?" Arliss said.

"Nossir. Not a word."

"You know anything about them bluevests he's got with him?" Arliss asked.

"Just Clarence, an' he's with us now," I said.

"You do what you want to, Rube," Arliss said, "but if'n I was you, I'd talk to Clarence 'bout them deputies. See if any of them boys has got sand an' if any of 'em is a real shootist. Good to know what to watch out for in case the bull busts through the gate."

"I'd figgerd on it," I said.

"I thought ya had," Arliss said. "How long before you git in the place here, ya think?"

"Couple a weeks, if I keep after it," I said. "Be nice to sleep without bein' jammed up in a place with four or five other folks snorin' away in rooms all around me. You mind if I use the team an' wagon to go git some pine?"

"Go ahead on, boy," he said. "Durn near anythin' I got belongs to you as much as me."

* * * *

I went on over to the livery an' caught up the team. Fer as big an' stout as them mules was, they was real agreeable. Just from bein' around mules, I was careful of 'em. I seen a big ol' Missouri mule pick a fella clean up off the ground by the shoulder one time. That ol' boy bled like he'd been gunshot. The mule jest stood there after he dropped him, ears back an' waitin' to see who was gonner be next. My daddy said that the reason you couldn't never trust no mule was because they was so smart, an' if one of 'em ever got the bulge on ya, ya might as well sell him 'cause you'd never be able to git ahead of him again. But I never had no trouble with Arliss' mules. They handled purty much like good mannered horses. Neither one of 'em ever tried to bite me or shook a leg at me or nothin'.

I had just finished hitchin' 'em up when Miss Harmony come in. She smiled.

"You makin' a run for it, Ruben?" she asked.

"Yes, I am," I tolt her. "I figger eight legs can take more steps than just two."

She laughed at that an' told me to write to her if I found work.

My mouth got sorta dry. "Miss Harmony," I said, "tomorrow bein' Sunday an' all, maybe you could see your way clear for you an' me to go for a buggy ride or somethin'. See some of the country an' waste a little bit a time."

"Are you saying that spending time with me is a waste?" she said.

"No m'am," I said. "That there is not what I meant! I'm just sayin' that…"

"I know what you're saying, Ruben," she said, grinnin' at me. "I would be pleased to waste a little time with you. Why don't I make up some fried chicken or something to take with us while we waste our time?"

"Why, that would just suit me right down to the ground, Miss Harmony," I said, "an' less aggravatin' than biddin' against Arliss for a box."

"If it's your pleasure then," she said, "why don't you come by tomorrow around noon.

"Noon it is," I said.

"Noon it is," she said, an' walked back toward the house.

* * * *

I clumb on that wagon then an' started off. Just as I passed the end of the barn, Homer Poteet's voice come floatin' my way out the mow door.

"Rube an' Harmony, settin' in a tree…" it said.

I popped the whip an' put them mules in a trot so I wouldn't have to hear the rest of it.

* * * *

I got lucky down at the yards. Turns out a riverboat had foundered on a sandbar upstream on the Missouri a ways an' they couldn't git it off, so they tore it up for salvage. I managed to git me two captain's chairs, a big ol chester drawers, a small table, a little-bitty table, a washstand with a pitcher an' a basin an' a lookin' glass, a full wagon of enough a tongue an' groove finished pine boards, already painted white, to do my ceilin' an' two walls at the front a Arliss' shop, a eight by twelve horsehair rug in blue an' black, some blue curtains an' brass rods for my windas, an' a real purty brass oil lamp that would hang from a wall on a big brass hook. It took me four trips to git all that stuff back to my place. Arliss come with me on the last three. I spent near forty dollars, but it was worth it.

*   *   *   *

The next mornin' I went up to the shack an' spent two or three hours settin' in some of the boards for my ceilin'. I went back to Miz' Clary's then an' washed up, shaved my face, brushed my teeth with salt, put on my cleanest pair a saddle pants, the brown striped shirt I'd never wore afore, knocked some of the dust offa my hat, slapped on a little Bay Rum, hitched up the Schofield, an' walked down to the livery.

I stepped inside the barn an' there was Willie, all saddled up, an' Homer Poteet, puttin' a saddle on a good lookin' little liver-chestnut mare that I hadn't never seen 'til then.

"Howdy there, Rube," Homer said to me. "Ya might check on your saddle an' make sure I got it where ya want it on his withers."

"Hi, Homer," I said. "What are ya doin'?"

"What does it look like, boy? I'm gittin' the horses ready for you an' Harmony to go on your ride. Ain't this chestnut a purty little thing?"

"I thought we was goin' in a buggy," I said.

"Reckon not," he said, reachin' under the mare to collect the cinch. "She brought this mare down here a little while ago an' asked if I'd saddle these two up for ya."

'Bout that time, Miss Harmony come walkin' in. She was wearin' what looked like a long skirt to me, but what turned out to be kindly a pair a pants with big ol' pleated legs. She was carryin' a canteen an' some saddle bags.

"Hello, Ruben," she said, smilin' at me. "Nice of Mister Poteet to saddle our horses for us, don't you think?"

"Yes, it is, Miss Harmony," I said, sorta confused.

"We have biscuits and bacon if we get hungry," she said. "Shall we go?"

She led that little mare on out. Homer, grinnin' like a damn possum, handed me Willie's reins an' punched me on the arm. "Now you two children have a good time an' play nice," he said.

I got out in the sunshine in time to see Miss Harmony swing up onto her horse. That's when I noticed that skirt was pants. I clumb up on Willie an' she reined her horse an' started off. I followed her on.

* * * *

We hit a wagon trail goin' west, an' she put that mare in a short lope. I eased up beside her an' we rode on that way a little as I watched her out of the corner of my eye.

"Miss Harmony," I said, "I got to say that you set a horse real comfortable like."

She laughed, her face shinin' in the sun. "Are you saying that I don't ride like a girl?" she said.

"I reckon I am," I said. "It speaks good for ya, I believe."

"You think so?" she said, an' touched the chestnut. That little mare took off. I give Willie my heels an' hissed at him. He laid back his ears an' done what he liked to do.

I had to check him back a little so he wouldn't pass the mare, an' we went on like that for a ways, afore Miss Harmony started laughin' an' reined her horse in. We dropped into a walk to cool 'em out some.

"That buckskin can run a little," she said.

"He's fast," I said, "an' quick, too. I git a choice, I'd just as soon have a quick horse than a fast one. I'm lucky with Willie. He's both. Yer chestnut is a purty thing. I like the color of her."

"She's easy to use." Miss Harmony said.

* * * *

We rode on that way for bit, then she turned off on a path an' I followed her. We didn't go mor'n a half a mile afore we come down a little slope. In the draw at the bottom they was a nice flat spot with a little sandy-bottom pool not much bigger'n two or three big dinner tables strung end to end, with a spring seepin' in one end an' a little trickle of a overflow out the other. A purty good size willa tree shaded it some. On down where the overflow went, maybe a hunnerd yards, was a grove a river birches. Everthin' else was knee-high grass except some gravel on the near side a that little pond.

"Ain't this purty," I said.

"I used to come out here to wade when I was little," she said. "My momma and daddy would picnic while my brother and I played in the water."

Miss Harmony got down then. I swung off, too. She looked at me. "You set us up a place to sit, Ruben. I'll gather some dry switches."

I took down my slicker an' spread it out in the shade, next to that spot a gravel. Miss Harmony come over with a big armload a dried up willa branches an' piled 'em up. I got some more an' she fetched her saddlebags. She pulled a rash a bacon in a bag an' some biscuits in a paper sack out one side, an' a little skillet an' a pine knot outa the other. I busted up some a them switches, set two rocks a little ways apart, put that pine knot down between 'em, an' built kindly a tent of them switches over it. The knot went off with one match an', right smart, we had us a little fire. She let it burn down some, then set that skillet on them rocks an' put five or six slices a that thick-cut bacon in. Then she commenced to bustin' up more switches. Willa switches burn up purty quick.

"I got to say it, Miss Harmony," I said to her. "You just ain't terrible girly, are ya?"

She laughed then, an' I had to join her. "I have never been accused of it," she said.

"The only other girl I really know around here is that Margie gal what waits tables in the Sweetwater. She's nice an' all, but she's as flighty as a canary. Chirps kindly like one, too."

That caused her to laugh again. "You have a way of getting to the point, Ruben," she said. "You and she kept company for a while, didn't you?"

"It's true enough that we went on a couple of walks," I said, "but I wouldn't call it keepin' company. She's a purty little thing, but it didn't take too long afore she kindly wore me out. That girl could talk for a week an' never git rid of a idea. I don't believe she ever said a thing I cared to listen to."

Miss Harmony was grinnin' an' pokin' that bacon with the end of a green switch. "Little too girly for you?" she asked.

"I believe she was," I said.

"I never had much of a chance to be a girly girl," she said. "My mother and older brother died of the wet lung in seventy-two. I started helping my father at the forge and in the livery then. He and I were all we had. I didn't have time to become a lady."   "I don't think you can become a lady," I said. "I think ya either are or you ain't. Whatcha choose to do or whatcha havta do don't mean much. Yer a lady all right, Miss Harmony. Ain't a speck a doubt in my mind about that. Looks right good on ya, too."

She fussed with the bacon for a while, then. I let the silence roll on, mostly 'cause I couldn't think of nothin' else to say. Purty soon, she turned the bacon, added more a them busted up switches to the little fire, an' spoke up.

"How's your house coming along?" she asked.

I tolt her about all that stuff I got from the riverboat salvage.

"You bought curtains and a rug?" she said.

"I did," I said. "I thought the blue in both of 'em might set each other off some. An' the white ceilin' will reflect lamplight quite a bit. The pitcher an' bowl both have a little blue in the trim, too."

"Why, Ruben Beeler," she said, "that sounds a little girly."

*   *   *   *

We et that bacon an' sopped them biscuits in the grease a little. When we finished, Miss Harmony went back to her saddlebags an' brung out a can a peaches an' a opener.

"Homer said you were partial to peaches," she said.

We speared them peach slices with willa switches an' took turns drinkin' the juice. I gotta admit that I believe I never enjoyed eatin' by a campfire more. When we finished, she rubbed the skillet out with sand, put it in the bag the biscuits had been in, an' stuck it an' that empty peach can back in the saddlebags. She had just set back down on that slicker when Willie pulled his head around an' started lookin' off down the draw toward that stand a river birches. I watched him some, an' he held his stare. Purty soon, he tossed his head an' pawed the ground a lick or two, then went back to lookin' toward them trees.

"What's the matter?" Miss Harmony asked me.

"Willie see's somethin' down in them trees," I said. "Stay set."

I got up an' walked over to where the horses was tied an' commenced to mess with my saddle bags while I shaded myself behind the horse an' looked down that way. A glint of reflected sunlight winked an' caught my attention.

"Miss Harmony," I said, "there's somebody in that copse a

birch trees down there that's watchin' us."

"All right," she said.

"We had a feller follow us the other night, ya know," I said.

"Homer told me, Ruben."

"I don't cotton to bein' spied on," I said. "I believe I oughta ride down that way an' see what this feller wants."

"Whatever you think is best," she said.

Slow like, I got aholt a the cinch an' tightened it back from where I'd loosed it when we stopped to eat. I moved up by Willie's head an' eased them reins from around the branch they was wrapped on. I flipped the offside rein up over his neck, took aholt of both of 'em, pulled his head around to aim him a mite, an' hissed at him. Willie bolted outa there like his tail was on fire. He made about three jumps afore I bounced up into the saddle an' he was at full speed, stretched out an' goin' for all he was worth. I hung on him low, an' we pounded toward them trees.

We was halfway to 'em afore that feller showed hisself an' got to his horse, two thirds of the way afore he got into the saddle. He went off down that draw as hard as he could go, with Willie gainin' on him. We warn't mor'n a hunnerd feet behind him an' his bay when he turned sharp to the right to climb up a cut an' git outa that draw. He was askin' too much a his horse. That bay tried to do it for him but slipped an' fell. He come off on the left an' hit purty hard. I didn't have to do a thing with Willie. He slid to a stop all by hisself. I kicked out of the stirrups an' lit on my feet, draggin' out the Schofield as I come around that bay while he was gittin' up. He jumped outa my way an' run off, clearin' my sight to the feller layin' on the ground. The fact that he was wearin' a blue vest didn't surprise me none. He was settin' up lookin' confused. His hat was off. I pointed the Schofield at him.

"You do one damn thing I doan tell you to do, mister," I said, "an' I will shoot you in both feet an' leave you out here to walk back. You hear me?"

He nodded, tryin' to ketch his breath.

"Ain't that nice," I said. "You leave that hogleg a your'n right where it is an' roll over on your belly."

He done it. I eased back by Willie, took my knife an' cut two a them latigo strips offa my saddle, an' come up behind that fella where he lay.

"Put yer hands behind yer back," I tolt him. He done that, too.

I tied his hands together behind his back, then tied 'em to the back a his gunbelt. I flipped him over an' took his Colt. He looked up at me.

"What are you fixin' to do with me?" he said. He was scairt. He needed to be.

"I'm thinkin' about strippin' ya nekked, whipin' ya with my rope a while, an' letting ya walk back into town that way," I said.

"I'm a deputy, yew sonofabitch!" he said.

"Not out here you ain't," I said. "I tolt yer boss I didn't want nobody followin' me around, an' he sent you out here, anyway. He knowed that if I caught ya, I'd git some upset, an' he didn't care. He's playin' a game with you, pard. Git up."

He flopped around some then got to his feet. I holstered my revolver an' took to the saddle.

"Walk," I said.

"Where to?" he asked.

"To town."

"All trussed up like this?" he said.

"You betcha," I said. "Just like that."

"What about my hat?" he said.

"Fuck yer hat," I said.

He looked at me hard for a minute, but then he started walkin'.

*   *   *   *

We hadn't gone very far when I saw Miss Harmony come up over a rise on the chestnut, leadin' a bay horse. She rode up an' smiled at me.

"Why thank ya, M'am," I said.

"You are very welcome, Sir," she said.

I helped that fella git in the saddle. Then, I took my piggin' string, put the loop over his head, an' tied the other end to the horn. I took his reins, got back on Willie, an' we struck off toward town. Miss Harmony smiled at him settin' there tied by the neck to the saddle horn like he was.

"Try not to fall off," she said.

*   *   *   *

We got back near town an' I thanked Miss Harmony for a lovely ride an' mentioned she might wanna go home.

"Not me," she said. "I'm going with you."

I figgerd she knowed her mind, so we rode through town an' down to the Sheriff's Office. Several folks watched us walk down the main street, an' a few of 'em tagged along. Yont was settin' out front when we arrived. He got to his feet.

"Arberry," I said, "I tolt you not to send anymore a yer hounds in my direction, an' here you throwed this mongrel at me. You can have yer dog back now. The next one you send will come home bleedin'. The one after that might not come back at all. You can keep the piggin' string."

I reined Willie around an' me an' Miss Harmony rode back the way we come.

Yont never said a thing.

*   *   *   *

We was most of the way back to the livery afore Miss Harmony spoke up. "You were a lot nicer to that deputy than you could have been," she said.

"Warn't his idea to come out there," I said. "He really didn't take no action agin us, just watched."

Miss Harmony grinned then. "Good thing we didn't go skinny dipping," she said

My face got hot as a pepper. She laughed until she had to kindly bend over a mite. When she looked at me, she started up again.

"Ruben," she said, "you are such a lovely shade of red."

I didn't know what to do with that, so I let Willie step out a little.

*   *   *   *

When we got to the livery, Homer was sweepin' up around the forge. He come walkin' over.

"I didn't expect the two of you back so soon," he said.

"Had to make a delivery to the sheriff," I said.

"One of his deputies came to spy on us," Miss Harmony said. "Ruben ran him down, tied him up, and took him back.

Homer looked at me. "Did ya now?" he said.

"I told Yont to leave me alone," I said. "He didn't."

"He'll look you up in a day or two," Homer said, "after he decides on his new tactics. Watch yerself."

I grinned at him. "I thought that was yer job," I said.

CHAPTER TWENTY-FOUR

I had too many feathers in my feet to settle down, so I left Miss Harmony at the livery an' come on back to my place. Arliss warn't nowhere that I could see, an' I set to workin' on my ceiling. In a few minutes, Homer come walkin' in. He looked around some an' smiled.

"Gonna have to be a heluva big bedroll to git all this shit in it when Yont runs you outa town," he said, grabbin' the end of a board an holdin' it up for me.

"That sonofabitch ain't runnin' me nowhere," I grumbled.

Homer got to grinnin' at me. I didn't like it much.

"I want a 'possum in here," I said, "I'll go shoot one."

He commenced to laughin' then. I glared at him, but it didn't even slow him down. Instead, watchin' him wipe his eyes 'cause of it got me kindly tickled, too.

"All right, Goddammit," I said, "I'll settle down."

"You should, Rube. A feller can waste a lot a hisself in bein' mad."

"Ol' Marion did fine with gittin' mad when he took off down that slope with that coach gun when we went at that Duncan bunch," I said.

"What?" Homer said. "Marion wasn't mad, boy. He just

comes to a focus, like. There wasn't nothin' else in the world for him right then but them outlaws an' what needed to be done. Wasn't no fear, wasn't no anger, wasn't no thinkin', wasn't no decision, just will. His will. When he gits like that, Rube, he is a force."

"I reckon I just don't understand that," I said.

"Ain't so, Rube," Homer said. "You understand it just fine. You just don't know ya do."

With Homer's help, I got the rest a my ceiling up afore dark.

*   *   *   *

I noticed a light burnin' in the shop an' I found Arliss at his bench, fussin' with a ol' Remington.

"Busted firin' pin," he said. "I'll fix it in the mornin'."

"Where ya been?" I asked him.

"I have been enjoyin' the company of the fair gender," he said.

I looked at him. He sighed an' shook his head.

"I been over by Houston House, boy," he said. "Out back."

It come on me then what he meant. "Oh," I said. "You been in there with the whores."

"I been in there with one of 'em at least," Arliss said. "I ain't as young as I used to be. Little gal calls herself Asia. She claims there's a new feller in town. Hard man by the name a Arkansas Bill Cole."

"Who's that?" I said.

"I heard the name before, but I don't know much about him. I think he's a bounty hunter or somethin' like that."

"Would Homer know him, ya reckon?" I asked.

"Most likely he would."

"Thanks," I said. "I'll go talk to him."

*   *   *   *

I was some hungry, so I went to the Sweetwater an' got a fried egg sandwich an' et it on the way to the livery. I found Homer settin' on a bench leanin' up against the barn, smokin' in the twilight.

"I thought I was shed a you for the rest of the day," he said. "What brings ya by, Rube?"

"Arkansas Bill Cole," I said.

Homer took a puff afore he spoke. "Where'd you hear that name?" he asked me.

"A whore over at the Houston House told it to Arliss," I said. "Claimed he was in town. You know him?"

"Not personal," Homer said. "I seen him once, over in the bootheel. Thin feller, near as tall as Marion. Was carryin' two black handled Colts in a double crossdraw rig. I heard he was a marshal once, then a law in Saint Louis for a spell, then took to bounty huntin'. Dead or alive warrants. Way I heard it, they was all mostly dead when he brung 'em in. Last I knowed of him he was down around Fort Smith, I believe it was. He's a shootist, I reckon."

"What do you supose he's doin' here?" I asked.

"Maybe," Homer said, "he's just passin' through."

"You believe that, Homer?"

He shook his head. "No," he said, "I don't think I do. Bill Cole don't go nowhere without a reason, I speck."

I set with him for a spell, but neither one of us said much.

It was full dark when I left.

* * * *

I was walkin' back to Clary's place when I come on Clarence Banks, out on patrol. I slowed down when I passed him.

"Clary's," I said. "Room four, upstairs."

Clarence never even looked at me. He just kept walkin'.

* * * *

I went upstairs, shed my boots, my gunbelt, an' my hat, checked to make sure my little ol' shotgun was on the nightstand by the cot, an' set. I didn't light no lamp or nothin'. Seemed like a hour went by, so I reckon it was only about fifteen minutes before I heard a little knock on my door. I opened it an' Clarence come in. The room was durn near pitch black.

"Two steps an' yer at the cot," I said. "Set yerself."

He fumbled around fer a second an' took his seat.

"I been lookin' for you," Clarence said. "Arberry's got a new man in town."

"Arkansas Bill Cole, I guess," I said.

"Yessir," Clarence said, "that's him. Arberry got aholt of him a while back, I hear. I didn't know he was even comin' 'til he showed up. Bounty hunter, I think. Come in from out around Lawrence in Kansas. Maybe Wichita."

"Did you meet him?" I asked.

"Nossir, I didn't," Clarence said. "I just seen him. Wears two Colts with black grips."

"How many deputies does Yont have?" I asked him.

"Used to have thirteen, then Mervin got knifed, then Wayne Combs got his head busted up, then you brung Fred Kessler in tied up on his horse. Sheriff Yont didn't like that one little bit. Run Fred off less that a hour after you brung him in. Told Fred if he saw him again, he'd shoot him hisself."

Clarence couldn't see my grin in the dark. "Any of you boys real pistoleros?" I asked.

"Couple think they are, but naw, no actual high standard slingers, I guess," Clarence said. "Some of 'em will stand with Yont though, I believe."

"So now," I said, "there are ten deputies, eleven countin'

Arkansas Bill Cole."

"I doan believe you could call him no deputy," Clarence said. "I was outside Arberry's office in the jailhouse when he give Mister Cole a blue vest to wear. Mister Cole tossed it back on Arberry's desk an' walked out. Once he got ouside, he laughed."

"Then we got Cole an' ten deputies to deal with," I said.

"You got nine deputies, Ruben," Clarence said. "I ain't agin' you boys. I'm fer ya!"

"I'm sorry, Clarence. I didn't mean nothin' by that. I was countin' heads, not intentions."

"I'll do anythin' I can for you an' Mister Arliss" he said." I'll keep my ear to the rail an' let ya know if'n I hear somethin' comin'."

"Thank you, Clarence," I said. "I know I can count on ya. If you cain't find me, tell Arliss if anything shows up."

"I shore will, Ruben," he said. "I got to go now, though. I'm 'sposed to be out on my patrol."

*　*　*　*

I laid on my cot starin' into the dark for a spell after Clarence left. I don't know how late I was up, but mornin' come early enough. I rubbed my eyes some, an' set up. After I got woke up a little, I looked out the winda. It was real cloudy an' rainin' purty hard. My slicker, as far as I knowed, was still out by that little pool. I'd plumb fergot it in all the excitement. I got on my boots an' hat an' went downstairs. I hustled out to the convenience, then run up, real quick-like, to the drygoods store. The feller there gimme a grin when I come drippin' in. His name, I had found out, was Elmo McCoy.

"Mornin' there, Mister Beeler," he said to me. "Rainin' is it?"

I looked at him, water ploppin' off my hat. "I doan know, Mister McCoy," I said. "I didn't notice."

He thought that was some funny, an' we stood there grinnin' at each other.

"I hear you and that Clarke girl brought one of Arberry Yont's deputies back yesterday tied up on his own horse," he said.

"That's the God's truth," I said. "That Harmony Clark is one tough woman when she gits riled up."

He grinned at me some more, then spoke up. "I got a extra cup a coffee in the back if you happen to know anybody that might want it," he said.

"Dammit, Elmo," I said, "it ain't good business to pick on no payin' customer."

"Excuse me, Sir," he said. "Lemme git you a cup a coffee."

He disappeared through the curtain an' I stood there, drippin'.

* * * *

I got me a frock coat in waxed lightweight canvas, went back to Clary's, put on the Schofield, an' walked to the Sweetwater. Warn't much of a crowd, 'cause a the rain, I reckon. I give my order to the tired lookin' dark-haired waitress an' purty soon, she set down a plate of fried potaters, ham, eggs, an' biscuits with honey. I tore into it, an' was just about done, when Arberry Yont stepped in outa the rain. He was wearin' one a them big ol' drover's coats with a shoulder cape an' was leanin' some to his left when he walked. I was curious what he might have hid under that coat. I loosened the Schofield under the table, toed out a chair, an' smiled at him.

"Mornin' Sheriff," I said. "Take a seat. I'll stand breakfast for ya if'n yer hungry."

He set an' looked at me for a minute, then kindly shook his head. "Ruben," he said, "I don't know what I am gonna do with you. I swear I don't. You are becomin' a thorn in my side, son, an'

I can't have it. I have lost two deputies because of you."

"Could be three," I said. "Maybe I knifed that one fella."

"I know better'n that," Arberry said. "You ain't the kind to sneak up an' stick a butcher knife in anybody. There's just those two."

"Sheriff Yont," I said, "You ain't lost two deputies 'cause a me. You lost them boys because a you. You didn't havta send nobody sneakin' around behind me. After the first time, I tolt ya I wouldn't stand for it, an' ya done it again anyway."

The waitress showed up with a cup a coffee for him. He took a sip, made a face, an' looked at me again.

"Ruben," he said, "I think you are a helluva young man, an' that is the truth of it. I'd take you on as a deputy in a heartbeat if you'd do it an' take orders from me. And now I hear that yer thinkin' about runnin' for sheriff. I need two more years in this town. Two more years. In two more years I'll be gone from this place an' in Jeff City. These folks can have this shithole back an' be welcome to it. I won't have no more use for it, period. But as it stands right now, I've already invested six years of my time in Deer Run. I cannot, an' I will not, give it up. Can you understand that?"

"Yessir I can, Arberry," I tolt him. "I surely can. But yer suckin' this town dry. That ain't right."

Yont shook his head an' sighed. "Then what are we gonna do about this, Ruben? What can we do?"

"That's purty much up to you, I guess, Sheriff," I said. "But while yer makin' up your mind about what to do, there is somethin' that you need to know. You ain't dealin' with just me. I ain't alone in this, not by a damn site."

His smile was kindly sad. "I got one more thing to try, then," he said. "I'm gonna reach under my coat, Mister Beeler. Don't git nervous."

He fumbled around for a minute an' lifted a buckskin bag with a drawstring top onto the table. It was heavy.

"In that poke are one hundred twenty dollar gold pieces," he said. "That works out to be two thousand dollars. Two thousand dollars is a lot of money. It's yours, Ruben, if you'll just let this whole thing go and leave town."

Yont was right. Two thousand dollars was more money than most folks ever saw in one spot. I eased the top a that poke open an' looked inside. Mercy. I reached in, took one a them gold pieces out, an' caught the tired-lookin' waitress' eye. I tossed the coin toward her an' she caught it.

"That's for my breakfast an' whatever the Sheriff wants," I said. "You can keep the change."

I turned back to Yont. He was starin' at me, level like.

I smiled at him. "Sorry, Sheriff," I said. "All that money is just too expensive."

I turned the bag over an' let them coins splatter out onto the table an' floor.

"Thanks anyway," I said, an' walked out.

CHAPTER TWENTY-FIVE

Arliss' eyebrows were up. "A hundred twenty-dollar gold pieces?" he said.

"Yessir," I said. "Two thousand dollars."

"And yer still here?"

"I am," I said.

He grinned at me. "Yer cylinder is short a round or two, boy," he said. "There wouldn't a been nothin' left a me but a puff a dust and the sound of hoofbeats!"

I laughed at him some.

"You know what this means, doncha?" Arliss said. "It means this mess don't have nowhere to go except trouble."

"I know it," I said. "Did it ever?"

"I reckon not. What are you fixin' to do?" he asked me.

"I think," I said, "that I'm gonna go set my stovepipe an' git that bottom collar put in."

"Oh, hell yes! That'll make everthing better," he said, an' went back to fussin' with that Remington.

*　*　*　*

I went out to the shed an' run a plumb bob from the stove to the ceiling an' cut a hole. Then I run that bob from the stove to the roof an' marked another hole. I put the pieces a pipe together, rememberin' to slide each piece into the one below it so I wouldn't have no creosote drippin' down the outside of the pipe. I got the bottom collar fit in an' everthin' ready to do the roof when it stopped rainin'. I was standin' on the porch, watchin' water run off the front eaves an' into my rain barrels, when Marion Daniels walked outa the back of Arliss' shop an' over to me.

"Howdy, Marshal," I said, steppin' back to give him some room.

Marion shook my hand. "I just heer'd that you turned down two thousand dollars to git outa town," he said, shakin' water offa his hat.

"Seemed like the thing to do," I said.

"Well, doan let it gitcha down, Ruben," he said. "Everbody makes mistakes. Homer know about yer meetin' with the sheriff this mornin'?"

"I ain't tolt him yet," I said.

"I'm goin' down to the livery," Marion said. "Why don't you follow along and we'll jaw a while."

I put on that frock coat an' went over to Miz Clary's an' got my little shotgun. I hung it on my gunbelt to the left side an' tilted the holster for a crossdraw. The coat hid it some. Then I went back out into the rain an' started off for the livery. After I walked a ways, I noticed my left boot seemed to be leakin' a little.

* * * *

By the time I got there, the rain had picked up agin an' it was really comin' down. Marion and Homer was just inside the barn door. I hustled over an' splashed in there with 'em.

"Toad strangler," Homer said.

Marion eyeballed me. "Where's your slicker?" he asked.

"Last I see'd it," I said, "it was layin' out next to a little spring pond west a here a ways. I forgot to git it when I trussed that deputy up."

"When you what?" Marion said.

"Miss Harmony an' me went for a ride Sunday an' stopped by a little spring to eat. This deputy was hidin' an' watchin' us, so I caught him up, tied him on his horse, an' delivered him to the sheriff."

Marion grinned at me. "The hell ya did," he said.

"Yessir," I said. "Miss Harmony helped."

"I bet that flew over like a brass owl."

"Deputy Clarence Banks said Yont run the feller off," I said.

"Arliss told me about your run-in with Yont this mornin'," Marion said. "I told Homer here while you was walkin' over."

"You turned down two thousand dollars just to stay here an' git shot full a holes?" Homer asked.

"Yes, I did," I said. "I like the company."

"Tetched in the head," Homer said.

"Crazier than a puppy with two peckers," Marion agreed.

We watched it rain for a while, then Homer spit tobacco juice out in the wet an' spoke up. "You tell Marion about Arkansas Bill Cole?" he said.

Marion took notice. "Bill Cole is around?" he asked.

"That's what our deputy tolt me," I said.

"Sheriff brung him in, I guess."

"Yessir," I said. "That's what Clarence said."

"Ain't that fine," Marion said. "If Arkansas Bill Cole is here, Piggy Wiggins ain't far away. Probably camped outside town somewhere."

"Who'd you say?" I asked.

"Piggy Wiggins. Runs with Cole regular. Your height, mebbe a little shorter. Goes about two-fifty. Got a red face, little blue eyes, a wide short nose that's kinda turned up so you look right up in it, an' he ain't got no hair. None. Not even eyebrows. Ain't never won no beauty contest that I know of. Pig is tough though. Nasty bastard. Bill Cole usta have some honor, but I speck the last ten years has wore most of it off him. I ain't seen him in five or six. If that sheriff has got them boys around, he's right serious. Pig Wiggins is a danger. Mean by nature. No doubt about that. Arkansas Bill Cole is a shootist. A fine one. Helluva pistoleer. Mebbe the best they is. Not a lot a doubt about that, neither."

"I wonder if it's too late to take that two thousand dollars," I said.

"Yer smarter than you look," Homer said.

Marion studied them clouds an' spoke up. "This here rain is fixin' to ease up some," he said. "Let's go to the Sweetwater an' git somethin' to eat. Ain't no reason we can't be seen together now."

Sure enough, in just a little bit things settled down some, an' we struck off. Marion stopped in Arliss' place on the way, an' leanin' up agin' the front window was a sign in black on yella about fifteen by twenty inches.

*   *   *   *

RUBEN BEELER
For Deer Run
SHERIFF
Low law Taxes
Honest Enforcement
vote for
BEELER

*   *   *   *

"Would you look at that?" I said.

"I had it printed up over in Jeff City," Marion said. "Gotcha fifty of 'em in cardboard like that an' three hundred black an' white notebook size on plain paper. You can set them big'uns in store windows an' such, and pass them little ones out to folks."

I was kindly embarrassed. "That makes me feel queersome like," I said. "I ain't never seen my name all out in the open like that afore."

"Git used to it," Marion said. "You owe me two dollars for them signs an' two bits for the wax paper bag they was carried in. I'll settle for a meal."

Arliss grinned at me. "Now that you are somebody," he said, "I'm gonna be right proud to be seen with ya. My friend Ruben. Got a nice ring to it."

"Too deep in here for me," Homer said, an' walked out.

The rest of us trailed him down to the Sweetwater.

*   *   *   *

Arliss brung one a them big signs with him an' headed back toward the kitchen with it while the rest of us set. Purty soon he come walkin' back, stuck that sign up in the front winda, an' come over an' joined us.

"It's official now," he said.

Margie come wigglin' over. "Good mornin' gents," she said. "We got chicken an' dumplins or fresh catfish an' broasted potatoes today. Both come with creamed peas an' rolls an' butter."

We all went for the catfish. While we et, we watched several folks walk by an' notice the sign. Couple of 'em got to jawin' at each other about it an' grinning. Mayor Eustice Forbes come by, seen it, an' studied on it some. Then he headed out, steppin' like he had business. Purty soon one a them bluevests walked up, looked at it, an' come inside. He picked that sign up an' started to

187

walk out with it.

"Hold on there for a minute, deputy," Marion said, an stood up.

The bluevest stopped and looked at him. Marion walked over to where he stood.

"What are you fixin' to do with that poster?" he asked.

The deputy swelled up a mite. "Well, I'm gonna take it with me if you don't mind."

Marion smiled. "There's the burr, son," he said. "I do mind. That don't belong to you. Why don't you put it back in the winda where you got it."

That deputy squared up on him some. "Just who in the hell are you?" he asked.

"I'm United States Marshal Marion Daniels, deputy," Marion said, an' stuck out his hand.

The bluevest took it an' Marion held on to him. "Now then," he said, puttin' on some pressure, "there's gonna be signs like that showin' up all over town. Me an' the Marshal Service would consider it a real favor if you'd take it upon yourself to be your duty to watch out for 'em. I don't expect any of 'em to be moved or damaged, son. Since it is now your responsibility to make sure nothin' like that happens, if anything does, I am afraid that I'll have to look you up, real personal like, an' discuss it with you."

The bluevest was kindly pale an' chewin' on his lip.

"I appreciate you takin' a interest in all this, boy, I shore do, an' I know yer gonna do a real good job."

Marion let go of him then, an' the deputy sagged a little. He collected hisself, put the sign back in the winda, an' walked out, wigglin' the fingers of his right hand. Marion set back down an' smiled.

"Nice young fella," he said.

*   *   *   *

We was on our second or third cups a coffee an' the rain had purty much give up when Elmo McCoy of the drygoods store come walkin' by. He spied that sign an' stared at it for a minute then looked in the winda an' seen me. In he come an' up to the table.

"Gentlemen" he said, "Elmo McCoy. Ruben, runnin' for sheriff, are you?"

"Reckon I am," I said.

"Well that's a breath of air," Elmo said. "Got any more a those posters?"

I grinned at him. "You fixin' to dress up yer outhouse are ya, Elmo?" I said.

"Maybe after you win," he said. "Can I get one for my window? Two would be better."

"In just a few minutes," I said. "I got some handouts, too."

"Wonderful," Elmo said. "I'll git my wife to pass 'em out at the church meetin' Wednesday night. You got enough, she can git her friend Effie to pass some out over among the Methodist heathens. Shame we can't all be Baptists. Got to have some folks that are willing to go to hell though, I guess."

That struck Arliss some, an' he laughed.

"I take it that you'd be a Baptist then, are ya Arliss?" Elmo asked.

Arliss shook his head. "I don't subscribe to no particular superstition," he said.

"Don't let my wife hear ya say nothin' like that," Elmo said. "She'd shoot Jesus at ya out of a shotgun if she could get him in the breech."

Homer snorted then an' Marion chuckled.

"I hate to wear out good company, boys," Elmo said. "I'll be gettin' on. By the way, Rube, that coat an' vest you couldn't return? New policy. Bring 'em by when you can. I'll trade 'em out for you."

"Thanks, Elmo," I said.

He looked out the winda. "Appears like it quit rainin'," he said. "Lord, I hope my wife is wrong. She told me this mornin' that she wished it wouldn't rain no more. If she's right, it's gonna be one damn long dry spell."

He left us then, grinnin' at him.

"He'll be a help," Homer said.

*   *   *   *

We walked back to Arliss' shop, but Marion passed it by an' headed for the back. "I wanna take a peek at yer place," he said.

We scraped as much mud as we could offa our boots on the edge of the porch, an' went inside. Marion looked around.

"This here is right nice, Ruben," he said. "You done some fine work in here. Gotcha some furniture, a woodstove, an' would you look at that? Stained glass on your windas an' a white ceiling. A fella couldn't want much more than this, I reckon."

"Thank ya, Marion," I said.

"They got any open rooms over where yer stayin'," he asked.

"Miz Clary is gonna have at least one I reckon. I'm movin' out."

"I'll take that one then. How 'bout you, Homer? You had enough a sleepin' in a barn?"

"I'll stay where I am, I guess," Homer said. "If things go to hell, wouldn't do for two of us to be too close together of a night. If they was to surprise one of us, they might git ahead a both of us."

We all stood there for a minute, then Marion went back out on the porch.

190

CHAPTER TWENTY-SIX

A little later that afternoon, I took that bag a signs an' handouts down to the drygoods store. Elmo McCoy met me inside the door.

"Helluva thing you're doin', Ruben," he said. "This town has labored under Arberry Yont's fist for too damn long. Good for ya."

"I brung all the signs an' papers I got, Elmo," I said.

"Why don't you just leave all that stuff here," he said. "I'll get a poster in every window along Main Street, over at the barbershop, down at the mill, the feed store, over in the yards, every place I can 'til they run out. I'll get those little flyers to the places that can pass 'em out to customers, and churches and the like. Get your name and the good news all over town. When you wanna give your first talk?"

"My first talk?" I asked him.

"Yessir," he said. "You got to do that. The election ain't for over two months yet. You are gonna have to speak three or four times between now and then. Keep your face an' words in front of the people. Walk around town sayin' hello to folks and such. It's called politickin', Ruben. Yont'll be out there doin' it."

"You mean I got to git up in front of a bunch a people an' talk to 'em about why I should be sheriff?"

"That is exactly what I mean," Elmo said.

"Lord," I said, "I never even thought about nothin' like that, standin' up in front of a crowd an' givin' 'em a speech or somethin'."

"You got a campaign manager?" Elmo asked me.

"A what?"

"Somebody to set up speeches and talk you up and go to businesses on your behalf and let you know what's goin' on in the community and make sure you are where you need to be."

"Nossir," I said, "I ain't got nothing like that."

"Well, you do now," Elmo said. "Me."

"You?"

"You bet, Ruben. I know that things like this have never crossed your mind, and why should they have? You are not a politician. That's part of your appeal. You're young, you're tough, you helped those folks that got waylayed by those bad fellas you shot, you have stood up to Yont, you're workin' on that little place a yours right here in town, you're likeable, and you're nice to people. We top that off with you talkin' from your heart instead of making speeches, with you dealing with people for the benefit of the town instead of yourself and what you can git out of it, and Yont is done for."

"Yont just ain't gonna set around an' let things slide on by, ya know," I said.

"No, he isn't," Elmo said.

"He's rough," I said. "He offered me two thousand dollars to leave town."

"Two thousand dollars!" Elmo kindly yelled.

"An' when I turned him down, he made it purty clear that since that didn't work, he was gonna find another way to git shed of me. He's even hired a couple a gunhands to come here."

"Still," Elmo said,"'if the town presents a united front…"

"This town has had years to present a united front an' it ain't never happened yet," I said. "Why the hell should it happen now?"

Elmo smiled. "You," he said. "You ain't a lot more than just a kid, but you have come in here an' shown more concern about this place than the folks that live here have in years. Yont has pushed this whole town around, but he ain't been able to push you. That there is an example, Ruben. And it has made some of these folks a little ashamed of themselves. Most people find it a lot easier to stick up for themselves if they have somebody who'll stick up for 'em. That is not only who you can be, son. In your heart, that is who you are."

"Sounds to me like yer the one who oughta be givin' a speech," I said.

Elmo chuckled. "These people don't need nobody throwin' a speech at 'em. They need somebody to talk to 'em and answer their questions and give a damn about 'em. That's you, Ruben. From the top a that big ol' hat of yours to the bottom of those dirty boots, that's you."

"Terrible nice a you to say that, Elmo," I said.

"You leave this to me, Ruben," he said. "We'll get it done."

I gotta admit, I walked outa his store thinkin' that we just might.

* * * *

The next mornin' I finished putting that pipe through my roof, an' tarred it up real good so they wouldn't be no leaks. I was just climbin' down the ladder when Miss Harmony come walkin' up. Her arms was loaded.

"Good morning, Ruben," she said, squintin' in the sun an'

looking all purty an' such.

"Miss Harmony," I said. "Ain't it good to see you this mornin'."

"I brought you a couple of house warming gifts," she said, an' put her burdens down on the porch.

"Well, what have you got there?" I asked her, walkin' over to take a peek.

"My father made you a boot scraper," she said, an' held it up for me to take.

It was a good'un. Solid iron with two scrapin' edges about three inches apart an' a heavy wire brush built into each side fer gittin' the mud offa the sides of the soles. It had four long legs on it, filed down into points, so a fella could push 'em down into the ground an' it'd stay put when he was draggin' his boots through it.

"This is just right," I said. "I doan believe I even seen one built this nice. You thank yer daddy for me. I'm right pleased."

She held up a worn ol' heavy wool saddle blanket. "This is for in front of your door to finish the job," she said. Then she lifted up about a six quart copper pot, all shined up, with a white enamel inside. Under the top, too.

"And this," she said, "will sit on your stove for beans or stew. It was my mother's."

"Oh, Miss Harmony, that there is fine, just fine. Look at it shine. I don't know what to say to ya. This is so purty an' bein' yer mother's an' all, I don't think a ever got anything as wishful as this is. Would you put it on the stove for me?"

"Of course I will, Ruben," she said, her voice kindly quiet.

I pushed open the door for her, an' she went inside.

I just stood there by the door an' watched her as she walked over to the stove an' set that pot on it. It was sorta like I was froze up standin' there. All of a sudden, I felt tears in my eyes. Miss Harmony see'd 'em an' come over to me an' put her hand on my arm.

"Why, Ruben," she said. "What's the matter?"

"Miss Harmony," I said, my throat all lumpy-like, "I ain't got nothin' that was my momma's, not hardly even a memory. To have somethin' that purty settin' in my place that come from you an' your momma, well, it just means a awful lot to me, I guess."

Miss Harmony put her arms around my waist then, an' leaned into me. We stood there for a spell, kindly swayin' back an' forth a little bit. Purty soon she pulled back an' wiped a tear from under my left eye an' smiled up at me. I smiled back an' she give a little laugh, then stepped away an' commenced to inspectin' my place.

* * * *

After a few minutes of lookin' around an' givin' me her approval, Miss Harmony went to the door an' stepped out onto the porch. I just couldn't give up on her, yet.

"Miss Harmony," I said. "It's comin' on noon. Would you be able to git a bite to eat with me down at the Sweetwater?"

"Since there's no stew in that pot yet, I guess I would," she said.

I lifted my gunbelt off the porch rail an' strapped it on.

"You carrying two guns now, Ruben?" she asked.

"The way things is, I believe it's prudent," I said.

"I've seen your poster," she said. "I believe it is prudent, too."

* * * *

She took my arm as we walked down to the Sweetwater. We took a table near the center of the room. We both had the catfish with greens an' cornbread. We was about halfway done when this fella come in. He was heavy-set, wearin' a faded ol' blue kerchief an' a faded ol' pink shirt that had started out as red. He carried a short-barelled Colt with a round cut grip in a cross draw an' a Bowie on the other hip. His hat was ratty an' rolled up in the front, an' he didn't hardly have no neck at all. He looked like he was sunburnt. His eyes was small an' wide set, an' his nose was broad an' turned up so you could see right up it if ya had the will to look. He didn't have no hair I could see, even above his eyes, an' his upper lip was so short, his top teeth showed. They was yella. Lookin at him, you could kindly tell what he smelt like. If ya had yer eyes closed an' smelt of him, I bet a fella could figger out what he might look like.

He took a little two person table just inside the door, an' looked around the room, grinnin'. When his eyes come on Miss Harmony an' me, he stopped lookin' an' stared. Miss Harmony an' me went on eatin' an' talkin' but he never broke his gaze until Miss Margie come up to his table. She didn't stay long.

"Do you know that man?" Miss Harmony asked me.

"No," I said, "but I know who he is. His name's Pig Wiggins. He's a killer. Arberry Yont brung him an' a fella named Arkansas Bill Cole to town. Cole is a pistolero. They're here to deal with me, I speck."

"We can go," Miss Harmony said.

"If you want to, we will," I said. "But we're not done with our dinners yet."

Miss Harmony smiled. "We can stay a little longer, I guess," she said.

Pig stared at us some more, then Miss Margie brung him some coffee. I didn't see real clear what happened then, but when she turned to walk away he leaned forward an' she squeaked an' jumped off from him. He laughed. I didn't like the sound of it.

I whispered to Miss Harmony to set still, then I raised my voice an' looked out the door.

"There goes Arliss," I said. "I gotta ketch him. I'll be right back."

I jumped up an' hurried toward the door. Pig watched me comin', but when I ignored him an' didn't change course none, he shifted his eyes back to Miss Harmony. I was at a trot when I turned on him.

I hit the front edge a his table with my hip an' all my weight behind it. The rear edge slammed back into his belly just below his ribcage. Hot coffee flew, an' some of it splashed on me, but it didn't make no difference. Most a the air in his lungs squirted out when the edge of that table drove into him like it done an' he couldn't git his breath. I kept my weight agin' him an' he started gaspin' like, tryin' to breathe but not havin' any luck. When his face started changin' color, I pulled away from the table, took his Colt, grabbed him by the kerchief, an' drug him outside. He was some heavy an' staggerin', still tryin' to breathe. When we got through the door, I let him drop. He laid there on the boardwalk, gaspin' like a carp. I knelt down beside him an' slapped his face. Them little blue eyes a his found me.

"We don't treat women in this town like that, Pig," I said. "I see you in here agin', I'll shoot ya. You can git your Colt at the Sheriff's office when you can walk. If you decide you wanna come at me, that'll be just fine."

He curled on his side then, holdin' his belly. I left him there an' walked around the corner an' down the way a piece. Arberry Yont was settin' at a desk when I walked in his office. He looked up an' seemed a little surprised.

"Your new dog shit in the Sweetwater," I said. "He does it

agin', I'll kill him."

I tossed that Colt on top a the desk, turned around, an' walked out.

*   *   *   *

Miss Harmony was still at the table when I got back to the Sweetwater. Piggy had took hisself off somewhere's. I set an' looked at her.

"Miss Harmony," I said.

"Mister Beeler," she said.

We smiled at each other for a minute. "Would you be kind enough to walk me back to the livery now, Ruben?" she said.

"That would be my pleasure," I tolt her.

*   *   *   *

When we got there, Homer was settin' on a bucket, smokin'. I let him know I'd met Pig Wiggins. When I finished the story, he stood up.

"I believe I'll walk back down to Arliss' place with ya," he said.

"That'd be right nice," I said. "I appreciate it."

He brimmed his hat at Miss Harmony. "M'am," he said, an' started off.

I grinned at her an' hurried to ketch up.

CHAPTER TWENTY-SEVEN

I moved outa Miz Clary's place that evenin' an' Marion moved in. When I tolt him about what happened with Pig Wiggins, Marion just shook his head.

"Ol' Ruben," he said. "Went right straight at him, did ya?"

"Yessir," I said. "I couldn't think a no other way to do it."

"I ain't sayin' you was wrong, son. Doin' whatcha done was probably the only way you could a got through it without bein' gunshot. Damn, boy, yer a pistol, you are."

I figgerd that was a compliment, so I didn't say nothin'.

"This gonna be the first night at yer new place for ya, is it?" he asked.

"Yessir. It ain't much of a house or nothin' but it's good enough for me."

Marion's eyes sharpened up some. "Well, it ain't no damn bug-filled soddy set out in the middle of the prairie someplace, drippin' mud from the ceiling on the dirt floor, now is it?" he said.

"Nossir," I said, "I reckon it ain't."

"Ya damn right it ain't," he said. "Ruben, a feller like you, at yer age, with his own house, money in the bank, a trade, an' settin' hisself up to be the sheriff of a town a over a thousand people, just ain't terrible common! Give yerself some credit, boy.

Lotsa other folks does. Now, git outa here. This ain't yer room no more."

I carried the last a what I had over to the shack an' put stuff away an' such. It was gittin' close to dark. I had just hung that brass lamp by the door an' lit it when there come a knock. It kindly surprised me.

"Hello?" I said.

My door swung open an' in come Arliss, Homer, an' Marion. Arliss was carryin' a bottle, an' Homer an' Marion was each carryin' a chair from up at the shop.

"Light another lamp, Rube," Arliss said. "This here is a house warmin'."

He reached in his coat pocket an' come up with five shot glasses. He set 'em on my table an' filled each one. I was some curious.

"How come they's five glasses an' just four of us?"

Right that minute, there come another knock.

"C'mon in," Homer yelled.

Through the door come Clarence Banks, complete with a badge, a blue vest, an' a smile.

* * * *

I was some foggy the next mornin'. I tolt ya before that I'm careful with drink, the one time I got drunk bein' so distressin' an' all. I didn't actual git drunk, but I could shore see it from where I wound up. I used the convenience an' walked up to the shop. Arliss had a Winchester '73 strung out all over the bench, peerin' at it.

"Durn fool lost count a how many shells he was puttin' in it, an' forced one too many. I got it apart without blowin' it up or nothin', but, Lord, it was worrisome there for a spell." He broke away from the rifle then an' looked at me.

"Talk about the walkin' dead," he said. "Rube, you ain't lookin' right comfortable."

"My head hurts some," I said.

"I speck it does," Arliss said, tryin' to hold on to a grin. "I can feel it throbbin' clean over here. Are ya fixin' to die, ya reckon?"

Right then it felt like somebody shot a arrow inta my left ear. I jerked from it an' closed my eyes for a second. "No, Arliss," I said, "I ain't gonna die."

Arliss give up an' full grinned at me. "I didn't figure you'd take the easy way out," he said. "Just a minute."

He walked off inta the back. His boots stompin' across the floor didn't do me much good. When he come back, he was carryin' a little brown bottle. He held it out to me.

"Take a swallow a this," he said, "then drink all the water you can stand an' go back to bed. "You'll feel some better when ya wake up."

I took the bottle an' smelt of it. "What is it?" I asked him.

"Laudanum," he said. "Some I got left from when I was shot. One swallow."

I took it. It didn't taste terrible good, but no worse than the inside a my mouth to begin with. Then I went to the bucket an' drunk two full dippers a water.

"Take to your cot, boy," Arliss said.

I went back to my place an' stretched out.

*　　*　　*　　*

I hadn't laid there very long when the sun come through the east winda an' the room shined over all gold like. That stained glass got to glowin', all green and yella, an' I couldn't hardly stand how purty it was. They was colors in that place I had never noticed afore. The copper pot was kindly lit up from the inside or somethin', settin' there on that black stove. I went to sleep

201

lookin' at it.

* * * *

When I woke up, I was terrible thirsty, but my head was considerable better. I drank a dipper, put on my hat an' boots, strapped on my gunbelt, an' started up to Arliss' shop. I hadn't took two steps out the door when my stomach kindly flipped an' it come to me how hungry I was. I passed Arliss place an' went straight to the Sweetwater. I had just started on my sausage, kraut, an' mashed potaters when Marion walked in. The second he come through the door, the whole place seemed to draw breath. That's the way it was with Marion. He was right noticeable, special with that marshal's badge on his vest. He seen me, come over, an' set.

"You breathin' are ya, Ruben?" he asked.

"Barely," I said, shovelin' in some more kraut.

"That's all right," he said. "Don't hurt for a man to git silly once in a while."

Margie come over, but he just asked for coffee an' pie. It come on me then that I'd only seen him actual eat a big meal a couple a times since I knowed him. I didn't say nothin' about it. I just kept eatin'.

When I finished up, Margie asked did I want some peach cobbler with cream. I said yes an' she went off to git it. Marion took a sip a his coffee an' looked at me.

"Saturday, Ruben," he said.

"What?" I said.

"Saturday evenin' around five, there's a big meetin' over at the new schoolhouse. They're gonna want to hear from ya."

"Who is?"

"The town," he said.

"The whole town?" I asked.

"A passel a fol,ks I expect," he said.

Margie showed up an' put that cobbler down. I warn't so sure I wanted it.

"You mean to tell me," I said, "that Saturday a bunch a folks is comin' to the schoolhouse to listen to me talk about bein' sheriff?"

Marion smiled. "That there is the jist of it," he said.

"Oh my," I said, an' kindly stiffened up, just starin' at the top a that table.

Marion shook his head an' reached over an' took my cobbler. He didn't say nothin' 'til he'd et both it an' his pie.

"It ain't gonna be so bad, Ruben," he said.

"I don't know if I can talk to a crowd like that," I said.

"That's why ya don't talk to the whole durn crowd, boy. Ya just talk to one person."

"What?"

"When you git up there, you locate one person on the left, one person on the right, an' one person in the middle. Those are the folks you talk to. Ya talk to one a little bit, then another one for a little bit, then the last one for a little bit. Then ya do it again. The crowd thinks yer talkin' to everbody, but ya ain't. Yer just talkin' to three people, one at a time. Takes all the pressure off. Then when it comes time for questions, you talk to that one person that asked ya somethin'. That way, it don't make no difference if there's a hundred people or a thousand people. You ain't talkin' to but one person at any given time. See?"

"That kindly make some sense," I said, lookin' around the table.

Marion chuckled. "I bet Margie would bring ya another piece a cobbler if ya asked her," he said.

* * * *

I was just finishin' my cobbler when the door opened an' I felt Marion stiffen up a little. Walkin' in the place come a fella near as tall as he was. He wore a black flat-brim hat with the front a the brim rolled down a little, a white shirt an' a buckskin vest. He was packin' two colts with black handles in a double crossdraw rig. His eyes was dark and slitted, he had a long thin nose, near no lips, a scar across this throat, an' he was terrible thin. He seen Marion an' brimmed his hat. Marion brimmed his an' toed a chair back. The feller smiled somethin' that warn't really a smile an' walked over. When he spoke, his voice warn't much more than a whisper.

"Marion," he said, when he got to us. He walked like his feet was sore. "Long time, no see."

"Been a while, Bill," Marion said. "Set."

He eased into the chair like he was delicate or somethin', an' nodded at me.

"Bill," Marion said, "This here is Ruben Beeler. He is a friend a mine. Ruben this is Arkansas Bill Cole. He an' I has knowed each other for a spell."

"Reckon yer the boy that took a pig to market yesterday," Cole said.

"Warn't much," I said. "Didn't have nothin' better to do at the time."

Cole glanced at Marion. "Thinks he's tough, don't he?" he said.

"He is," Marion said.

Cole looked back at me. "Are ya?" he asked.

"Ask yer pig," I said.

"Kinda tired a that pig," Cole said. "Done me a favor if ya kilt him."

"There's always next time," I said.

"There always is, boy," Cole said. "Or the time after that."

"How ya been, Bill?" Marion asked.

"I ain't got no dirt over me yet," Cole said. "Still marshalin' are ya?"

"Never could find a honest job," Marion said. "I heard you was in town."

"Surprise ya?" Cole asked.

Marion smiled. "Not much. You always was too damn fond of a dollar."

"Ever now an' then," Cole said, gittin' to this feet, "a feller has got to spend one or two of 'em. Buy hisself a new pair a britches."

"I reckon so," Marion said.

"Like this young fella here," Cole went on, noddin' at me. "He's gittin' a little too big for the one's he's wearin'."

We watched him walk out through the door an' I felt myself sag some.

"He scare ya, Ruben?" Marion asked.

"A little," I said.

Marion smiled an' nodded his head. "Me too, boy," he said.

CHAPTER TWENTY-EIGHT

I stopped by Arliss' shop on the way back to my place. He was at his bench fussin' at a Sharps. I tolt him about meetin' Arkansas Bill Cole.

"Cole won't come at you, boy," he said.

"He won't?"

"Not right off. He'll take a run at Marion first. He sees Marion as his biggest threat."

"I reckon he does," I said. "Marion can handle him though, can't he?"

"I ain't never seen him in motion," Arliss said, "but he's got a helluva reputation. He's a shootist, Rube. A damn good'un. Could go either way I speck."

Hearin' that kinda news set me back some. I changed the subject.

"That Homer's gun?" I asked.

"Durn near," Arlis said. "It's a forty-five seventy cartridge conversion. His is a forty-five ninety. And this'uns barrel's four inches shorter. Had a cartridge rip open in it sometime or other, and the breech got scarred some. Hard to git a empty out of it now an' then. I've had the thing for near a year. Got it on trade for a Henry. I'll sell it some day an' make a profit. Elmo's lookin' for ya."

"He is?" I asked.

"Yessir. He was by here a little while ago. Wants to see ya."

"Oh hell," I said. "All right. I'll go up that way."

Arliss smiled at me. "Ain't lookin' forward to talkin' in front of a crowd much, are ya?" he asked.

"Truth be told, I ain't, Arliss," I said.

"Kinda like wadin' a crick, Rube," Arliss said. "A feller hates to do it, but once ya git in there and git started across, it ain't so bad."

"I got it to do, I reckon," I said.

"Never know, boy," Arlis said. "Ya might even like it."

*　*　*　*

Elmo McCoy was arrangin' some dishes when I got to his drygoods store. He stopped all that an' come over to me when I stepped in.

"Ruben," he said, "guess you heard about the meetin' on Saturday."

"Yessir, I did. It come up purty quick like, didn't it?"

"That was Mavis' doin'," he said. "My wife, Mavis. She took some a them handouts to church last night, an' folks just jumped on 'em. Same thing happened to her friend, Effie Gossard, over in that Methodist bunch. Them two hen's got to cacklin' at each other and made the rounds after those church meetin's and this mornin' and set it up. Folks is real interested in you and what you have to say. Everybody is tired a Arberry Yont. I've passed out fifty or more of those flyers myself. You've been good for business. Quite a few folks that don't usually drop in much have noticed the posters in the windows and come inside. Most of 'em bought somethin' while they were here."

'Bout that time, two ladies that were lookin' around noticed me an' nodded in my direction.

I nodded back an' said, "good afternoon, ladies." One of 'em come over to me.

"Mister Beeler," she said, "me and my Dan are looking forward to hear what you have to say at the meeting Saturday."

The other one spoke up from where she was lookin' at some bolts a cloth, that she an' Cecil would be there, too. I thanked both of 'em an' me an' Elmo drifted toward the counter.

"I gotcha set up at the barbershop for Saturday morning," Elmo said.

That took me by surprise. "Beg pardon?" I said.

"You get in the barber shop around ten on Saturday. He'll cut your hair and give you a shave. Then his bathtub is reserved for you at eleven."

"A bathtub?" I said.

"Yessir. He's got two in the back."

"I been in a washtub," I said, "but I ain't never been in no bathtub."

"You'll love it," Elmo said. "Set up so you can lay back and soak for a spell, with all the hot water you want. When you get out of it, there's a shower so you can rinse off. Your clothes will be there wainting for you."

"My clothes?"

"That's right," he said. "I gotcha a dark gray shirt with a thin light gray stripe and a white padre collar, and gray saddle pants with black panels in the seat and down the inside of your legs. Your suspenders are black."

"I don't wear suspenders," I said.

"You will for the talk," Elmo said. "Make ya look a little older. And I want you back here early afternoon so we can discuss the meeting." He walked over to a rack a hats an' picked one out. It was dark gray with a low, kindly flat, pinched crown, an' a flat brim rolled down some at the front an' the back. He handed it to me. "Here," he said, "try this on."

"I got a hat," I said.

Elmo glanced up at my headgear. "You ain't runnin' for cowboy," he said. "You're runnin' for sheriff. Try it on."

I warn't happy about it, but I put it on. It didn't fit as good as mine, but when I went over to the lookin' glass an' studied on it, I was some surprised. It looked kindly good.

"See there," Elmo said, "makes you look a little more mature. You get to be in office, you can wear whatever you want, but you'll have that hat on when you go up to talk. Then you'll take it off, set it on the desk, an' run your fingers through your hair. We don't want you to look like you're hidin' under anything. That'll give the men a honest impression of you, and the ladies will like seein' you act so open an all. Can't ignore the women, Ruben. Their husbands mostly do what they're told."

"All this for just one talk?" I asked.

"More than that," Elmo said. "We are turnin' young Rube, the carpenter, into youthful Ruben, the sheriff. I know what I'm doin', son."

"I speck you do," I said, "but ain't I gonna look terrible fancy?"

Homer smiled at that. "You don't need no cutaway coat or no brocade vest with a watch chain, two pearl-handled six-guns, and a gold tooth. You do need to look a little more like you mean business. I'll set you up with another couple of shirts and a extra pair a pants after the meetin' on Saturday."

"How much is all this gonna cost me?" I asked.

"You bring back that coat, vest and shirt you never used and we'll call it square. With the extra traffic I've had in here, I'm coming out ahead."

Them ladies come up with some stuff, an' I moved outa the way. The one that spoke to me first put some change on the counter an' turned toward the door. Then she looked at me an' spoke up agin.

"If you don't mind me sayin' so, Mister Beeler," she said, "that's a good hat for you. Right handsome. It brings out the gray in your eyes."

I was kindly surprised an' I felt my ears git warm. "I don't mind at all, M'am," I said. "Kind of you to say so. Thank you."

She flashed her eyes at me an' smiled. "Brings out the red in your ears, too," she said. "We'll see you Saturday."

I watched her leave an' turned back to Elmo. He was grinnin'.

"I rest my case," he said.

*   *   *   *

I was kindly restless on Friday. I fussed around my place a while then went down to the yards an' got me two more a them captain's chairs an' a not too big armoire for hangin' things in. That afternoon I walked over to the livery. Verlon was at the forge an' Homer was pumpin' the bellows for him.

"Dammit, Rube," Homer said, "don't you be tellin' nobody you seen me doin' honest work. It'll ruin my reputation!"

"Your secret is safe with me," I tolt him.

Verlon spoke up. "You all set for Saturday night?" he asked.

"Tell the truth," I said, "I'm scairt to death."

"Can't help with that," Verlon said. "Anything else I can do for ya?"

"Nossir. I' thought I'd ketch Willie up an' go for a ride. Maybe see if that slicker a mine is anywhere near where I left it."

Verlon nodded at Homer, an' Homer turned to me. "Believe I'll tag along with ya," he said. "Nice day an' that gray a mine ain't been under saddle for a while. If he doan git rode regular he gits a mite peevish."

*   *   *   *

My slicker warn't nowhere to be found near that little pool. We rode the draw down an' come on it, tangled up in them river birches where that fella was spyin' on Miss Harmony an' me. That big rain we had musta washed it down that way. I shook it out an' it didn't seem no worse for wear.

"Hear you met Arkansas Bill Cole," Homer said.

"He come in the Sweetwater when me an Marion was in there," I said.

"He scare ya as much as the meetin' comin' up?"

"Damn near," I said.

"My money's on you, Rube," he said. "When things scare ya, just take 'em on one at a time. You ain't in this alone."

"That mean yer gonna talk to the crowd with me?" I asked.

"Yer damn shore alone in that if yer countin' on me," he said.

"Maybe not, Homer," I said. "I'd like it if you, an' Marion, an' Clarence was to come by Arliss' place about a hour before the meetin'. I got a idea that might ease them folks minds a little bit. I know most a them has been in Yont's harness for so long they're afraid of the whip. I'd like to help with that."

"I'll see to it," he said.

I tied that slicker behind the cantle, an' we headed back. The whole ride, Homer never stopped lookin' around, searchin' the hills for sign.

CHAPTER TWENTY-NINE

I didn't stop an' see Arliss or nothin' on the way back. I just went to my place an' stewed. I fussed around, set out on the porch a while, an' worried. It was gittin' late when I figgered I should be hungry, even though I warn't, so I walked up to the Sweetwater to git a bite. Once I got out on the street, I come to notice two bluevests sorta movin' along with me on the other side. I done my best to ignore 'em.

The Sweetwater was mor'n half full. I set an' asked for the pintos an' pork. While I set there an' made myself eat, folks kept lookin' at me some. Several nodded at me an' smiled. Two or three of 'em even walked over to my table to tell me they'd be at the meetin'. It was right strange. I warn't usta much attention an' it vexed me some but, to tell the truth, it was sorta pleasant like, too.

When I left an' went back outside I knowed I was bein' watched. I could feel it on me. I looked up an' down the street, but I couldn't spot no bluevests or nothin'. Then I come to look into a little alley across the way, an' there, on the edge of the dark, I seen Homer leanin' up agin a water barrel holdin' his big ol' Sharps. He brimmed his hat at me an' I went on. I gotta admit it made me feel some better.

*   *   *   *

I didn't sleep no good that night, wakin' up a bunch a times, waitin' for mornin' like a fella does when he's too restless to rest. A little after ten in the mornin' I showed up at Culver's Barbershop an' Bath House. The barber there was about twice my age an' bald. He wore a white apron an' sleeve garters, an' grinned real big when I come in.

"Mister Beeler," he said, "I been expectin' ya. Take yer hat off an' git in the chair, sir, an' we'll git ya cut back some."

"Thank ya, Mister Culver," I said, hangin' my hat on a rack.

"I ain't Culver," he said. "Culver has been dead for years. My name's Davis. Lionel Davis. I took the place over after he passed. I just ain't never bothered to git a new sign."

I got in the chair an' he put that sheet thing over me an' got everthin' adjusted to his likin', then went to work. The whole durn time he cut on my hair, he never shut up. I ain't terrible sure he even slowed down enough to take a breath. He talked about the weather, he talked about his wife an' her church doin's, he talked about the cost a feed, he talked about me, he talked about the way people was talkin' about me. He never quieted hisself for a heartbeat. He did slow down a little when he was usin' that razor on my throat, an' I was purty glad a that.

My hair had got some long. When I saw myself in the glass at the end a things, it sorta looked to me like my head had shrunk.

"There ya are, Mister Beeler," he said. "We gotcha slicked up now. Took enough offa ya to weave a small blanket, yessir. Now if ya wanna grab yer hat an' come on in the back with me, we'll git that trail dust knocked offa ya, too. Elmo McCoy was in a little while ago an' dropped off some duds for ya. You don't owe me a thing. It's all been took care of."

I set in that high-back copper tub in water to my chin for

near a hour. When that water come to git cool, I'd just pull up on a little plug down by my knee an' let some out, then pull this chain hangin' there, an' hot water would run out a pipe comin' through the wall an' right into that tub. They was cakes a soap back there too, on a little shelf in easy reach. That soap was some softer than lye, an' smelt like flowers or somethin'. When you'd use it, it would lather right up an' foam. Then they was these brushes with long handles for easy gittin' to spots that woulda otherwise been some hard to reach. I set in there 'til I was fair wrinkled up, then pulled the plug an' let that water run out. The more water that left, the heavier I got. By the time that tub was empty, I felt like I weighed as much as Willie.

I got out a the tub an' went in this little stall-like arrangement with a swingin' door. They was a faucet kinda thing comin' outa the wall about head high that had a round front on it punched full a tiny holes. I pulled on a chain hangin' there, an' cold water shot out an' hit me right in the face. I jumped from the chill of it, but it got warm then an' I rinsed off from head to toe. I don't believe I ever got so clean afore in my whole life.

I dried myself off on a couple a big towels an' run a comb through what was left of my hair. I got dressed, used a damp towel to wipe my boots down some, an' strapped on my gunbelt. They was a long bag hangin' on a wall hook that had my new clothes in it, an' that hat hangin' beside it. I grabbed that bag an' that hat, an' headed out the back door. I hustled down alleys an' such until I got back to my place. I knowed that Elmo wanted me to put them clothes on after I got my bath, but I just wasn't ready for that yet.

Back home, I stripped down an' washed up a little after havin' them dirty clothes on an' all, then I got dressed in the ones that Elmo give me. Them pants was built like the ones I had, with that extra layer where a fella come into contact with the saddle, but where the pants was gray, that extra layer where it come across my butt an' down the inside a my legs was black. To tell the truth, I thought it was some stylish. My other saddle pants was made outa canvas, but these new ones was softer brushed cotton or somethin'. They was right gentle feelin' an' had some comfort to 'em, an' they had a seven button fly. I'd never heard a such a thing.

I got into 'em an' tightened up that little belt in the back to where they snugged up nice. Then I put on that new shirt, tucked it in, buttoned it all the way up to that stiff white collar, got into them durn suspenders an' adjusted them to where they didn't vex me too much, an' put on that hat. From what I could see in the glass on my washstand, I didn't look too bad. I didn't look exactly like me, but then I did, too. I put what I needed in my pockets, strapped on the Schofield, took a deep breath, an' walked up to see Arliss.

* * * *

When Arliss seen me comin' up through the back, his eyebrows went up an' he grinned.

"Rube!" he said, "by God, boy, don't you look purtiful! I got to admit, you look some older and a little set on somethin'. I think Elmo done ya proud."

"It all feels kindly funny," I said.

"Don't make no difference," Arliss said. "It takes a team a while to get used to new harness. You'll adjust quick. Where ya off to?"

"I gotta go see Elmo," I said. "He wants to talk to me about tonight. I'll be back by four so I can git with you, an' Homer, an' Marion, an' Clarence."

"We'll be here, Rube," he said.

I started to leave then, an' Arliss spoke up.

"By the way, boy," he said, "I really do like that hat."

*   *   *   *

Elmo like to wore me out. He had a lady workin' for him so when I got there he took me into the back an' started in on me. Some a what he said stuck, but most of it come at me so fast I couldn't ketch aholt of it. It just flew around the room an' flapped out the winda like bats. I stuck it out though, an' done my best to agree with everthin' he said. It went on for quite a spell, but eventually he slowed down.

*   *   *   *

When I escaped I noticed I was some hungry, but the way my stomach was jumpin' around, I knowed I shouldn't eat nothin'. I went back to Arliss' place an' kilt time while he worked on settin' a new trigger in a ol' ten gauge Greener. After a while, Marion showed up. He looked me over.

"Ya look like ya mean business, Ruben," he said. "That there shore cain't hurt. Good for ya."

Homer an' Clarence come at the same time. Homer looked at me an' smiled, but he didn't say nothin'. Clarence was the big news. He warn't wearin' no badge, an' the blue vest was gone. He grinned at me.

"Hi, boss," he said. "What are we fixin' to do?"

CHAPTER THIRTY

Everbody else went to the schoolhouse around half-past four. I waited until near five afore I walked over. There was people everwhere, inside, standin' around outside an' such. Several buggies an' horses was tied out front, an' a feller could hear the buzzin' a the crowd a half a block away. Four or five bluevests stood around the edge a things. Elmo was hangin' around outside the door lookin' nervous. He brightened up some when he seen me an' come hustlin' over.

"We got a mess a folks here, Rube," he said. "More than two hundred. Probably close to three. The room is packed. Now that you're here, these people outside will squeeze in. I'll go up front in a minute and introduce you. Then you come on up. You remember what I told you?"

"Ever word," I said.

Elmo looked at me for a second an' grinned. "The hell you do," he said. "This is your meetin', Ruben. Yours. You'll do fine."

He took off then. I watched the stragglers go in an' I stepped up into the door an' waited.

* * * *

The tables an' such had been carried outside to make more room. The benches were moved up close to the front an' in the center for the women to have a place to set. The rest of the room was standin' space for the men. The teacher's desk was pushed back an' a low crate was in front of it. Purty soon, Elmo walked to the front of the room an' stepped up on that crate. The place quieted down.

"Ladies and gents," he said, "most of you know me from my drygoods store. I'm Elmo McCoy. I am here this evening to introduce a young man that I have come to know, to like, and to respect. This young man, I have learned, while acting as a deputy United States Marshal, was among those who took down the Duncan gang over by Gasconade earlier this year. It was he who saved a traveler an' his daughter from death and worse just outside of town less than a month ago. On at least two occasions, he has acquitted himself well within our community by dealing with men of low character who insulted our women. But more than all that, he also did the finish carpentry in this very room in which we gather."

That comment got folks laughin' some an' lookin' around.

"Now it seems," Elmo went on, "that this fine young man has taken an opportunity to do right by our community. This gives our community the opportunity to do right by him. I am very pleased to introduce to you, Mister Ruben Beeler. C'mon up, Rube."

I'll be durned if they didn't clap for me! I walked on up there, thinkin' about how crossin' a crick warn't so bad once ya got yer feet wet, an' turned around an' looked out across that room at all them people lookin' back at me. I just stood there for a minute, then I took my hat off an' put it on the desk. Then I run my fingers through my hair an' stepped up on that crate. The place got quiet, an' my mouth got dry. I seen Miss Harmony settin' in the middle of that covey a women, smilin' at me. I don't know why I done what I done, but I done it anyway.

"Miss Harmony," I said, "yer lookin' right purty this evenin'. Are ya doin' all right?"

"I'm fine, Mister Beeler," she said. "How are you?"

"I'm plumb scairt," I said. "An' that's the truth."

She laughed, an' the crowd laughed, an' I laughed, an' all of a sudden, I felt better.

* * * *

"Folks," I said, "I ain't never stood in front a so many people afore in my life. I'm grateful that all of ya come out this evenin', an' right surprised that all a you would do that just to hear me talk. But since ya did, I will.

"It was not intent that brung me here to Deer Run, but circumstance. But I'm here, an' I like it. I have a place here now, I've called bingo here, I have found work here, I have come to know some good people here, an' I believe I might even have a lady friend here."

The crowd laughed a little at that.

"I live here," I said. "Arberry Yont offered me two thousand dollars to leave this town. I'm still here. He brung Pig Wiggins an' Arkansas Bill Cole in to run me off or kill me. I am still here. I like this place, but there are things in this community that I don't care for at all. There are things here that distress me some, an' most of 'em wear blue vests. Almost ever person an' ever business in this town has to pay tribute to Arberry Yont an' his gang. There is a big difference between a tax an' a tribute, just like there is a big difference between a group of law enforcement officers an' a gang a thieves. The plain truth is, this town is on the wrong side a them differences.

"To keep a sheriff an' some deputies don't come free. They deserve to git paid for a job a work like anybody else. But, if yer payin' this bunch ten dollars a month, you should only have to pay one. If yer payin' these robbers fifty dollars a month, you should only have to pay five. You are payin' ten times more to Yont an' his gang that you should have to pay, an' that kind thing needs to stop!"

The room come alive then, with clappin' an' some whistles. When it settled down, I went on.

"This town deserves a mayor that can find his way out of a crowd a three. This town deserves a city board that works for the city instead of the city workin' for them. You people deserve to git outa Arberry Yont's harness, an' out from under his lash!"

Agin the crowd took off. I waited 'til they settled down.

"If you good people elect me sheriff, yer law tax will git cut by ninety percent. You'll be glad to see a deputy on the street. You'll be free to elect the city officials you want, an' vote the crooks an' carpetbaggers outa office. But that has got to start with the sheriff. The plain truth is, if you vote me in, you vote him out. We need to git shed of him folks, an' them bluevests that run with him. To do that, you need my help an' I need yer help."

When the crowd got quiet, a fella near the back a the room spoke up.

"Yont ain't gonna take to this much," he said. "Ain't no tellin' what he might do!"

"Yessir," I said. "You are exactly right. He's got deputies outside right now, an' Lord knows who else. That's why I ain't in this alone. Come on up, boys."

From different places in the room, Marion, Homer, Arliss, an Clarence worked their way through the crowd an' lined up in front a where I stood on that box.

I give the crowd a minute to stop whisperin' an' spoke up. "Here we got U.S. Marshal Marion Daniels," I said. "We got ex-

U.S. Marshal Homer Poteet, we got gunsmith an' shootist Mister Arliss Hyatt, an' we got ex-Yont deputy Clarence Banks. These men an' me have all been authorized, by way of the United States Attorney General, the governor of the State of Missouri, an' the Supreme Court of the State of Missouri to be commissioned as officers in what is knowed as the Missouri State Special Police Force. Let's put 'em on men."

While the crowd clapped an' cheered, we all took out our new badges an' pinned 'em on.

"There it is, folks," I said, when things got quiet. "Now you got the real law on yer side. You got the Missouri State Police. The rest of it is up to you. My thanks to all of you for comin' out. Have a good evenin'."

I lifted my hat up off the desk an' put it back on.

*   *   *   *

I took a half a hour or more to git the place cleared out. Folks kept comin' up to me wantin' to talk an' shake hands an' such. It got plumb silly is what it done. Finally things broke up an' I was standin' outside next to Marion when Elmo come up.

"It couldn't have gone any better, Rube," he said. "It just couldn't have gone any better! You need to get over to the Sweetwater and get a bite to eat. Let folks see you an' say something to you. It's real important you be out in the public right now."

"All right," I said. "I'll do it."

"Wonderful!" he said, an' run off.

I looked at Marion. "You hungry?" I asked.

"You go on," he said. "Me an' the boys'll spread out some. Wouldn't be smart for all of us to git too close together right now."

I had broke away from a couple more people an' started

walkin', when I seen Miss Harmony standin' out by the road. I went over. She looked at me an' smiled.

"You said you thought you had a lady friend, Ruben," she said. "Is that true?"

I grinned an' looked up the road a little. "I hope I do," I said.

"Well," Miss Harmony said, "I guess anything is possible. Nice hat."

I watched her git up in their little buggy with her daddy an' drive off.

*   *   *   *

While I walked on to the Sweetwater it come to me that there warn't gonna be no more meetin's or speeches. This thing would play out afore it ever got near to election time.

CHAPTER THIRTY-ONE

When I got over to the Sweetwater, it was plumb near full. Just inside the door was that little table that Pig Wiggins had set at. I took it an' leaned my chair back agin the wall. Lord. I hadden et nothin' all day, nor slept much the night afore neither. Plus, I'd been like a snake in a skillet, worryin' about that meetin' for near two days. When I hit the chair an' leaned back, most a the stuffin' just leaked right out me. Miss Margie an' another gal was tearin' around the place like they was on wheels, tryin' to keep up with the extra business. Margie seen me, dropped what she was doin', an' hustled over.

"Ruben Beeler," she said, "folks in here been talkin' about you an' that meetin' tonight. Sounds to me like you got this whole town in your pocket!"

I smiled at her. "That there will wear off soon enough," I said.

"I don't know," she said. "You are the topic of every conversation. We got some nice beef roast with new potatoes and carrots. That sound good?"

"Have ya got any pie or cobbler?"

"We do," she said. "We have some blackberry pie and we have some blueberry cobbler."

"Miss Margie," I said, "if you would bring me two pieces a that blueberry cobbler in one bowl with some cream on it, a cup of coffee, an' a bowl of sugar, I would surely dance to your next weddin'."

She dimpled all up an' just looked as purty as a bluebird. "How 'bout my first one, Ruben?" she said. "Would you dance to that?"

"Why Miss Margie," I said, "have you got a weddin' comin' up?"

"I do," she said an' giggled. "Around Christmas sometime. We ain't set the exact date yet."

"Well, who's the lucky fella?" I asked. "Do I know him?"

"You do," she said, beamin' at me. "It's Clarence."

"Clarence Banks?" I said.

"That's him. He sure does think a lot a you, Ruben. To tell the truth, so do I. I think you are a fine man and you always was a gentleman to me."

"That's nice of you to say, Margie," I said. "I believe you to be a good woman an' I think highly of your intended. I feel like he's my friend."

"Thank you, Ruben," she said. "Now don't you go blabbin' this around. Me an' Clarence ain't announced nothin' yet."

"My lips are sealed," I said.

"At least until I git that cobbler here," she said, an' scooted off.

She had just stepped away when a fella an' his wife, on the way out, stopped to tell me how much they liked my talk an' such. Purty soon, another fella stopped on his way out, then another fella an' his wife. It become regular. Durn near everbody that left the place, spied me settin' there an' stopped. I appreciated they was all happy with what they heard an' such, but I kindly started feelin' like a preacher at the end of the service. I shouldn't a set right by the door like I done. In a little bit, Margie brung me my cobbler.

"There you are, Ruben," she said. "No charge, it's on the house. You just set right there an' enjoy it. You look a little tired."

"If I go to sleep an' fall outa this chair," I said, "git Clarence to carry me home, will ya?"

She giggled an' bounced off. That gal had so much energy, I got even more tired just watchin' her.

I like my pie sweet, so I dropped a spoonful a sugar on the cobbler an kindly mashed it all up in the cream. Since I was eatin', most folks just smiled or nodded as they left, instead of stoppin' to talk. That cobbler an' sugar give me some energy, so I flagged Margie down an' asked for a half order of that roast. The place was about two thirds empty an' I was near through my meal when Clarence walked in. He noticed me.

"Howdy boss," he said. "I didn't know you was in here. I'll go back out on patrol."

"Set down, Clarence," I said. "Take a load off. I'm just finishin' up."

He set an' looked at me. "Anythin' goin' on?" he asked.

I couldn't resist. "Just that Margie gal," I said. "I been settin' an watchin' her. She shore is a purty little thing. Terrible easy on the eyes."

Clarence didn't know what to do with that. "You, uh, you an' her usta keep company didn't ya?" he said. "Wadden she the one you was with the night you knocked that feller off the boardwalk?"

"Yes, she was," I said. "Lookin' at her like I been, an' watchin' her walk around, I'm thinkin' I oughta start up with her agin."

"Uh, Ruben," Clarence said, "about that. Uh, me an' her,

well, uh, we..."

I couldn't keep on with it. "Rest yourself, Clarence," I said. "Me an' Margie never did keep company. We just talked some an' went for a couple a walks. I think she's a fine girl an' I think you are a lucky man. Just a few minutes ago, she confessed yer plans for Christmas time. She also made me swear to keep it a secret. I only told you 'cause I thought you maybe already knowed about it."

Clarence got the color of a strawberry an' ducked his head, grinnin'. I stood up an' dropped a dollar on the table.

"I appreciate ya, Clarence," I said. "Have some roast on me."

It was near full dark when I got outside, an' a light breeze outa the north had cooled things down some. All in all, it was a fine night.

*　　*　　*　　*

I took my time walkin' home, stopped an' jawed with Arliss for a spell, then went to my place. I lit a lamp an' fussed around for a while, then blowed the light out, stripped down to my skivvies, made sure the little shotgun was on the nightstand next to me, laid back, let out a sigh, an' woke up. I think I was just too plum tired to sleep. I tossed an' turned for quite a spell, an' then, just as I was finally droppin' off, I heard Homer yell.

"Right there you sonofabitch, or I'll put a hole clean through ya!"

Then they was a gunshot, then that big ol' Sharps roared.

I come outa the bed like it was on fire, grabbed that little shotgun, an' tore out the door.

"It's all right, Rube," Homer hollered, "he's down!"

I went around to the east end of the place, the only wall where they wasn't a winda, an' there was Homer, that Sharps tucked up under his arm, a Colt in his right hand.

"I think he's all they was," he said. "I didn't see nobody else."

Bout that time, Arliss come trottin' up in his bedclothes carryin' a lantern. There, layin' on his side on the ground was a bluevest I didn't know. Beside him was a tipped over two gallon can a coal oil an' a box a matches. A Colt revolver was about a foot from his outstretched hand. There was a hole through his chest an' out his back that had just missed his badge.

"Fixin' to set yer place afire," Homer said. "Not no more."

Clarence come runnin' up, half outa breath, gun in hand.

"Holster yer piece, Clarence," I said. "It's all over. You know this fella?"

"Yessir," Clarence said, lookin' down at him in the lantern light. "His name is Clyde Franklin."

"All right," I said. "Don't nobody touch nothin'. Clarence, you go git the Sheriff. Not a deputy, but Yont. Wake him up if ya need to, but git his ass down here to investigate this shootin'."

Some other men from out in the street had showed up, after hearin' the shots an' all.

"Homer," I said, "keep these fellas on hand. They got here quick enough to verify that nobody moved nothin' nor tampered with no evidence. I'll be right back after I git some pants on. Arliss, go git dressed afore I arrest ya for bein' indecent in public."

I was back out in just a minute, boots an' pants an' gunbelt on, with another railroad lantern. Three or four fellas was standin' around, waitin'. Homer was settin' on the porch with his feet up on the rail, smokin'.

"Howdy, Rube," he said. "How ya doin'?"

"I'm fine," I said. "You all right?"

"He hit me, but not much. Just a little bullet burn on my arm right below my shoulder."

There was a rip in his shirt, but hardly no blood that I could see, even holdin' that lantern up close.

"You need to go to the Doc?" I asked.

"Aw, hell no," he said. "I'll just pour a little whiskey on it an' it'll be fine. Special if I don't use all the whiskey on my arm."

"Thanks, Homer," I said. "You saved my place an' maybe me, too."

"Nothin' to it," he said. "Slow night an' all."

"Arberry is gonna be some pissed off," I said.

I could see Homer's grin by the light of the lantern.

"See," he said, "somethin' good can come outa almost anythin'."

CHAPTER THIRTY-TWO

A couple a bluevests come walkin' up, one tall an' kindly thick, the other one shorter an' thin. The big one stomped up to me.

"What the hell is goin' on here?" he holler'd.

"Been a shootin'," I said. "Clarence Banks is on the way to git your boss to investigate."

"Who's that layin' over there?"

"Fella name a Clyde Franklin," I said.

"Clyde Franklin? By Jesus, he's one a our'n!" the bluevest yelled.

"Not anymore," I said.

"He's dead?"

"Looked like it to me," I tolt him.

"Well did ya even fuckin' check him?"

Homer, his feet still on the rail, spoke up. "Didn't need to," he said. "It was my Sharps that hit him. That gun kills buffler with one shot. A human don't stand no chance at all."

The big fella turned on Homer an' snarled. "So you done it!" he said.

"Yessir," Homer said, spittin' a little piece of tobacco off his tongue. "I give him first shot an' he took it. He just warn't no good at it."

"So that's it, is it?" bluevest thundered. "You just gonna start killin' us off?"

Homer grinned. "Don't have to," he said. "You fellers could always run away."

That big fella was almost in a rage. "Oh, you dirty bastards! I wanna see him!"

He started toward the body then an' I stepped in front of him. "Why don't you shorten up yer reins, mister," I said. "Ain't nobody here touched anythin' over there, an' you ain't goin' to neither. Let's just wait for Yont."

He went to push by me then, so I grabbed that shotgun outa the crossdraw an' smacked him right smart on the elbow with it. He howled an' fell down, clutchin' at his arm, but bounced up purty quick. That arm I hit wouldn't work at all, an' he went for his Colt with his off hand. I stepped up an hit him a helluva lick on the other elbow. He howled agin' but kept his feet, both arms hangin' loose. I lifted his Colt an' took a quick glance at his partner, but that fella was just standin' there, watchin'. The big one was so mad he was almost in tears, but there warn't nothin' at all he could do. I speck that made him some madder. He started in cussin' me, an' I spoke to him, soft like.

"If you don't shut up, the next hit you git is gonna be in the mouth," I said. "I ain't got no sympathy for the fact you cain't protect yourself."

His partner spoke up. "For chrissakes, Irwin," he said, "shut the hell up. It's embarrassin'."

He settled down some, an' went off a ways, his arms loose like an' danglin'. I walked over to his partner.

"Thanks," I said. "He's hurt, but he ain't broke. His arms'll work in a while." I handed him the big fella's Colt. "Hold this for him, will ya?" Give it back when he's gone from here."

"I will," he said. "You coulda hurt him a lot worse."

"I thought about it," I said.

He grinned at me an' walked over to where his partner was still kindly hoppin' around. I went back to the porch an' set on the rail. Homer chuckled an' smacked me on the leg with the back of his hand.

"Right purty," he said. "You ever consider a career in law enforcement?"

*   *   *   *

It took Yont about ten minutes to show hisself. He come bustlin' up with Clarence an' two more bluevests.

"What the hell is goin' on?" he yelled.

Homer took his feet offa the rail an' looked at me. "I got this," he said, an' stood up. "Howdy, Sheriff," Homer went on. "That ol' boy layin' dead over there come to Ruben's place carryin' a jug a coal oil. I watched him splash some a that coal oil on the wall a Ruben's house. Then, I'll be damned if'n he didn't reach into his pocket an' take out a box a matches. Bein' a experienced law enforcement officer, I come to a conclusion. Since ol' Rube over here is fixin' to kick yer ass somethin' terrible in the upcomin' election, an' since this ol' boy layin' dead was one a yer little posse, I concluded that his behavior an' the articles he had with him represented to Mister Beeler an' his home serious threat, doncha see? I announced my presence an' requested that the dead feller over there cease an' desist his hateful activity. He took exception to my innerference an' drawed his handgun. Then he aimed it at me an' fired it. He mostly missed. In a effort to end his felonious activity an' protect my own life, I aimed my Sharps at him an' fired it. As you can see, I didn't miss. We have kept the scene secure for you to look over,

231

knowin' you'd be concerned an' all. One a your pups attempted to interfere an' invade the scene. Officer Beeler here wouldn't let him. That's about it, wouldn't you say, Officer Beeler?"

"I speck so," I said.

"Now there are two or three gentlemen over there," Homer said, noddin' toward them boys that was waitin' "that come on the scene right after it happened. They can attest to the fact that everthin' is just as it was. I'm sure that yer investi-by God-gation will arrive at the same conclusions as ours has. I am just terrible sure a that, Arberry. Ain't you?"

Yont walked over to the body an' looked around a little bit. Homer set back down, propped up his feet, an' rolled another smoke. He'd just set fire to it when Arberry come back.

"I can't see anything to dispute what you told me," he said.

"That's some good police work, Sheriff," Homer said. "Why doan you git aholt of the undertaker an' git that fire-startin' piece a shit drug off?"

Yont stomped away then, his two deputies trailin' along behind him.

"Hey, Homer," I said, "you ever consider a career in law enforcement?"

CHAPTER THIRTY-THREE

Things got kindly quiet for a couple a days. I took duty in town durin' afternoon an' evenings, Homer patrolled durin' the evenin' an' night, Clarence took days, Marion come an' went as he pleased, an' Arliss? Arliss was just Arliss.

Miss Harmony an' me went for a buggy ride one mornin', down by the river. We come back to the livery, turned out the team, an' was considerin' a bite to eat at the Sweetwater, when I heard a shot come from down that way. I took off an' hustled in that direction. When I come on the main street, I seen three fellas carryin' another fella as fast as they could around the corner an' into the Doc's office. I went over that direction an' up the steps, bein' careful 'cause there was so much blood.

The doc was bendin' over the fella, rippin' open the leg of his pants, high up on the thigh. Blood was pumpin' outa him in spurts.

Oh, Lord. It was Clarence. He was white as a sheet.

The doc got a strap around his leg up by the crotch an' tightened it down, then commenced to fussin' with the wound. Purty soon he stood up, shakin' his head.

"There ain't nothin' I can do for him, boys," he said. "That bullet plumb ruined that big artery in there. There just ain't nothin' I can do."

"Is he dead?" one a them fellas asked.

All of a sudden, that blood flow just quit.

"He is now," the doc said.

The office door crashed open an' Miss Margie come tearin' in, squallin'. She threw herself on top a Clarence, clutchin' at him an' callin' his name. Then she just broke down into cryin'. It was pitiful seein' her like she was, an' him like he was.

That fella spoke up agin.

"I seen it," he said. "She was with him, walkin' down by the Houston House. There was a feller standin' there that said somethin' to her. This fella here stepped up an' the other fella just pulled an' shot him. Just like that. They wasn't more than three feet apart. Then he went in the saloon."

I took Miss Margie by the shoulders then, an' kindly eased her up offa Clarence. She stayed bent over some, holdin' herself an' moanin' like. I urged her to the door an' out onto the landin'. I seen Miss Harmony comin' up the way, an' she seen me. I settled Miss Margie on the steps, an' she set there, still bent over, but quiet, an' I went back inside to talk to the witness.

"You seen the fella that done the shootin'?" I asked.

"Yessir."

"You know him?"

"Nossir," he said. "I seen him around town the last few days. Squat feller. Got a face that looks sorta like a hog. Smells sour."

I looked down at Clarence agin' an' noticed his holster was empty. Somethin' scratched at my mind. "This man pull his gun?" I asked.

"Nossir," the fella said. "He never had the chance."

I started for the door just as I heard Miss Harmony shout fer me. I busted out on the landin' an' she looked up at me. "Margie ran off," she said, pointin' down the way. "Ruben, she's got a gun!"

I headed down them steps to chase her, but my foot went out from under me, slippin' in that blood, an' I fell them last two steps. I smacked my knee purty hard an' that slowed me down quite a bit. I got to my feet an' went on, as fast as I could. I come around the corner an' seen her runnin' down toward the Houston House. She had a block an' a half on me. I give it all I was worth but it warn't near enough.

I was still half a block behind her when she darted into that saloon. I run on an' heard a gunshot, followed real quick by two more. I pulled my Schofield, busted through them swingin' doors, an' had to step lively to one side to keep from trippin' over Margie where she lay on the floor. It was that side step that saved me, I reckon. Pig Wiggins was right there, not twenty feet away. He got off two shots at where I warn't. I got off one at where he was.

That bullet hit him in the throat an' rocked him back some. He started to raise his piece an' I shot him agin, this time in the belly. He sat down on the floor then, pink foam flowin' out his mouth an' blood runnin' down his neck, lookin' confused. Then them little pig eyes a his found me, an' I couldn't stand it. I shot him agin', dead center chest, an' he flopped over on his back, his right leg twitchin' an' his heel thumpin' on the floor.

I heard them doors bang open behind me an' Marion say "Ruben?"

"I'm all right," I said, an' turned to Margie. She was layin' on her back, hit twice in the chest, Clarence's handgun layin' a couple a feet away. I lifted her head an' looked down at her.

"Clarence?" she said, an' the light in her eyes went out. Just like that.

* * * *

Miss Harmony was waitin' outside when I walked out. She put her arms around me an' we hung onto each other for a spell. Marion come out after talkin' to some folks an' findin' out what happened. The three of us stood there, not sayin' much while the undertaker come an' went. As the hearse pulled away, Arkansas Bill Cole come down the street on horseback. He turned his bay in our direction an' stopped.

"I heard what happened, an' I doan hold with it," he whispered. "Bad business, boys. I'm done here. See ya on down the trail."

"Better not," Marion said.

Cole brimmed his hat an' touched the bay into a short lope. We all just stood there an' watched him ride away.

Nobody said nothin' fer a while, an' I noticed Marion's jaw twitchin' some. Purty soon, he spoke up.

"By God, Ruben," he said. "This here ends today."

He walked off then, an' I follerd him.

* * * *

Arberry Yont was settin' at his desk when we come in his office. He stood up real quick an' started to say somethin' an' then there was a hole in his face where the top a his nose usta be, an' the blast of a gunshot slammin' offa the walls. As Yont hit the bookcase behind him an' slid to the floor, Marion put his Colt back in the holster. I swear, I never seen him draw, cock, nor fire. It was that fast. It was just that goddam fast.

"That'll do it," Marion said.

I walked around the desk to where Yont lay, lifted his revolver outa the holster an' tossed it on the floor.

"I'm a witness," I said. "I seen him pull on ya."

"Damn right you did," Marion said, an' walked out.

CHAPTER THIRTY-FOUR

Deer Run made me temporary sheriff until I could git voted in at the election. A bunch a fellas left town. In what usta be Yont's office, I found a little safe set into the floor under a rug. Took me a while, but I prised it open. Inside there was near sixteen thousand dollars. I give Marion, Arliss, an' Homer each a thousand an' kept a thousand for myself. The rest I passed onto the consolidated churches old folks fund. Homer went back over to Gasconade County, an' Marion went back to marshalin'. About three weeks after I took office, two fellas by the names of Hank Buford an' Emory Nail showed up with a note from Homer sayin' they was good men an' needed work. I hired me two new deputies on the spot. Miss Harmony an' me kept on keepin' company, an' she made me try to start callin' her just Harmony.

A couple days after I was formally elected, I asked Arliss if I could borrow the wagon.

"Rube," he said, "I'm gittin' tired a givin' you permission to use that wagon. I have tolt ya that it's as much your'n as it is mine. Take the durn thing!"

"Thank you," I said, grinnin' at him.

He eyeballed me some. "Whatcha need it for?" he asked.

"I gotta go down to the yards an' git me a mess a lumber."

"Why the hell do you need lumber?"

Arliss," I said, "if you must know all my business, I'm fixin' to build a bedroom onto my little house."

Ya see, Miss Harmony an' me had been talking some, an' had reached a agreement. It warn't gonna be just me an' Arliss anymore.

Author's notes

Save an author; write a review.

I would love to know what you think about DEER RUN TRAIL. Ratings and reviews are a great way to applaud (or boo) an author, so please consider leaving a review for DEER RUN TRAIL on any retailer site.

For more information regarding other titles in this series, please visit my website, www.ironbear-ebooks.com or visit us on our FACEBOOK page, Ironbear eBooks.

Go to http://www.ironbear-ebooks.com to sign up for our newsletter, WRITER'S BLOCK. (Ironbear sends out our newsletter once per month. We promise not to swamp you with emails. And, we will never share or sell our mailing list. To me, that's just wrong.)

Please continue to the next page to read the first 4 chapters of the next book in the TRAIL series, NODAWAY TRAIL.

Thanks,
David

PREVIEW

Saddle up with Ruben again as the saga continues when he and Marion ride the...

NODAWAY TRAIL
Book 2

CHAPTER ONE

I was settin' in front of the Sheriff's Office thinkin' about gittin' me somethin' to eat when he come ridin' in on that big ol' roan a his. I watched him git off an' wrap a rein around the rail. He favored his back some. The roan got busy with the trough, an' he clanked his way up on the boardwalk, them Mexican spurs a his lettin' a fella know evertime his boots hit. I hadden seen him in over a year, not since me an' Harmony got hitched. He eased down in a chair beside me an' I noticed a scar on his left cheekbone that wadden there afore. His big droopin' mustache had gone near total gray. He put a ankle on a knee an' squinted at the street for a minute.

"Sheriff," he said.

"Marshal," I said.

We set there for another minute afore he grinned an' slapped me on the knee.

"Ruben, gawdammit!" he said, "are ya alright?"

"I believe I am, Marion," I said. "How the hell are you?"

"I'm trail tired, boy," he said, "an' that there is the straight of it. What's the Sweetwater got on special today?"

"Are you so feeble ya cain't even walk over an' find out?" I asked him.

"Mebbe you outa come with me in case I fall over and cain't git up."

"Maybe I should," I said. "We got laws agin' folks layin' around in the street in this town."

Marion grunted an' stood up, then walked off down toward the corner on them godawful long legs a his. As usual, I followed along behind.

*   *   *   *

We took a table near the back an' the owner, a fella name a Hershel, come over.

"Rube," he said. "Marshal. We got some extra nice catfish today with green peas an' fried potatoes, or chicken stew an' cornbread."

We both took the catfish an' stayed purty quiet until after we et an' got coffee. Marion stirred a little brown sugar inta his.

"Miss Harmony alright?" he asked.

"Fixin' to have a baby," I said.

"The hell she is!"

"Yessir. Miz Clary says it'll be a spell yet. Prob'ly November sometime."

"Ain't that fine. You got a kitchen built on that place a your'n yet?" he asked.

"Nossir," I said. "After Harmony said she was gonna have a baby, her daddy wanted us to move into his place down at the livery. Nice big house, plenty a room. Even got that pump from the cistern right there in the kitchen. So we done it. I help out with the stock an' on the forge some. So does Harmony. Cain't git her to quit. We give my place to Arliss, it bein' right behind his shop an' all."

"Nice of ya," Marion said.

"Ol' Arliss has been plumb good to me. Least I could do."

"How's the sherrifin' business goin' for ya?" Marion asked me.

"Them two fellas that Homer sent over has worked out real good as deputies. Town's mostly quiet these days. Got a fair council an' Elmo McCoy's the mayor now. How's the Marshalin' trade doin'? I notice ya got a new scar."

Marion touched his cheek. "There was nine of 'em, Ruben," he said. "But I got all of 'em with five shots."

"It took ya five?" I said. "You must be slowin' down some. Ol' age ya reckon?"

Marion grinned at me. "Last fall," he said, "I was over in Gasconade tryin' to keep Homer on the straight an' narrow. I was standin' out by the rail in front of the Sheriffs Office next to that jug headed roan a mine when a horsefly or somethin' got up on his ear. He tossed his head my direction an' the shank a his bit smacked the hell outa me. Knocked me on my ass. The doc had to put seven or eight stitches in the damn thing. Said it give me a concussion. I doan know about that, but I had a helluva headache for a couple days."

"Homer alright?" I asked.

"He was then," Marion said, "but I doan know about now. I swung through Gasconade on the way here, but he was off chasin' somebody somewheres. Horse thief, I believe it was."

We set there for a spell, quiet-like, while I waited for him to git to the point. Marion doan git in a hurry much, unless it's called for, then he gits around right smart. Putry soon, he spoke up agin'.

"You reckon them deputies a your'n could take care a this town with you gone for a while, Ruben?" he asked me.

"I reckon," I said.

"An' Miss Harmony," he went on. "You s'pose she'd be alright if you left for a spell?"

"That baby ain't supposed to be here afore November," I said. "She's with her daddy, Verlon. Harmony's tough, Marion. Whatcha need?"

"Quite a spell ago," he said, "even afore the war most likely, come a feller up by the Missouri north a Saint Joe in Atchison County name a Clovis Waxler. Set hisself up a ferry business gittin' folks across the river. Rumor has it he had two boys an' some of his wife's kin hangin' around a few years later. Now an' then, a couple a folks an' their wagon would disappear, or some little pole boat wouldn't show up down river when it was supposed to.

"Eight or ten year ago it was believed that two a his nephews, last name a Siebert, held up a bank over by East Saint Louis. The Pinkertons got after 'em but lost 'em in the Missouri Breaks. After a year or two, they give up. That whole mess was supposed to be hangin' around up near where that ferry usta be, out in the sticks runnin' between Atchison and Nodaway Counties. Month or two ago, his sons, Jack an' Jim, is believed to be the two men that got with a couple a whores in the Blue Island saloon on the north side a Saint Joe, kilt one of 'em with a knife, an' cut the other one's ear or nose off, an' sliced her up here an' there.

"Some County Sheriff formed a posse an' took off after 'em. Like most possies, once a couple a them fellers got shot an' the sheriff was kilt, they lost heart an' give up the chase when the bunch run for Nebraska or Iowa. When shit like that happens, the mess falls to fools like me. You done good when you come with me an' Homer when we went after that Duncan bunch. You've done yerself proud here. I could use ya, Ruben. I hate to wade into this mess all by myself. A course, you'd be a deputy marshal agin'."

"When do we leave?" I asked him.

CHAPTER TWO

After we et, Marion went by the shop to visit with Arliss a spell, while I walked down to the livery. Verlon waived at me from the forge. Harmony was in the kitchen poundin' on a pile a dough to make bread. She set the dough aside under some cheesecloth, wiped her forehead with her apron, an' come over an' give me a kiss. I thumbed some flour offa the end of her nose an' grinned at her.

"Been snowin' in here?" I asked.

"One of us has to work a little bit," she said, throwin' a grin back at me. "What brings you home in the middle of the day?"

"Marion's in town," I said.

"Oh! Well ask him over for supper. We haven't seen him since we got married."

"I will if ya want me to," I said.

"Why wouldn't I want you to," she asked. I followed her to the outside stove where she checked the fire an' oven.

"Well," I said, "he wants to borrow me for a while."

"What for?"

"He's got some business to take care of over north a Saint Joe a ways," I said, "an' he wants me to ride along. He figgers that two of us would be some better than one a him."

"The two of you would be better than four or five of most men," Harmony said. "If he needs your help, of course you have to go. You wouldn't feel right if you didn't."

"I don't want ya gittin' worried about me an' all," I said.

"Ruben Beeler, my worries are my worries," she said. "There is nothing you can do about them, and precious little that I can. You don't need to worry about me worrying about you. Marion needs you. You go ahead along with him. Hank and Emory can take care of things here."

"You don't mind it if I go?" I said.

"Yes, I do," she said, "but not as much as you'd mind it if you didn't. Understand?"

"I reckon I do," I said.

She smiled at me. "Then I reckon," she said, "that I don't want to pound that dough out again. Get out of my way. Ask Marion over for supper. Arliss too, if he wants to come along."

*　*　*　*

On my way to Arliss' shop I run across Hank Buford an' told him I'd be leavin' for a while in a day or two an' that if he needed help to git aholt a Arliss or Verlon Clarke to fill in. He said he would an' he'd make sure to tell Emory in case I missed him. I went on then, an' found Marion in the shop talkin' to Arliss.

"Marion tells me you an' him is takin' to the trail, Rube," Arliss said.

"Whenever Marion wants to go," I said.

"I'm restin' up for a day or so, Ruben," Marion said. "Take a day to git what truck you need in shape and some chuck for us. You still got that packhorse?"

"Still do," I said.

"Good," Marion said. "I'd just as soon stay on the trail as much as we can. We'll leave enough tracks as it is without ridin' through ever town we see."

"Suits me," I said. "Harmony would be right pleased if'n the two of you would care to set with us for supper this evenin'. Last I seen her, she was fixin' to stick a couple a loaves a her sourdough in the oven. The ones she puts a little cinnamon in an' glazes with honey. Verlon's got a ham or two in the smokehouse that should be about ready. Might be a hard meal to miss."

"'Bout half-past five seem good, Rube?" Arliss asked.

"Make it six," Marion said. "I need to git Miz Clary to do a little laundry for me, an' I'd like to git down to the barbershop for a haircut and a tub a hot water. Might be a while before I can git to that kinda thing agin'."

*　　*　　*　　*

The next day I set to cleanin' my guns an' lookin' after my horses an' tack. Verlon trimmed up my packhorse an' put fresh shoes on him. I put on a new cinch, as the ol' one was gittin' a little thin. I'd had one break on me once an' I didn't care for it. It was deep spring an' Willie was gittin' a little grass fat. A trip would shape him out an' drop some weight. I went over to the general store an' got some flour an' cornmeal, some dry beans, some salt-cured bacon, half a dozen cans a peaches, coffee, one a them plugs a dried tea, some jerky, brown sugar for Marion, some peppermints an' four a them little boxes of Gayetty therapeutic papers. Harmony always kept 'em in the outhouse an' I'd got some used to 'em. They was a luxury, sure enough, but they was a damn site more useful than a corncob or a handful a moss an' leaves.

I stopped by an' seen Elmo at the dry goods store an' got me a nice pair a buckskin chaps. If we was gonna be ridin' the river any, I wanted somethin' to turn briars an' thorns. I also got me a new slicker as mine was leakin' at the seams, a wax-treated ground cloth, an' a spool a stage line in case we might need to string us up a shelter a some kind.

I was fixin' to go collect the buckboard to pick up all my truck, when I seen Verlon comin' down the street in his with some bags a feed. I flagged him down an' loaded up my stuff an' he saved me a extra trip. Back at the livery I packed up my panniers, added my three pound axe to the load, an' finished up gittin' what we needed for the trail.

That night, Harmony didn't have a lot to say an' hung onto me quite a bit while she slept. It was worrisome an' kept me awake more that I mighta liked, but I let it go. I knowed she was some upset I was headin' out with Marion an' all, an' I didn't feel no need to add to her discomfort none. She did fix us a big ol' breakfast a ham an' eggs an' fried potatoes, an' sourdough biscuits an' gravy. I didn't figger I'd git that good a breakfast for a while, so I et as much as I could hold an' still swing a leg over a horse.

I had them panniers strung up on my pack saddle an' was putting a skillet an' coffee pot in one of 'em when she come out with a sack a them biscuits for us. I got everthin' closed up, an' was tossin' a blanket on Willie when Marion caught up his roan, an' saddled up. Arliss was on hand. We said goodbye to him an' Verlon, Harmony gimme a kiss an' a hug, an' about a half hour after daybreak, me an' Marion took out. We wasn't more than a hour gone when clouds gathered, the wind picked up, the temperature dropped, an' it come to rain.

I wonder how come it is that a fella can feel wetter in the rain than if'n he jumped in the durn river? It never did rain terrible hard, but the wind kindly drove it at us, turnin' some of it into a mist that snuck down collars, up sleeves, an' into eyes an' ears 'til the two of us was shiverin' from it. It wadden but the middle a the afternoon afore we come on this little creek an' got down next to it an' up agin' a high bank that cut the blowin' from the northwest an' give us a windbreak. Marion rooted around in some brush that had collected in a bend at high water, lookin' for some dry wood while I hobbled the horses an' strung that groundcloth to give us a little roof to set under. Between the saddles an' the panniers offa my packhorse, I fixed us up a place to lean back out the weather an' dug a pine knot out the pack about the time Marion showed up with a armload of small stuff that was not too wet. That pine knot got them sticks goin', an' purty soon we had us a fair camp an' fire. I got some water outa the crick an' put coffee on an' a pot to boil an' handed Marion a peppermint stick.

"I thank ya, Ruben," he said, leanin' back an' puttin' that stick between his teeth. "Ain't it fine how a stick a peppermint can take the edge offa unfair day like this one. It's the little things that can make the biggest difference, I guess."

We'd set there a hour or so an' I'd put some beans in the pot an' a piece a bacon when he had to go piss. He durn near fell down tryin' to git up. It embarrassed him I believe, an' he limped off a little ways. When he come back, he grunted when he set down, an' screwed his face up some. He beat his hat on his knee a lick or two to git the water offa it, put it back on an' stared into the fire.

"Now before you even ask, boy," he said, "me and the roan took a fall this past winter over by Sikeston. There was a foot a snow on the ground and I speck that softened up things some, but I hurt my back down low a little. Wasn't long afore I had some shootin' pains down my ass plumb to the back a my right knee that was worrisome. Got to where it kept me up of a night and I couldn't hardly walk. I went to a doctor over that way and he rolled me around on the floor pullin' on that leg and pushin' on my butt four or five different times. Felt right foolish, but it helped quite a bit. I git around alright with it now, 'cept once in a while it hangs up on me. Wet weather seems to aggravate it some."

"I believe that horse a your'n has had all a you he wants," I said. "First he slaps you upside yer head an' knocks the hell out of ya, then he tries to cripple ya fallin' down. Maybe ya oughta git a mule."

Marion rolled that peppermint sick around a minute afore he spoke up.

"I believe," he said, rockin' his head a little from side to side like he usually done when he was gittin' cocky, "that little tin star you been wearin' for a spell has turned you into about three-quarters of a smartass."

I grinned at him. "Anything's possible," I said.

Marion rooted around in a pocket under his slicker for a minute.

"Well," he said, "I reckon this'll only make matters worse."

He tossed somethin' silver at me, an' I caught it. It was a U.S. Deputy Marshal badge.

"Do you swear to uphold and the rest of all that?" he asked me.

"Yessir, I do," I said.

"Alright then," he said, sinkin' a little lower into his set. "Good to have ya along, Ruben. Doan let the fire go out."

He pulled his hat down low over his eyes an' sighed, what was left a that peppermint stick twitchin' a little.

*　　*　　*　　*

I woke up afore daybreak the next mornin' an' freshed the fire. The rain had stopped overnight, but it was still cool and windy. By the time Marion got up, I had coffee hot an' bacon on to go with Harmony's biscuits. Marion headed out to do his business an' I give him a box a them Gayetty therapeutic papers. He looked at 'em, quizzical like.

"What the hell's this?" he asked me.

"Well, it ain't a handful a wet leaves," I said.

When he come back, he didn't say nothin' about them

papers, but he didn't give 'em back neither.

CHAPTER THREE

Our third night on the trail we camped four or five miles outa Saint Joe. The next mornin' Marion left me at camp an' rode to town. I had me a cup a tea an' brown sugar, an' et all but the last two a them biscuits, then squared everthin' away so we could git on without much fuss. While I was waitin' on Marion, I took a little ride down toward the river an' found a couple a boys fishin'. I got offa Willie an' tied him to a saplin' an' walked down the bank to where they was.

"You boys doin' any good cuttin' down on the fish population?" I asked.

The little 'un spoke right up.

"We got us some catfish, mister," he said. "Five of 'em."

"The heck ya do," I said. "Lemme see."

He pulled on a rope they had tied off to a root an', sure enough, they had three mudcats, a little channel, an' about a five pound flathead.

"Would ya sell that flathead?" I asked.

The little fella studied on me for a minute, squintin' in the sun. "How much?" he said.

"You got the product," I said. "You set the price."

He thought that over an' said, "two-bits."

"You got change for a dollar?"

"Neither one a us got any money, mister. You ain't got two bits?"

"All I got is a dollar," I said.

He studied on me agin' afore he spoke up.

"If'n you ain't got nothin' to eat," he said, "I'll give ya that channel so ya don't go hungry."

I grinned at him. "How 'bout I trade you my dollar for the flathead," I said.

He blinked at me. "A whole dollar?"

"Take it or leave it," I said.

He took it.

*   *   *   *

I rode back to camp, freshed the fire, an' put a chunk a bacon fat in the skillet to cook down. While that was sizzlin', I took out my Barlow an' cleaned the fish, throwin' the guts away from camp 'cause a flies. I dipped that catfish in some a the cornmeal an' had just laid him in the skillet when Marion come back.

"Ain't no town law on hand," he said, puttin' a little slack in the roan's cinch. He walked over an' looked down at the fire.

"Catfish, ain't it?" he asked.

"It is," I said. "Flathead."

"Where the hell did you git a catfish?"

"You ain't noticed that big ol' river just west of us?" I asked.

Marion thought that over for a little bit, but he didn't let no question git away from him. He didn't let none a his half a that catfish git away from him neither.

*   *   *   *

After we et, we rode around Saint Joe an' come back at it from the north side. I went on in with the packhorse an' run across the Blue Island Saloon on the edge a town. It was a rickety buildin', long an' narrow, with a floored tent attached to it on the east side servin' fatback an potatoes an' such. I hooked that little shotgun on my belt, made sure my badge was covered up, an' went in.

There wasn't hardly but six or seven fellas in the place. A couple a hayshakers was takin' turns drawin' cards an' hollerin' at each other at one a the tables. I went up to the bar an' this heavy set fella come up an' asked me what did I want.

"Shot a whiskey," I tolt him, "an' it better be in the bottle it come in."

"You'll git what everbody gits," he said, reachin' under the counter.

I smiled at him. "Mister," I said, "if I figger it come outa a tub in the backroom, you'll git a bath in it afore I leave."

He stopped his reach an' took a bottle offa shelf behind him, poured a shot, an' set it down.

"Two bits," he said.

"Thank you," I said, an' dropped the money on the bar just as Marion walked in, his badge showin'. He took up space about six or seven feet from me. I ignored him. Them two fellas playin' cards quit they're yellin' an' got quiet.

"Yessir, Marshal," the fat fella said. "What can I do for ya?"

"You had a couple a whores in trouble a while back," Marion said. "One kilt an' one with her nose or ear cut off, I hear."

"One was kilt," he said. "Bled out. The other'n had her nose an' face sliced up some an' got beat on or somethin'."

"Know who done it?" Marion asked.

"I wasn't workin' that night," the fat fella said.

"I didn't ask if you was workin' that night," Marion said. "I asked if you know'd who done it."

The fella licked his lips. "Nossir," he said, "I don't. Some folks talked, but I doan remember what they said."

Marion smiled at him an' leaned his elbows on the counter. "You think maybe," he asked, "if you was on this side of the bar you might have a little better idea?"

The fella started to take a step backwards an' Marion had him by the shirtfront, just as quick as that. "Do ya?" he asked.

"I doan know, Marshal," the fella said, kindly shrinkin' down some.

"Let's see," Marion said, an' just hauled him over the bar like he wadden any heavier than a loaf a bread.

Marion, as calm as you please, stood there, holdin' that fella like he was one a them kids on the river. "Now then," he said, "how's yer memory?"

"Honest, Marshal," the fella said, "I wadden here. But I heer'd it said it was them Waxler boys, Jim an' Jack. They took off an' the sheriff over in Nodaway county set after 'em with a posse, but two or three fellers got shot an' he got kilt. The Waxlers an' them are a wild bunch. They purty much used to own Atchison an' Nodaway counties. That's all I know. Honest."

Marion turned loose a him then. "Thank you for your cooperation, sir," he said. "That cut up lady here today, is she?"

"Yessir, she is. Upstairs. Room four. Nobody with her that I know of."

"Reckon I'll go up an' have a talk with her, an' anybody else I care to," Marion went on. "I doan speck to be bothered none. That alright with you?"

"That's fine, Marshal," the fat fella said, wipin' some sweat off his face with a sleeve.

Marion turned away then an' climbed them steps. If he had a bad back, I sure couldn't see it.

As soon a Marion got outa the room, them two hayshakers lit a shuck. I sipped on that shot for a spell an' finally Marion come back down an' walked out. I finished the shot an' got another one. I waited a couple a minutes, took the shot an' stepped outside. Soon as I got on the off side a Willie I spit that whiskey in the dirt, mounted up, grabbed the packhorse's lead rope, an' set off. Marion would be waitin' for me on down the line.

*   *   *   *

I stopped at a livery on the way out an' filled our water bags from their cistern, then kept Willie at a easy canter an' caught up to Marion in about three miles.

"There was two fellers in there flippin' cards," I said. "They lit out when you went upstairs."

"Musta got tired a playin'," Marion said.

"That's what I figured," I said. "When we camp tonight, let's build us the biggest fire we can. Maybe hire somebody to hang around an' play the mouth harp or the fiddle. What the hell do we havta worry about?"

Marion smiled. "Settle down, Ruben," he said. "You'll git a sour stomach."

CHAPTER FOUR

We hit some heavy brush for a while, but it broke up after a ways. I rode up beside Marion.

"Was that lady hurt some?" I asked.

"Quite a bit," he said. "She's healed up most a the way, but she ain't never gonna be right. Nobody took a knife to her. A feller did cut on the other one's neck an' she died from it, but the one I talked to got hurt tryin' to help her friend. She come at the ol' boy with the knife, an' his sidekick flung her across the room. She went face first inta a lookin' glass on a dresser agin' the wall. That glass busted up inta splinters when she hit it. She ain't but about twenny years old. Doan know if she ever was purty, but she damn shore ain't now. Said her name was Charity. Wasn't no charity in what that feller done to her."

"She know the names a who done it?" I asked.

"Says she don't," he said. "Said they was just a couple a hard cases she'd never seen before. May be true. She's plumb broke down about it, though. Scared right through. This other gal I talked to claimed it was boys from that Waxler bunch, but she wasn't sure which ones. That's just what she heard a couple a the other whores say. None a them other girls would talk to me."

"This Waxler got a ranch up thisaway?" I asked.

"He's got somethin' up this way," Marion said. "I doan know if the old man is even still alive. Way I heer'd it, he never was mor'n a pirate on the river anyway. Shit, boy. He prob'ly come up here before the war. This was some rough country in them days. Oglala injuns was still raidin' this far south an' east of their territory. Cheyenne was burnin' out settlers. Dakotas was raisin' hell west a here a ways. Wadden no law a hardly any kind.

Couple a big ranches tryin' to get started, raisin' horses though, not cattle. Homesteaders an' squatters scattered around. It was frontier. Waxler an' some a his kin show up an' purty much just take what they want an' hold onto it with a gun. In them days, Nebraska City was a piss-pot. Lincoln wadden much better. Hell, Omaha wadden mor'n a wide spot on the trail, saloons an' whores. Liquor an' fuckin' has always paved the way for the rest a the herd, Ruben. Neither one a them things is exactly whatcha might call polite society. Folks that come up through that time, an' profited from it, doan got no plans to change anythin' unless they is give a real good reason. Kinda like a pack a wild dogs. They got their territory. As a rule, ya cain't just wade in there and gentle 'em down so they'll trail along behind the wagon. Most times ya gotta run 'em off or shoot 'em."

"You think them fellas that took outa that saloon was some a the bunch?" I asked him.

"You ever watch a pack a wolves?" Marion asked.

"Nossir."

"There's usually a dog an' a bitch in the middle of it," he said. "Them two purty much run things. Everbody else sucks up to 'em. Then ya got the rest a the pack. They got a order to 'em. Rank an' file, just like the goddam army or somethin'. Like generals an' colonels an' majors an' captains, right on down to privates an' new recruits. Everbody down the line wants to move up the line. To do that they gotta git noticed doin' somethin' by command an' prove they do a good job. Sometimes in a wolf pack there'll be one or two strays hangin' around the edge a things, tryin' to figger a way into the bunch so they doan havta go it alone. Could be that's what them fellers was at the saloon. If I recall, they was fair young. Might be they seen a chance to go runnin' to a captain or a major with the news that I'm out here sniffin' around, an' git themselves noticed some."

"If that's the case," I said, "somebody's gonna know we're comin'. Then maybe somebody on up the ladder might wanta come look us over."

Marion smiled. "Or do somethin' to get a boost on up another step or two," he said.

"Well, ain't that just fine," I said.

"Be some easier if they was three of us," Marion said.

"Be some easier if they was thirty of us," I told him.

He thought that was kindly funny an' chuckled a while. "Ol' Ruben," he said.

"You spent time watchin' wolves?" I asked.

"Some," he said. "When I was yer age, back afore the war, I spent time watchin' injuns. Them an' wolves operated along the same line. Them injuns didn't have to be taught it like our boys. They was born to it. That's why we never could whip 'em in a fair battle. We could out gun 'em, but we damn shore never could out fight 'em. I never did feel sorry for no injun. That don't make no more sense than feelin' sorry for the wind. But I damn shore feel sorry for what we done to 'em. Seems to me like preachers an' politicians cain't never leave nothin' alone. Hell, Ruben, we even give 'em bad blankets and such so they'd git the fever or the pox an' die from it. We done the same thing to the injuns that we done to the bufflers. Them big shaggies never stood no real chance neither. Injun or buff, mebbe it was just their time, but the way it come about was terrible wrong. Damn shame, Ruben. Damn dirty shame."

*   *   *   *

We stayed on the trail all day, never mor'n a mile or two from the river, chewin' on jerky now an' then. Later that afternoon we come on a open flat for a ways, studded up with

new growth river birches an' thorn bushes an' such, nothin'
mor'n four or five feet high. Marion turned toward the river then
an' stopped next to a gravel bar in grass about a foot tall. Willie
flushed a rabbit an' my packhorse took exception an' got to
dancin' around some an' give me a little rope burn through my
shirt. Marion swung down an' looked up at me.

"You git done playin' with them horses," he said, "why doan
you go ahead on an' make camp?"

"Some early ain't it?" I asked him.

"Lemme borrow your rifle," he said.

I pulled the Yellaboy outa the scabbard an' handed it to him.

"Tend to the roan for me. I'm going for a stroll," he said, an'
walked off down our backtrail.

I pulled saddles an' packs an' hobbled the horses after I led
'em down for a drink. They went after that grass like it had gravy
on it. They was some dry wood above the high water mark an' I
carried a bunch of it in an' built a fire. 'Cause we had enough
time, I put on a pot a beans an' got the flour out for fry bread.
We still had two or three hours a good light left when them
beans started to boil. I tossed in some bacon an' salt, then added
a little molasses an' let 'em bubble.

It was a purty place. Had a nice breeze from the south,
hardly no cloud in the sky. I got one whiff of a skunk from God
knows how far off. Unusual that was, gittin' skunk scent in the
daytime. I set there an' watched a big ol' heron along the river
bank, now an' then grabbin' a little fish an' slidin' it down that
long neck. I coulda easy had us a rabbit, but I didn't wanna fire
off no gunshot, Marion someplace out there like he was an' not
knowin' I was only shootin' at a critter. Instead, I opened one a
them cans a peaches, leaned back agin' my saddle, an' et half of
it, puttin' the rest aside for the marshal.

Musta been a couple a hours go by when Willie tossed his head an' looked off toward the south, twitchin' his ears. He snorted once, then relaxed an' went back to the grass. Marion was comin' back I figgerd, or Willie wouldn't a been so calm about it. Sure enough, a few minutes later he come walkin' into camp. It come on me then that I didn't hear them Mexican spurs a his. I took notice an' seen the rowels was tied up with little pieces of rawhide. He leaned the Yellaboy agin' the backside a my saddle an' grunted as he set down.

"Beans an' bacon in about a hour," I said. "Half a can a peaches open for ya. Coffee's hot."

"Thanks, Ruben," he said. "If they come in, them three fellers might git here in time for the beans."

"Three fellas?" I asked.

He nodded. "A mile or so south. I figger they trailed us from town. I was them, I'd circle an' come in from the north. That way my horses could git scent first an' not be shy, an' it wodden be so plain I'd been trailin' nobody."

"Whatcha reckon they want?" I asked him.

"See who we are. Maybe try an' git the bulge on us. They most likely know why I was in town. I speck two of 'em was the fellers in the saloon. They got any guts, they'll come in to size us up. If'n they don't, they might come at us after dark. If the third one is like them other two, they ain't nothin' but kids. Kids usually ain't got a lotta experience. They git nervous an' maybe figger they got somethin' to prove. They is more hazardous than dangerous. Hazardous can shore enough put a feller in the ground, though."

Marion got up an' moved his saddle farther away from where I was settin', fetched that can a peaches, an' stretched out agin'.

He et a peach an' grinned at me. "Wanted to put a little more distance between us," he said. "Wodden want one a them fellers to hit me just 'cause he was tryin' to shoot you."

*　*　*　*

They come in outa the northeast after we et an' it was gittin' on toward sundown. Three of 'em. Number one was a big fella with a black slouch hat an' a black kindly holey beard. He was carryin' a silver-lookin' Colt with a gold hammer an' shiny white grips in a crossdraw. Number two was kindly heavy-set wearin' a ol' gray hat with a ragged brim an' a string comin' down around his neck from it. He was packin' another Colt in a side holster by his left hand on a gunbelt lined with bullets. The third fella didn't have no hat. He was little an' skinny with wiry carrot hair, freckles, an' light-colored quick eyes. He had what looked to me like a ol' Colt's Dragoon shoved down in his pants. That revolver musta weighted five pounds. If it hadn't been converted, it was a cap an' ball. Their horses wadden much. I eased my scattergun down beside my leg. Marion didn't move at all. When they got close, number one spoke up.

"Howdy," he said.

Marion nodded to him.

"Me an' my frens had a long day. Could you spare a cup a coffee for some travelers?"

"Wouldn't turn no man away from coffee that had his own cup," Marion said. "It's on the fire. Help yerselves. That little bag layin' there has got some brown sugar plug in it, if'n you got a taste for sweet."

"Thank you, sir," number one said, gittin' down an' collectin' a cup from his saddlebag.

The other ones got down, an' number two got his cup. One an' two poured coffee an' squatted across from us, number three just stood behind 'em an' watched. They was all young, none of 'em older than me.

"Where you fellers headed?" number one asked.

Marion yawned an' scratched his neck. "Omaha mebbe," he said.

"What's in Omaha?"

"Hell, boy," Marion said, real cheerful like, "they's a whole bunch a shit in Omaha. Ya ever been there?"

"Nossir, I ain't," number one said.

"I recommend it," Marion went on. "If'n I was you, I'd finish my coffee an' head up that way. Ain't hard to find. Just go back the way ya come an' keep on goin'."

"You sayin' you want us to leave?" number one asked.

"No," Marion said. "I'm just sayin' that it might be safer for ya in Omaha than it is here."

Number two spoke up. "Well, yer about a hard ol' stump, ain't ya?" he said.

Marion smiled.

"Son," he said, "I was twenty-three year old the last time my daddy kicked my ass. It was a lesson of value. It taught me to never confuse age an' ability. Might save you some grief if you was to take heed. Omaha is lookin' better for you boys all the time."

It was then that number three went for his gun. Marion shot him before he even cleared his belt. He fell over backwards an' I raised the scattergun an' leveled it at them other two. Neither one of 'em moved a inch. The one on the ground commenced to wheeze an' twitch. Number one spoke up.

"You sonofabitch!" he hollerd, "Yew shot Bucket!"

"Who?" Marion asked, his Colt pointed between the two that was left.

"Bucket, Goddammit!"

Marion grinned at him.

"Safe to say," he said, "that bucket is leakin' some. He'll settle down an' git quiet in a minute. Meantime, I'd appreciate it if you two boys would take out your revolvers an' toss 'em, real gentle like, over to this side a the fire. A course, ya doan have to. My pard over there can easy git both of ya with that little shotgun a his. Doan make me no never mind. The more the merrier. I ain't gonna dig no holes anyway."

Them guns come over the fire in short order. Marion picked up the shiny Colt an' looked it over while I kept the scattergun on them two.

"This here is a nice piece," he said. "Pearl handles, all engraved, nickel plated with a gold trigger and hammer, 'bout a eight inch barrel." He looked at number one. "This your'n?"

"You know damn well it is," number one said.

"Bullshit," Marion grunted. "Ain't no way a web-footed river rat like you ever had half the money in one spot to git a fine piece like this. You took this offa somebody, most likely after you backshot him."

He stepped over the fire, grabbed number one by the throat an' lifted him up on his tippy-toes.

"Mebbe I oughta give this Colt back to ya an' let ya come at me with it, boy," he growled. "You want it? You want yer smokepole back, you chickenshit sonofabitch? You wanna drag leather agin' somebody who's facin' ya?"

Marion held him there for a minute, eye to eye, an' then just kindly tossed him away. Number one hit the ground gaggin' with snot runnin' outa his nose an' wheezin'. Marion looked at number two. Two was terrible pale an' shakin' some.

"Pick up that dead bucket over there an' tie him to his

horse," he said. "Then you an' that coward mount up an' git out. I ever run up on either one a you agin', I'll kill ya. My name is Marion Daniels, boy. I am a United States Marshal. I can see like a hawk an' scent like a hound. Anybody in that bunch you'd like to run with wants to try me on, tell him to bring a shovel an' a friend to use it. You got two minutes to git that snot-covered asshole up an' git out a here. Doan fergit to take that redheaded bucket a shit with ya. I doan want him stinkin' up my camp."

We watched 'em ride away, an' Marion tossed another piece a wood on the fire.

"Hey, Ruben," he said. "We got any more a them peaches?"

* * * *

For more information regarding other titles by David R Lewis, please visit the website, ironbear-ebooks.com. While there, be sure to sign up for our monthly newsletter, WRITER'S BLOCK.

* * * *

49517492R00152

Made in the USA
Middletown, DE
18 October 2017